Gangsta Shyt 2

CATO

**Lock Down Publications
Presents
Gangsta Shyt 2
A Novel by *CATO***

Lock Down Publications
P.O. Box 870494
Mesquite, Tx 75187

Visit our website at **www.lockdownpublications.com**

Lock Down Publications
Like our page on Facebook: Lock Down Publications
@www.facebook.com/lockdownpublications.ldp
Cover design and layout by: Dynasty's Cover Me
Book interior design by: Shawn Walker
Edited by: Tumika Cain

Acknowledgments

To my ONLY son, Malcolm Ismail Ali Owens and my daughter, Sheena White; To my nephews: Drae Ross, Donte Marriott, and Gabriel Steele; To my niece: Kayla Steele; To my sister: Evelyn Owens, To my cousin Carol Hollinger and to all my other family members whom I love. I dedicate this book to you. I do this as an inspiration and example to them that they will dream big and reach high.

I also want to acknowledge and thank some of my greatest supporters. Terrence Jackson, Candice A. Rose, and Joy Mitchell who gave me my namesake.

To Lockdown Publications for giving me the opportunity to share my pen with the world. I want to also thank my editor, Tumika Cain, a true godsend.

Rest in peace and in love to my parents: Thomas Owens Jr. and Patsy Owens

Chapter 1
The King Has Returned

Under a beautiful fall Indian summer sky, an entire section of a remote strip of beach in Panama City, Florida was packed with people fully dressed in formal wear. The security detail, dressed in tuxedos, walked about with a wary eye and units on their faces. Their heads rotated from side to side, scanning east and west, as if they were early warning radar systems on high alert from some unknown ominous threat looming in the horizons.

The male guests, some dressed in full gangster suit attire and others in tuxedos as well, stood around congregating amongst themselves, while others had their wandering eyes fixated on the female congregation nearby. Their laughter and cat calls that let everyone know what was on their minds could be heard from one end of the private strip of beach to the other.

The females, who wore dresses and skirts, were huddled up and taking part in their own animated chatter. Some of them made their own cat calls and hisses directed towards the men. The clear distinction between the hood rats and the upscale females could be clearly distinguished in the manner in which they interacted and carried themselves. The hood rats were loud and sought attention, and the latter were reserved, classy, and respectful.

The DJ sounded off on the ones and twos, while the chefs gave a last minute viewing of their delectable varieties of food that sat on top of the long buffet table situated underneath the huge canopy. The cake, which cost about five racks, had a huge gold crown in the middle studded with diamond and ruby fondant and sat atop a table with the inscription, "Welcome Home King Tony." Indeed, this scene had all the pomp and spectacle of a King returning home from a military campaign or a mission of diplomacy to resume ruling his kingdom.

When Tony and Sugar finally arrived, holding hands, it was as if the President and the First lady themselves had graced the event with their presence. All eyes were on them as the King and Queen had finally returned to their throne. When Genie saw them, he walked up and greeted his best friend with a brisk hug.

"Well, y'all finally made it, I see," Genie said.

"Yeah bruh. We finally here," Tony said, looking at Sugar with a raised eyebrow. "Somebody wanted to stop at damn near every store we passed by on the way here." Sugar gave him a hard, but playful punch to the arm.

"Yeah that's right!" She popped her neck. "I think I earned the right to stop at each and every one of those stores I laid eyes on. But I was considerate. We only stopped at five." She chuckled. Genie laughed.

"And yes. You did earn that right," Genie said, before giving her a kiss on the cheek. "I'm just glad y'all could make it to your old man's celebration."

"No, my brother, it's our celebration," Tony said. "This is also your silent coronation, kid. This thing we built is now in your hands."

"And I could never repay you for this, bruh." Genie bumped Tony's fist. "Hell, I could never repay you for any of the shit you've done for me in two lifetimes. If it wasn't for you, I wouldn't be here to see any of this." To say that Genie owed a debt of gratitude to Tony would be an understatement. He felt he owed him his life.

"No need to thank me for any of that, bruh. If it wasn't for you, we wouldn't be where we are standing today. This thing we, as in you and I, we built together, my brother. So it's only right to transfer it all over to you."

"Much love and respect, homey." Genie said as he embraced him, wanting him to know just because he was taking over there was still room for him. It wasn't about an ego trip. Everything about the organization stood for brotherhood and loyalty and that wasn't about to change just because there was a shift in authority. "Remember, this organization is still at your disposal. Macky Boy and the soldiers got your back."

"No doubt. Speaking of Macky Boy, where is that young nigga at?" Tony looked around. "I see a lot of new faces I don't recognize, but I don't see him."

"Yeah, we have a whole new crew, including the muscle, with the exception of a couple of the stand-up cats Macky wanted to retain."

"Well, I wanna thank the youngster personally for what he did."

"You already know where he's at, T. He's making sure security is tight although he's the new Capo." Tony and Sugar laughed and shook their heads at the same time.

"Has anyone told the youngin that he been promoted? Don't we have another cat over the muscle now?"

"Yeah, we have a cat Macky handpicked personally from his hood, named Cassadine. But Macky claim he still have to groom him some more."

"Okay," Tony said, smiling. "Well, let me go holla at him before this party gets started."

"Aight, T. But let me holla at you real quick about something," Genie said before they walked away from Sugar.

"Be right back, Baby Girl." Tony kissed her on the cheek.

"Okay, Bae. I don't wanna be around y'all niggas anyway," she joked. "I'm going over here with the rest of the ladies."

"Okay boo." Tony smiled. "Enjoy yourself."

"What's up, Genie?" Tony turned to Genie and said with a serious look.

"T, I didn't wanna mention this in front of Sugar, but the reason why Macky ain't visible is because he got some Intel that there may be a possible assassination attempt on you today."

"Real talk?"

"Yeah bruh."

"Any idea who's coming at us this time?" Tony searched his mind trying to think of who could have issue with them enough to attempt an assassination.

"He was told it could be the Colombians?"

"The Colombians?"

"Yeah."

"Why would the Colombians be beefing with us?"

"I'm not sure, T. But Macky is convinced that this threat is real enough to take every precaution. This is why he is with the muscle right now."

"You know, Genie, the only thing I can think of is that business with Ocho Rios. He was a Colombian, but he wasn't really connected after he broke away from the cartel to do his own thing."

"Yeah well, it could be a relative. Then again, bruh, we have shut shit down for a lot of people who had things on lock for a while. It wasn't just Natty Boy and the syndicate niggas we put out of business."

"This is true, Genie. I'm going to step off for a minute and call Armando. He might be able to give us some insight on this shit."

This unwelcomed news of a possible beef with the Colombians concerned Tony so much so, he immediately called his plug, Armando, to see if he had heard or knew anything about it. The last thing he needed in this new direction in his and Sugar's lives was for some gangsta shyt drama to take place.

On the third ring Armando's receptionist picked up.

"Hola."

"Hola. Armando, por favor."

"Si. Who's speaking?"

"Tony."

"Si. Si. Hold on momentarily, sir." Seconds later a voice spoke into the phone.

"My friend! How are you?" Armando said, enthusiastically.

"I'm good, Mando. I'm just glad to be off Rikers."

"Oh of course, my friend. Armando is also delighted that you are home. I was very saddened to have heard about your ordeal. I wish that I could have done more to help. If you had gone to jail here in Mexico or even Colombia, you would have been within my reach."

"I know, Mando. It all worked out for the best. My woman held everything down in my absence."

"Si. Si. Your woman performed incredibly, my friend. I have never witnessed anything like that nor have I ever heard of such a thing. It was the stuff that legends are made of. She is a boss in every aspect of the word."

"Yes. If it wasn't for my baby, I would be finished. But Mando, what I called you for is because of some shit I heard just a minute ago."

"And what is that, my friend?"

"I just received word that the Colombians are planning to hit me and my people."

"What?" Mando said, standing up with a classic Cuban cigar in his hand.

"Yes. And I figured you could give me some insight on this."

"My friend, why would the Colombians want to fuck with you?"

"I'm not sure, but I have a couple of theories, such as that business with Ocho. Wasn't he a Colombian?" Tony asked as he surveyed the beach far and near with a wary eye.

"Yes. He was, in fact, Colombian, my friend. But this fat fuck Ocho was not loved by the Colombians after he broke away and started dealing with their Peruvian rivals."

"Okay. But does he have any relatives or friends who would have taken his death personally?"

"Well, yes. As a matter of fact, he has a half-brother and a sister who perhaps would have not appreciated what happened to him. And both are very dangerous people who head their own cartels. My friend, allow me to make some quick inquiries into this matter."

"Okay, Mando. I appreciate it."

"Yes, my friend. It will only take a minute. I will call you right back." After Tony hung up the phone he again scanned the area back and forth before heading towards Macky Boy and Genie who were both standing away from the crowd flanked by the soldiers who were on heightened alert.

"Mr. Stallworth!" Macky Boy said smiling, walking towards him with an extended hand.

"I don't want a handshake, Youngster. Give me a hug," Tony said as he gave his protégé a tight, manly embrace. "I want you to know that I am forever indebted to you for what you did in my absence."

"Don't mention it, sir. I did what I did because that is how I'm cut. Death before dishonor."

"True. Now what is the deal on these Colombians? Genie mentioned to me they have some beef with us."

"Yes sir. I just got word of this today. Otherwise, I would have informed you much earlier. The Colombian broad I've been kicking it with is a cop with the NYPD. She told me that she got word that some Colombian cartel leader put a hit out on a big time drug dealer by the name of Antonio Stallworth. Now I haven't had time to get this confirmed, but I take this seriously, sir, as should you."

"No doubt, Macky. Good work though. I know you will keep things safe for us."

"Oh yes sir. No doubt. Like I said, sir, if I had known about this much sooner, I would have suggested that this party be cancelled."

"It's cool, Youngster. We'll be good. In the meantime, I'm going to make some more inquiries into this."

"Okay sir. I'm going keep things safe."

"I know you will, son. But again, I am appreciative for everything you've done."

"Thank you, sir. That means a lot to me. Thank you for having the trust and confidence in my abilities." The two embraced before Tony walked over to his woman, and Macky Boy walked over to his soldiers to give them further instructions.

"Sweetie, I guess I may as well tell you."

"What's that, Bae?" Sugar said, looking him in his eyes.

"I was just informed that there may be a possible assassination attempt on me."

"What! Really? Any idea who it could be? I thought we took care of all our enemies."

"Yes. And I'm not exactly sure who these people are. I'm waiting to hear back from Mando. Besides, there will always be enemies out there, declared and undeclared, in this life we chose."

"Damn! This is why I wanted you out of this life, Tony!" Sugar said, shaking her head. Although Sugar didn't mind the gangsta shyt, in no way did she see it as a permanent way of life. Naturally, it wasn't conducive to the family life that she had envisioned.

"I know, Baby Girl, I know. I have a feeling that this is just a case of the past rearing its head in the present.....some shit that has more to do with yesterday than the here and now. Whatever it is, we will handle it."

"Okay. This event should have been postponed if that is the case." Sugar frowned.

"We just received the Intel. But listen, Baby Girl. We will handle it, alright? So just chill." The frustration was obvious in Tony's voice.

"Okay. I'm chilled. I'm the last person out here who is afraid of the gangsta shyt popping off. I just wanted this to be a drama free day where we could relax, turn up, and enjoy ourselves."

"I know, Baby Girl. And it will be. Everything will be fine." Tony placed a reassuring kiss on her lips. "I'm going to step off for a minute, Baby. Be back in a second."

"Alright, Bae. Keep your eyes peeled," Sugar said as he walked away. Seconds later Tony's phone rang. It was Mando.

"Hey, my friend, I have some info. You were right. There is a bounty on your head."

"Okay. Did you find out who it could be?"

"Yes. It is Ocho's sister. His brother, Raul, washed his hands of Ocho some time ago and therefore didn't take his death personal. His sister, however, she was close to him. In fact, she is his full sister. Meaning, they had the same mother and father, while the brother, Raul, only shared a father with Ocho. This sister, however, is said to be ruthless. I have heard much about her."

"Damn!" Tony said. "Okay. Was there any word on the when and the where?"

"No, my friend. You know better than anyone how these things go. It won't be something announced."

"Yeah, I know." Tony said, looking down at the beach sand.

"Si, but Tony, I want to reiterate that this bitch is sadistic. She likes people to know her work. Her killers use nothing smaller than AK-47s for the jobs. Typically, they use 50 caliber machine guns and flamethrowers to make things messy. And they are bold. No matter where you are, if they will come at you they will stop at nothing to get you."

"I understand," Tony said as if he were deep in thought to himself. "Well, thank you, Mando. If you hear anything else on this, please get back with me."

"My friend, if I hear anything, you will know right away. In fact, if I find out where this bitch is, Mando will take care of everything himself."

"Thank you, Mando." They ended the call. Tony gave another scan around the area, but this one had a distant look to it. This news was cause for concern to say the least. Everyone knew the longstanding vicious reputation of the Colombians.

Although the threat of an assassination plot loomed over the festivities, everything went on as planned. The women, including Sugar, all danced in rhythm to *Wobble* before the DJ put on the *Cupid Shuffle* as the men looked on with their eyes glued to the many big booties shaking and wiggling with each movement of their owners. Macky Boy and the soldiers totally ignored the women and the music as they scanned the private beach owned by Tony's politician friend. Macky Boy's men looked like the FOI brothers in the Nation of Islam. They were sharp, disciplined, totally wary and in tuned of their surroundings to protect their leader at all costs. The only difference between them and the FOI was, these men were armed with assault rifles and small arms.

When the DJ switched the music from line dancing to old school and finally to a mixture of Young Jeezy, Yung Thug, and Lil Wayne, the younger females in the crowd bum-rushed the makeshift dance floor to twerk and shake what their mommas gave them. Every pair of male eyes was trained on them, even the eyes of a couple of the disciplined soldiers got in an occasional peek. While everyone focused their attention on the party, Macky and Tony seemed to be the only ones who noticed the helicopter that had flown overhead and disappeared behind the sand dunes. When it didn't reappear again, that seemed to dismiss anything ominous or threatening about it, especially since heli-copters made frequent flyovers all the time on the public beaches a few miles away.

After a couple of hours had passed and although nightfall had begun to set in, the party goers weren't the least bit discouraged. The party continued to rock on and did not let up nor did it miss a beat. When it became too dark, the wait staff lit the torches to provide some light and warmth as the northern winds that had begun blowing off the Gulf started to bring in a slight chill. The flames from the torches that jutted up towards the sky enhanced an already beautiful scenic view the beach had to offer. The flick-ering orange and red flames could be seen for miles around as the crowd of people including others within the organization accom-panied by their guests began to file in. One of the former workers from Tony's last regime, King, who now controlled an entire bor-ough in Queens, walked up to his former boss and gave him a warm greeting.

"What's up, Tony?" King said as he gave him a tight, manly embrace. "So glad to see you back on the turf, my brother."

"Likewise, King. Good looking out while I was away. You, Memphis and Macky were the only ones who didn't switch out on us. For that, I'm appreciative."

"Yeah, kid. We just don't roll like that. Yonkers cats are death before dishonor."

"No doubt. How is shit going for you in Queens? I heard you been working the hell out of it," Tony said with a smile.

"Yeah, well, you already know. King gotta keep that paper coming and keep his hustle tighter than Stud pussy. But none of that would have been possible without you putting us on like you did, bruh. You could have been greedy and kept shit on lock, but instead you put it in our lives and made sure everybody ate. I'm here to tell you that the current state of the streets was never like it is now in my lifetime. And you know I've been out here chasing a dollar for a minute. It's all good out here, bruh. Gravy!" King said as he gave Tony some more dap.

"I feel you, King. But I only provided the product. You and the other cats made shit happen. Big ups to you and much respect," Tony said. Just as they were about to embrace again, a spatter of some warm, unknown fluid hit Tony's right cheek. When he looked down, brain matter and blood were all over his dark pink shirt, and when his eyes shifted to King, he was making his final descent to the ground. When he hit the dirt with a thud, he lay there with his eyes open staring up at Tony, and his body writhing in a death spasm. It was as if everything happened in slow motion. When Tony got his bearings and caught a glimpse on his right through his peripheral vision, the man sitting on a raft just barely in sight from the sand dunes was taking quick aim at him.

"Get down!" Tony yelled as he hit the beach sand.

The assassin's bullet missed its mark and hit one of the waiters in the shoulder. His serving tray of drinks he was carrying took flight as he let out a yell before crashing to the ground in agonizing pain. When Macky Boy and his soldiers realized what was going on, a loud chorus of machine guns rang out in Tony's direction and raked the beach sending sand and debris several feet into the air. Four errant bullets tore through the torso of a female, who was caught directly in the line of fire, before she could flee for her life. She was killed instantly. Macky Boy quickly returned fire in rapid succession without letting up as he ran towards his boss without any regard for his own life, killing the gunman who had honed in on Tony.

As the other assassins moved forward on rafts, and some on foot, spraying the beach with their assault rifles amid the frantic people who screamed and scrambled for safety from the flying

heat rocks, Genie yelled out to Tony, "T!" he screamed from behind the buffet table where he and the others were pinned down.

"You alright, bruh?" Genie then chambered a round in his
Glock 40.

"Yeah, I'm alright!" Tony yelled as he pulled his two gold-
plated four fives from their holsters. "Where is Sugar?"

"I'm okay, Bae," Sugar yelled out in the midst of the constant
deafening gunfire, as she remained low and crouched down
clutching her nickel-plated .38.

With the assurance that his Queen was okay, Tony stuck his
twin four fives out and rained a hail of bullets in the direction of
the assassins, hitting one of them in the face just as he stuck his
head up to fire. When the bullet came into contact with his jaw
that tore away a massive chunk of flesh and bone, the assassin
stood fully erect holding the horrific gaping wound in his face. A
final .45 hollow point from one of Tony's gold-plated pistols hit
him in the forehead that ceased any and all movement.

Meanwhile, Macky Boy and the soldiers unleashed a deadly
barrage of gunfire, giving Tony cover as he quickly darted low
across the beach and dove behind a sand dune as if he was back
on the battlefield Afghanistan.

When one of the soldiers let off a few shots from his HKK
and made a fatal attempt to cross the beach that was turned into
a virtual no man's land, a long flame burst out of nowhere that
engulfed his body into a burning inferno. He screamed briefly
before the fire melted him down into a fetal position. His fully
consumed body lay there burning on the water's edge. Before the
masked executioner behind the flamethrower could rain hell
down on another soldier who lay wounded and trapped out in the
open from a bullet wound to his leg, Tony leaped forward from
his position out into the open and shot the masked man once in
the chest and finish the deal with a quick follow up shot to his
right eye, that blew his eyeball out of the back of his head. After

making his final descent to the ground, he lay there face down in the sand with his hand still clasping the flamethrower.

"Genie! Get the girls out of here!" Tony yelled as he again took cover. Genie followed his instructions by gathering the frightened women together and began leading them to safety.

"Get all the way down low to the ground and crawl to the cars!" Genie yelled to the frantic women. As they quickly crawled through the sand towards the vehicles as he instructed, a machine gun burst hit two of the females trailing behind, killing one and wounding another. When one of the assassin's popped out of nowhere and was about to fire on an unsuspecting Genie, who had his back turned ushering the females to safety, Sugar shot him twice in the temple and once in the chest before his lifeless body hit the ground.

"Die muthafucka!" she yelled angrily before she grabbed the wounded female and began dragging her to safety behind with Genie and the others.

"Macky Boy!" Tony yelled. "Lay me down some cover fire!"

Following his boss's instructions, without hesitation, Macky Boy and the soldiers simultaneously sprayed the sand dunes with a relentless deadly hail of lead poisoning that gave Tony a chance to slip in behind the assassin's position. Noticing Tony had flanked the killers and got the drop on them, Macky Boy motioned for his men to cease fire to avoid hitting him. When the assassins raised up to return fire at Macky Boy and the soldiers who had taken cover, Tony hit them off with his four fives and kept firing until they were all dead. The three remaining assassins, a couple hundred yards away, realized that their mission was foiled, tried to escape, but were cut down by Genie's Mac 11.

The entire area reserved for Tony's coming home celebration was now littered with the scattered bodies of the assassins and some of Tony's entourage. The serenity and ambiance of the area were now replaced with death and carnage. The once coarse white beach sands were now stained and clumped up with coagulated blood, intestines, flesh, brain matter and other small body parts. The once salty ocean air was now fouled by the smell of gun smoke and burning flesh. It had the scene of a massacre right out of Hollywood. While Macky Boy and the soldiers cautiously conducted a thorough walk through to make sure the assassins were all dead, Tony and Genie met up with their pistols still in hand, which were still hot from the intense gun battle.

"You alright, T?" Genie asked as he holstered his Glock and held his Mac 11 down by his side.

"Yeah, I'm okay," a clearly exasperated Tony replied in a low voice. "Sugar and the girls?" Tony's heart rate was now approaching normal as his adrenaline began to decrease.

"They're all good. I got them out of here. Well, not all of them," Genie said, looking down at the body of a dead sister whose beautiful brown eyes stared wide down at the sand. "We gotta get out here, T, before the Pigs come." Genie clutched Tony's shoulder. The look on Tony's face said what he elected not to verbalize. He hadn't seen this much death and destruction since he was in a heated battle in Kandahar, Afghanistan. As Tony holstered his .45s, a calm and collected Macky Boy walked up.

"Mr. Stallworth, we should leave now, sir," he said softly as he looked around warily for any more danger. While Tony walked stoically to the white Expedition, where his Queen was waiting in safety, he thought to himself, *As soon as I was resolute on leaving this life, there is some unknown force in the universe trying to pull me back in.*

Chapter 2
A Transfer of Power: Genie's Coronation

Early the next morning, Tony and Genie flew to Bogota to see Armando, personally. There were two reasons for the visit: the incident last night on the beach and the transfer of power, which was Tony's plan to knock out two birds with one stone.

"Hello, my friend," Armando said, as Tony and Genie stepped off the helicopter, Armando's muscle armed with Uzis flanking him.

"What's up, Mando?"

"First and foremost, I want to express my regret and condolences for what happened last night at your homecoming celebration. I have my sources working on finding that bitch as we speak," he said. "She has security up the ass, but eventually we will find this cunt."

"Yes, there is no doubt in my mind we will find her," Tony replied, "but I have another purpose for coming here on such a short notice."

"Oh no? What else brought you here, my friend?"

"We are transitioning. My best friend, brother and right hand man here, Genie, will now assume all power in my organization. I know this is sudden, but I made the decision while I sat in jail." Armando smiled.

"I understand, my friend. When it is time to walk away, it is time to walk away. And we should never look back at that point. I look forward to hearing about your new life and working with your brother here," Armando said before he shook Genie's hand.

"I look forward to working with you as well, Armando," Genie said as Tony looked on with a smile.

"Now to the business of this bitch, Elvira," Armando said. "Come with me."

After they reached Armando's ranch, he had several pictures of Ocho's crazy ass sister spread out all over a table. He even had pictures of her half brother, Raul, the late Ocho, and other family members.

"This is Elvira Rios, aka *perro loco,* or crazy bitch." Armando said as Tony and Genie began looking through the pictures.

"*Perro loco,* huh?" Tony asked as he looked down at one of the pictures of Elvira hugging a female who was dressed in a NYPD police uniform.

"Yes. Crazy bitch," Armando replied before taking a puff of his Cuban cigar. "And she earned that name well. Although she was a woman, she had the utmost respect from the other cartel leaders who were all men. And in order to achieve that, she had to be vicious, more so than the men." Tony seemed to be fixated on the picture with the female cop in it, and Genie noticed it.

"What is it, bruh?" Genie said under his breath.

"This girl in this picture. She's NYPD."

"Yeah. That is definitely an NYPD uniform she's wearing," Genie said. Armando began to take a keen interest in it also.

"Yes, my friend. That is Elvira's niece," Mando said. "Ironically, she's a cop in New York. And rumor has it, she leaks info to her aunt."

"Armando, can I take this picture with me?" Tony asked.

"Si, si, my friend. All those pictures are yours to take. We must find this bitch ASAP, my friend. She will be relentless in hunting you down. If she can't get to you, she will bring harm to your family or your wife's family. This is her reputation."

"I will find this bitch before it gets to that. That, I can assure you." Tony continued to stare at the picture of her and her niece. The picture he held in his hand switched on the proverbial light bulb in his head as he recalled Macky's words out on the beach.

The Colombian broad I've been kicking it with is a cop with the NYPD.

CATO

Chapter 3
In This Life, You Either Kill or You Die

The next evening back in Brooklyn, Tony and Genie met up with Macky Boy.

"Come in, Youngster," Tony said as he sat back in his office chair. Genie who sat next to him took a sip from a silver liquor flask.

"Mr. Stallworth, I want to apologize for that incident on the beach. If I had known a few hours earlier maybe none of that would have went down." Macky felt partly responsible for the incident on the beach. Protecting his boss and Sugar was something that he took deadly serious, even if it meant sacrificing his own life.

"Hey, Youngster, there was nothing you could do. Those things happen in this life we chose. Death is a part of it. But just imagine if you hadn't known anything at all. Shit would have been a whole lot worse for us all. At least we had some time to prepare for what was coming and deal with it," Tony said, not blaming the youngster at all.

"True." A sense of relief came over his baby face.

"Macky Boy, who did you say told you about this hit?"

"A girl I been kicking it with. She's a cop with the NYPD."

"This cop?" Tony said as he pushed the picture of the female in an NYPD uniform across the table to him.

"Yes sir. This is her," a stunned Macky said, staring at the picture. "What's up? Was she behind the hit?"

"I'm not sure," Tony said as he sat back in his chair. "But that other bitch in the picture was. I know this for a fact. It's your girl's aunt." The youngster stood there for a moment stunned before dropping down hard in the chair, still staring at the picture he held in his hand.

"Macky Boy, I have a question for you and I want you to think long and hard about this because it's very important. Right now I don't have any reason to believe your girl was involved. But did you mention to her about the coming home party?" The youngster didn't take his eyes off the picture when he answered

"Yes, sir, I told her that I was deejaying the party. She thinks I'm a DJ and a physical trainer," he said in a low voice with his eyes still trained on the picture.

"Okay. But she doesn't know you work for me then?"

"No," he said in a low voice.

"Okay. Chances are she didn't know, because if she did, they would have hit me much sooner," Tony said as the youngster continued to hold the picture in his hand staring at it.

"Don't take it hard, Youngster. It wasn't your fault and you are not to blame. Neither is your girl, because again, I have no reason to believe your girl was involved. However, you are going to have to fix this. And I'm going to leave it all up to you to handle it like you think it should be handled," Tony said, placing his hand down on his shoulder before walking out of the office. Genie too walked over and grabbed his shoulder to console him before exiting the office.

"I will handle it," the youngster said under his breath as he continued to look down at the picture. "You have my word on that."

***

The following Saturday was Colombian Independence Day in New York. The original date was July 20, but the Colombian immigrants celebrate it on November 11. It was a little over 205 years ago from this day, Colombian patriots stirred the population of Bogotá into street protests against Spanish rule. The Spanish Viceroy, under pressure, was forced to agree to allow for a limited temporary independence which later became full and permanent. This celebration was marked by drinking, dancing, reenactments of the near bloodless revolution, revelry and of course, food. Lots of food, such as tamales, chorizo, empanadas, Colombian coffee, yuca congelada, tapas, arepas, soups made with chicken, and a delicious chilled, blended drink made of milk, sugar, and a fruit known as curuba.

Every year Nicola's family came to visit for this holiday that was like American Independence Day. When her parents immigrated to New York back in the early sixties, they had lofty dreams for their future child who would be born nearly two decades later. Nicola's father, who was a blue collar factory worker and upright man who was hell bent on not becoming another drug trafficking Colombian, worked sixty to seventy hour work weeks to make sure his family wanted for nothing. He bragged to his friends and co-workers that his little daughter, who wore pigtails, was going to grow up to be a Supreme Court justice. If he had lived long enough to see that she would instead become a cop, he would have been just as proud. What he would not be so proud of was his cop daughter's close association with one of the black sheep of the family - his cocaine kingpin sister Elvira.

Elvira Rios, or *perro loco*, was the type of individual who made grand entrances whenever she visited her family. Meaning, whenever she came into her relatives homes, she came bearing expensive gifts. In fact, any time she showed up it was better than Christmas for her people. At the last family gathering, which consisted of mostly distant relatives and people who were more so friends from their nation than close kin, she gave them all five racks a piece before she left. This was her way of maintaining their loyalty. With her full brother Ocho's demise, her niece, Nicola, was the only person in the entire world who she truly cared about, and she made sure she didn't want for anything.

CATO

When Nicola was going to quit the force to attend law school, Elvira convinced her to stay on and climb the career ladder so she could have an insider within the force who could give her valuable information about anti-narcotics operations and drug stings. To seal the deal, Elvira gave her niece a quarter of a million dollars in cash, on top of the brand new 640i BMW.

The contrast between Nicola's character and her late principled father, was obvious in her demeanor and even in her conversation. Perhaps Nicola's father working himself into an early grave, forever shaped her worldview. And it didn't help when her grief stricken mother who had never known another man other than her father, followed him into the grave less than six months later. With their deaths, Nicola would later come to despise his blue collar, nose to the grindstone approach to life.

"Auntie, I want you to meet my new boyfriend and this time I won't take no for an answer. Every time you come to visit, you always seem to avoid meeting him," Nicola said before placing a kiss on her aunt's cheek.

"Nicola, I will only meet him if you are serious about him. I don't want to be meeting people who are not going to be around long."

"Oh, auntie, he's such a keeper! He's so wonderful to me!" the tall shapely girl, who had a juvenile infatuation in her eyes, said. "I would be a complete fool if I wasn't serious about this man."

"Is he Columbian?" her aunt asked with a serious look on her face.

"No, but he is part Dominican."

"Okay. And what is the other part?" her aunt asked. Nicola laughed.

"Black."

"Black?" Her aunt stood there with her hands on her hips.

"Yes auntie. His mother was Dominican and his father was black. What difference does it make anyway?"

"It makes a big difference, but you are too young to see and understand these things."

"Oh, auntie, when you meet him, you will see what I'm saying."

"Okay. Well, at least he's not white. Does he speak Spanish?"

"Yes, he speaks it fluently. Better than me and you, in fact."

"Okay. That's a plus. Never be involved with a man who don't speak your language and can't identify with your culture. If so, and you bear his children, there will be a clash within the home."

"Like I said, auntie, he's part Dominican so he was raised in the Latino culture."

"Well, that's good. As long as you are happy, that is the most important thing to me," her aunt said before placing a kiss on her face and flopping down on the sofa. "Now when do I meet this wonderful man of yours?"

"He should be here any minute now. He really wants to meet you."

"I want to meet him too. But he should hurry up. I'm hungry," the large-sized woman, who had the look of a one of those Amazon women, said. Her size would intimidate any female and even most men. The look on her face spoke of a hard upbringing. Though she smiled often, donning her partially gold fronts, there was a no nonsense aura about her. For those who knew the look, there was something deadly about this woman.

While Nicola finished getting dressed, there was a ring at the door.

"Who is it?" her aunt asked looking through the peephole.

"Mack."

"Nicola, there is a Mack at the door for you."

"Okay, auntie, that's my boo. Let him in." Auntie opened the
door and let the young man with the baby face inside.

"How are you, ma'am?" the young man said smiling.

"I'm fine. And yourself?" she asked, studying him closely
with her piercing eyes.

"Oh I'm good. I'm Mack," he said extending his hand.

"I'm Elvira. Nicola's aunt. Nice to meet you," she smiled and
said leaving his hand hanging in the air. "Nicola will be out in
just a minute. Have a seat." The young man sat down at the
kitchen table and shyly looked straight ahead.

"So, my niece told me a lot about you. What do you do?"

"I am a professional DJ."

"Professional DJ?"

"Yes, ma'am. I own my own business."

"So what exactly does a professional DJ do?"

"I DJ parties, weddings, baby showers, funerals and any other
event you can think of."

"Funerals, aye?" she quipped with a grin. She thought about
how many funerals she made happen over the years.

"Yes, ma'am. Funerals," the youngster said.

"Hey boo boo!" Nicola said to the youngster as she entered
the kitchen and kissed him.

"Hey, love, you look beautiful, as usual," he said after he
stepped back and looked at her.

"See, auntie. This man knows how to treat me. He's always
complimenting me." Nicola would have liked nothing better than
to finally win the approval of her aunt, who was hard pressed to
accept any man she ever kicked it with. In her eyes, no man was
good enough for her niece who was more like the daughter she
never had.

"I see," the aunt said, looking at her boyfriend with a wary
eye.

"So are we ready to go to the parade?" he asked.

"Yes, we are," the aunt interjected. "I need to eat before I become angry."

Mack and Nicola laughed. "Well, let's go!" Nicola said excitedly before the three set out for the Independence Day parade.

When they arrived, the festival was well underway. The gold, blue and red colors of the Colombian flag on clothing, hats, ribbons, ticker tape and floats gave the event a colorful spectacle. In the backdrop, there was the popular Colombian la salsa music and people cheerfully dancing to its beat. There were men walking in groups smiling and throwing out candy to the excited kids who moved about in a sort of feeding frenzy trying to catch as many pieces as their small hands could grasp. There were young women strutting down the parade route dressed in skimpy cheerleading costumes in their national colors, while the smiling school children dressed in school uniforms, rode their homemade floats and mock cars. Miss Colombia, dressed in her pageant clothes, walked gracefully and proudly ahead of her entourage. This was indeed a joyous day of pride for the Colombian people.

Inside a restaurant along the parade route, Nicola, her aunt, and her boyfriend ordered lunch.

"Wow!"Mack said. "I've been to a Dominican parade in Harlem before, but it was never this live."

"Yes. This is one of the busier parades in New York," Nicola replied. "Can you excuse me? I'm going to run to the women's room."

"Okay sweetie," Mack said before they kissed. The aunt now trained her attention on the youngster for a little interrogation session.

"So this is your first time attending this parade I take it," Elvira said.

"Yes, ma'am. I was going to attend last year with Nicola, but I had an event to DJ."

"Okay. I see. How long have you two been seeing each other?"

"A little over a year," Mack replied.

"A year, aye? Are you planning on marrying my niece?" she asked bluntly.

"Of course. I have one more payment left on her engagement ring. But don't tell her. It's a surprise," he said smiling.

"Ohhh okay. Muy bueno. I am delighted to hear this. Nicola is like my own child. I'm sure you know I raised her after her parents died."

"Yes, she told me all about you. She thinks the world of you."

"And I think the world of her too. I want you to keep that in mind when or if you ever get the urge to fuck over her or mistreat her in any way. I would take something like that very personally." The look on her face was stern.

"Oh no doubt. You have nothing to worry about. I love your niece more than I love breathing air." Elvira laughed as she thought to herself. *If you really do value breathing air, you better not fuck over my niece.*

"Okay. What have you two been talking about? Me?" Nicola said as she returned to the table. Her aunt and Mack laughed.

"Yes, I told her how much I love and adore you," he said before placing a kiss on her cheek.

"Yes, it is so nice to see that you have someone who loves you," her aunt said smiling.

"I told you, auntie. My boo love me and I love myself some him."

"That's wonderful. Now where is the waiter with our food?" she said, looking impatiently towards the kitchen. No sooner than she inquired about the food, the waiter was coming around the corner with a huge serving tray of food.

"My apologies for taking so long. We are short on help due to the festival," he said as he served them their food. "Is there anything else I can get you?"

"No, we are good," they all replied. The heavyset waiter then walked off and headed into the kitchen.

"He looks like your uncle," Elvira whispered to Nicola before she placed a plantain into her mouth. Elvira thought back endearingly about her upbringing with her chubby brother who would often get picked on and she would have to fight his battles for him.

"Uncle Ocho? You think so?"

"Si. Only Ocho was a bit heavier," the aunt said as she made the rest in peace hand gesture in the air.

After they finished their lunch, they headed out to the parade which was now going strong. As they walked down the parade route, everyone's eyes, especially the small children, seemed to be fixated on the scary looking Grim Reaper figure dressed in all black, who walked alongside a Jesus character who carried a makeshift wooden cross, and who wore the crown of thorns on his bleeding head. The scene symbolized the crucifixion event and the Reaper as the bringer of death.

After hanging out and taking part in the revelry for a couple of hours, the aunt was ready to take it in. Her protests regarding her feet begun to become more frequent and vocal. She candidly admitted that she wasn't as young as she once was and therefore couldn't hang out like she used to.

When they finally returned back to Nicola's apartment, the aunt collapsed on to the couch and let out a sigh of relief. She was exhausted.

"Are you okay, auntie?" Nicola asked.

"Si. I'm okay now," she said as she exhaled. "I should have had that surgery on my poor feet years ago when my physician suggested it. And the weight I have gained does not help matters.

I used to work out daily, now I can only ride the exercise bike a half hour at a time."

"Have you tried water aerobics or swimming?" Mack asked.

"Sometimes in my pool back in Bogota."

"Yes, low impact workouts are the best option for you."

"Auntie, my boo is also a physical trainer," Nicola said, looking at him admiringly.

"Hmmm. You are just full of surprises, young man," auntie said with a discerning eye. "What other surprises do you have in store for me?" She smiled at him while rubbing her feet. Mack laughed.

"Now it wouldn't be a surprise if I told you, right?" he joked. "Well, sweetie, I'm going to tear out," he said to Nicola.

"Okay, Bae," she said before placing a kiss on his lips.

"It was really nice meeting you, Auntie," he said, holding her hand. The aunt seemed to let her guards down.

"Likewise, son." After they embraced, Mack exited Nicola's apartment.

"So what do you think?" Nicola asked.

"What do I think of what?"

"My boo!" she said smiling. "What do you think of him?"

"He's okay. A little too touchy feely, but I think that's good for you."

"Aww, auntie. No one is good enough for me in your eyes. He's too touchy feely," she repeated and laughed. "You never were the affectionate type."

"Well, that is not entirely true. I used to be once upon a time. But growing up in the slums of Bogota may have contributed to that. Perhaps this is why I don't have a man." Elvira's life during the years after leaving America was marked by violence and abuse, once being raped by a cartel boss who she would later assassinate after she rose to power to form her own cartel. It was after his killing in which used a flamethrower to roast him alive that she became known to all her rivals as perro loco. And she carried that name proudly.

"You would probably end up killing him anyway," Nicola quipped. "Oops. I'm sorry, auntie," she said before placing her hands over her mouth. "That came out wrong."

"That's okay." Auntie gave a half grin. "You are probably right. I just never met a man who could deal with me, with the exception of one," she said as she thought about her last husband who she caught fucking her pretty young maid. She'd turned out to be his side bitch. Her mind reverted back to the night she walked into their honeycomb hideout cabin in the Andes Mountains. She recalled the shocked looks on their faces, just before she began squeezing off shots from her revolver. She smiled wickedly while rubbing on her sore feet. She left them right there in the cabin, making it their tomb. That was ten years ago and it is a good chance that their mummified corpses were still there, since this cabin was in a remote place that no one knew about except for the deceased and the wifey.

"Auntie, you should go back on the dating scene. Maybe an American man would be better for you."

"Hahaha. So you think the Colombian men are no good for me, aye? American men," she repeated. "You sound like you want your auntie to go catch a murder case, because that is exactly what would happen if I got me an American man. My temper is too bad, and they are too disrespectful. You already know how I feel about that."

"Yeah, I know. But really, since you have only dated men from the homeland, you should try something new. Who knows? Maybe you will find your boo who will soften you up some."

"Niece, let me explain something to you that you may be too young to understand. When you are my age and been through the things I have been through in life, the last thing you want to do is complicate matters. Bringing a man into my life on anything serious at this point, will do just that. Where I am in my life right now, whatever I want, I buy it. If I want a man for some companionship, I call an escort service. I have no desire for anything more. Besides, I have dated an American before."

"Really? When?"

"While I attended college here at Columbia University. We were classmates."

"Wow! Really, auntie? I didn't know you attended Columbia!"

"Si," she said smiling.

"Wow! My father never told me about that."

"Of course not. Your father disowned me before you were born. Have you noticed he's never mentioned much about me other than something negative?" Nicola put her head down. She knew all too well that her aunt had been a taboo subject under her father's roof.

"Yes. He never mentioned you other than to tell me how he didn't want me to turn out like you."

"Si," she smiled and said. "It's okay. Hector was just like that. He was the most honest man I have ever known, and the most self-righteous. But he meant well. I was his baby sister, who he at the time, thought was his daughter. Again, this was before you were born."

"Why did papa become disappointed in you?"

"He didn't like my boyfriend for starters."

"But why?"

"Well, first of all, my boyfriend was black."

"What?" Nicola was shocked since her aunt was always admonishing her about dating within her race and ethnicity.

"Si. Si. He was black. Dark as night," she said smiling. "But that really wasn't why he disowned me. My boyfriend, Shaka, was a black militant and your father was the type of immigrant

36

who didn't want to make waves here. He felt since he was in America that he had to be the patriotic type and Shaka was just the opposite. This caused them to clash constantly."

"But that still doesn't explain why he would disown you, auntie."

"His disowning me came later."

"Well, what happened, auntie? At what point did he disown you?" The aunt smiled.

"Shaka, who was as sweet as he could be at times, had anger issues that he couldn't overcome, especially when it came to me. He was extremely protective over me. One night, while we were at a party off campus, a Latino gang member, who had been giving me a hard time about dating a black man, groped me. When Shaka found out about it a fight broke out. The gang member's friend hit Shaka over the head with a beer bottle while Shaka was beating the shit out of his vato," she paused for a second seemingly to gather her thoughts. Her body language and tone had begun to change as she relived the incident.

"While Shaka was on the ground trying to regain his faculties, the gang member who groped me, took out a switchblade and was about to stab him, when I stabbed him in his neck several times with a blade Shaka had given me for protection. I was out of my mind that night at the thought of that *puto* harming the man I love. Everything was like a blur. Well, the gang member died shortly thereafter, and your father who feared he and your mother would be deported, ushered me out of the states back to Colombia."

"Wow auntie! So this is why he was so upset with you all those years." Elvira laughed.

"Si. Along with my criminal lifestyle as he termed it, that I would get into much later in life. That one incident forever changed the course of my life. Not long after that, the gang member's vatos seeking retribution, murdered my Shaka. My dreams of one day returning to the states to become a lawyer and having a life with Shaka was forever destroyed. So I turned to the streets. I did what most young people in my barrio were doing. I became involved in the cocoa trade. I climbed my way up the ranks by being ruthless, more so than anyone else, and I had to be being a female. Hence the name I was given *perro loco,"* she said laughing. "I guess after killing that *hijo de puta* who groped me, taking life became easy for me, especially a man's life."

"I never heard this story you just told me." Nicola was stunned at what she had heard. Her father was silent on his baby sister.

"Of course you didn't. And it was good that you didn't at such a young age. This is why I am so particular about who you are involved with romantically. I like your boyfriend, but there is something about him. My instincts tell me that there is much more to him than meets the eye. Something I cannot put my hands on."

"There really is, auntie. But it is all good," Nicola said before placing a kiss on her aunt's cheek. "The room is ready for you whenever you want to retire. "I'm going to rest for a few hours before I have to go to work. See you later, auntie."

"Okay, niece. I'm going to sit here for a while before I turn it in." Not long after Nicola went to her bedroom, her aunt drifted off to sleep right there on the couch. Between the flight and the parade, the day was obviously taxing on her large, 6 ft 5, big-boned frame.

After Nicola put on her NYPD uniform and strapped on her service pistol, she headed for the door. Before exiting, she smiled, kissed her sleeping aunt, and placed a comforter over her huge frame and walked out.

Around two a.m. the two bodyguards, who had been standing posted up outside the brownstone apartment, had long retreated to the car to escape the winter chill. Inside their ride they listened to *Bon, Bon* by Pit-bull while enjoying the heat emanating from the car's vents that provided them with the warmth the wool trench coats could not. These were the same two men who had been keeping a watchful eye on their boss while at the parade earlier that day. The stone cold crimson masks they wore on their faces, gave them away.

When a red Kia, driven by a black female, slightly bumped their ride from the rear, pissed and startled at the same time, they quickly stepped out to investigate. The beautiful red-boned sister who rear ended them smiled and began to profusely apologize, which almost immediately disarmed them and put them at ease. While they assured her that everything was alright while getting in a few flirts in the process, the unmistakable sound of two shots silently zipping through the air, via a silencer, that struck one of the men in the head and the other in the neck rendering him immobile. While his life blood squirted between his fingers, he twisted and turned on the pavement in pain holding his neck with a look of terror and desperation in his eyes.

A masked man calmly emerged from the darkness and finished him off with a series of quick shots that ended his ordeal. It was quick and humane. The female driver who had crashed into their ride, cranked up her car and gave a smile and an approving nod to the masked man, dressed in all black, before she slowly drove away. The masked man then trained his attention on the bodies of the two men. One by one, he dragged them out of sight underneath their car which was still running, before proceeding on to the apartment complex across the street.

After inserting a key into the apartment door, he carefully twisted the doorknob before it creaked open. Pausing to scan the living room and not seeing anything, he proceeded on his mission. Standing stealth in the dark hallway that lead to the two bedrooms, the masked intruder stood there pondering his next move as he waited to hear any movement such as snoring, a flushing toilet, or anything that would indicate the location of his target. Suddenly, there was movement in the kitchen that sounded like someone was rummaging through the fridge for a late night snack. Hearing this, the intruder crept ever so slightly towards the kitchen. When he reached the entranceway, he saw a large-sized woman bent over halfway perusing through the fridge. Standing there with his pistol in hand, he locked in on his target. As she stood there looking inside the fridge, her instincts alerted her to his presence. Turning around slowly, she faced him.

"Hola," she said smiling with her back to the opened refrigerator.

"Hola," the intruder replied. His calm tone and demeanor belied his mission. He was serene, casual and even displayed a courteousness. This intruder was definitely a professional and Elvira knew it.

"I take it that you are here for me?" she asked as she closed the refrigerator door.

"Si," the intruder said, nodding his head.

"May I have a seat?"

"Si." He cautiously watched her sit down at the kitchen table.

"So am I the only one you are here to see?" she asked.

"Si."

"Okay. That gives me comfort. May I ask why you are here to see me? I'm just curious." She sat back in her chair trying to appear at ease. Before answering, the intruder pulled out a chair and sat down in it across from her. He then pulled off his ski mask, revealing his identity.

"Like I told you earlier today, you are full of surprises," she said smiling.

"The incident on the beach last week," Macky replied stonedfaced.

"Oh. Okay. I see. You know, years ago when I was a young ambitious wildcat of a woman, I would have handled that thing

personally, like I have always done. But having money makes
you lazy....so much so, you have others to do your dirty work for
you," she said with a chuckle. "So this is nothing personal,
right?"

"No. The only thing that makes it personal, other than the fact
I like you, is your niece."

"So no harm will come to her?" she asked with an inquisitive
look.

"No, of course not. She's totally not in this," Macky responded as he sat back in the chair wearing his own relaxed look
with the gun pointed at her chest.

"Okay, bien buena," she said with a calm look on her face.
This seemed to put her at ease. She was now totally resigned to
her fate.

"But I have a question for you," he asked. "I have to know
this to keep Nicola safe."

"And what is that?"

"Was there anyone else involved that I should know about?"

"No. My half-brother refused to avenge Ocho's murder. So it
was left up to me. It was my right to do so. This is our custom."

"So your brother wasn't involved in any way?"

"No, not at all. He doesn't have the balls I have."

"Okay. Your niece is safe. I will marry her and she will have
my children. I hope that puts you at peace."

"Si. I am at peace." She smiled. "However, I have one final
request." Macky nodded his head.

"Sure."

"In the chest. I want to be pretty when I go see the Virgin
Mary." Not long after she closed her eyes to await her fate, three
shots cut through the air and into her heart, killing her instantly.
It was quick, perhaps painless and humane. The impact and dead
weight of her huge frame caused her body to collapse to the floor,
sounding like a sack of bricks. Macky Boy then calmly stood up,

put his ski mask back on and left the kitchen. Before exiting the apartment, he took a hammer and pried open the doorframe to make it appear there was a break in. He then disabled the one video camera out in the apartment's hallway and took it with him before he disappeared into the night.

The killing of Elvira, was something that had to be done, because that is exactly what she was going to do to his boss, Tony, whom Macky swore his loyalty, allegiance, and life to. No matter how torn he was in killing a woman who meant the world to the woman who meant the world to him, he had to handle his business like the soldier he was. It was always death before dishonor. He knew in this instance, the law of the streets dictated that, in this life *you either kill or you die.*

Chapter 4
Let's Take a Trip to the Motherland

When the plane finally landed sending Tony's heart rate down to normal, the all black cast on the tarmac was an impressive sight to see, along with the all black cockpit and crew. This is how one knew he was in the Motherland - black folks doing their own thing, which was something Tony and Sugar could fully relate to since they too were independent masters of destinies. Back home in their kingdom, they were King and Queen.

After Sugar and Tony grabbed their luggage, they were chauffeured off to their hotel suite. When they arrived, they were pleasantly surprised at the beautiful scenery in the backdrop of the hotel, which sat on the water exactly as it was advertised. The sun seemed so close to the water's surface, as if it was sitting right on top of it.

"Ohhhh, Tony!" Sugar said as her eyes lit up. "This is absolutely beautiful!"

"Yes it is, Baby Girl. And it should be given the price tag they hit a nigga with," he quipped.

"That's okay. Never mind about the price tag. We have millions that are just sitting there in the bank some crackers are making use of to make the next billion dollar business deal. Besides that, it was well worth it to come here. And you better be quiet, because if I like it enough, we will buy this bitch," Sugar said with a diva look on her face. Tony laughed.

"Alright now, girl. Don't be going crazy over here with your spending," he said, as they walked into their room where surprisingly, the song *Differences,* by R&B artist Ginuwine, was playing from the room's speakers. After the bag boy laid down their bags, he looked at Tony, smiled, and said, "If there is anything else you need from me, here is my calling card."

"No, sir, that will be all for now," Tony said before tipping him a crisp twenty spot, which caused his eyes to light up. He folded it, stuffed it into his pocket, and exited the room one happy Liberian. One American dollar was worth about forty in this nation founded by freed slaves that had endured two brutal civil wars in the past 20 years, that nearly tore this mineral rich nation asunder.

"Alright, don't mess with me," Sugar warned. She was in full diva mode, which was actually something that drew Tony to her. Her feistiness was a turn-on for him. He smiled and threw a pillow at her, starting a pillow fight.

"Okay. Okay. I won't mess with you." He ducked from the pillow she threw back at him, then ran up and grabbed her before throwing her gently down on the bed and began planting kisses all over her face. Soon the action on the bed extended into the bathroom and into the bathtub. After undressing and getting into the shower, they resumed where they had left off. With their bodies intertwined, they began kissing wildly. The time in jail away from his woman seemed to ignite Tony's sexual passions and vice versa. Sugar was just as stoved up and horny, if not more than, her old man.

The way they carried on was as if they had been apart for decades. Soon the kissing traveled back to the bedroom where Tony laid Sugar down and began running his tongue up and down her hips and then over her six pack before he ended up at her grand prize, that had already swollen with excitement. Soon the position changed into the 69. The muscles in Tony's face tensed up every time Sugar softly twisted her tongue around the head and base of his manhood.

While they did their thing, a beautiful rare bird the size of a sparrow, with rainbow colors, landed on the balcony and sat there taking in an eyeful. After the 69 had run its course, Tony laid down on his back in anticipation of an extended head session.

With his muscular dick, with a slight curve in it, stood firm pointed up towards the ceiling, Sugar laid down on her stomach, cradled it with one hand, gently cuffed his balls with the other and began slowly licking the sides of it while she stared intently into his eyes, which had now begun to roll from the greatest pleasure that a woman could give a man - slow, wet, soft, passionate head.

Sweet nectar dripped incessantly from Sugar's well-groomed, well-shaved pussy from the excitement that came from pleasing her old man. The one thing that turned her on just about more than anything was to take in a mouthful of his chiseled manhood. When Tony opened his eyes, she gave him another visual by letting his dick pop in the corner of her mouth and allowing it to slowly slide back into her jaw, followed by her soft pink tongue that snaked in and around it. The effect was a popping sound that could be clearly heard throughout the room.

"You like that, Bae?" she asked in a low, sexy voice. He replied with his eyes. The sight of his manhood pushing out her cheek every time she thrust her head forward in rhythm was more than he could take without blowing out, so he signaled for her to hold up. Smiling, and marveling at her work, Sugar leaned over and kissed him before slowly mounting him. Gently holding his rock hard manhood in her hand, she lined it up with her sweetness. As she bore all her weight down on him slowly, inch by inch of him traversed inside of her. Once she could not go any further, her eyes tightened.

When she her hips began a slow and methodical roll, her nearly shut eyes peered out of the balcony doors at the beautiful, foamy ocean waves that seemed to crash onto the shore in sync with her sensual movements. As the old school joint, *Baby, I'm For Real* by The Moments, played from the speakers, she caught a rhythm throwing her pelvis forward. As Tony tightly held her well-oiled ass, that was shiny from the baby oil he smeared all over it, her eyes were now narrowed to tiny slits from pleasure as the dick started to hit its mark. Noticing the feathered spectator who was twisting its head from side to side in curiosity, Sugar smiled and nodded her head in Tony's direction to alert him to its presence. Tony looked at it and smiled.

"Let's give the nigga something to really watch," he said, before he climbed on top of her and began pushing himself deep inside her sugar walls. With each thrust, Sugar moaned. The build up inside of her was real. When she finally squirted her juices all over his manhood, leaving a puddle on the sheets, she bristled, wrapped her legs tightly around his back and pulled him to her in a tight embrace with her eyes closed shut tight. While she continued to hold him tightly, Tony could feel the pulsation of her vagina throbbing and gripping around him tightly as it continued to release its load.

After stopping briefly to change positions, she placed her knees down on the bed, lay on her chest and arched her flawless brown ass up in the air before Tony settled in behind her and began putting in work. With each deep thrust, the smacking sound produced by his pelvis slamming into her voluptuous ass every time they came into contact, could be heard so loudly around the room, the bird went crazy with excitement as if it knew exactly what was taking place. When Sugar became too loud, the bird became startled and flew away. After a couple hours of intermissions, climaxes, switching, changing and rotating positions, Tony and Sugar collapsed into a deep sleep, the type of sleep that only comes after an intense session of lovemaking.

After waking up from their sex-induced slumber and getting dressed, Tony and Sugar embarked on a romantic stroll down on the beach. As they walked hand in hand along the shore, they passed by couples who were mostly foreigners either on vacation or there to take advantage of the new opportunity made possible by the election of Liberia's first female President, Ellen Johnson

Sirleaf. The new so-called era of stability produced by an American-educated President elected to office, brought in potential foreign investments from all over the world who were looking to exploit the Liberian people in another century. There were now so many lucrative opportunities Tony was considering exploring some type of investment himself. Little did he know he would soon find his investment opportunity from an unlikely source, in an even more unlikely hustle.

Later on that night, they attended a concert of local African musicians who played everything from traditional African music to African American R&B, which was surprising since neither group had ever been to America before. The one thing that Tony and Sugar noticed that African American and Africans had in common was rhythm. Rhythm is a testament to African roots, which every human being on the earth derived from. Everybody in the place had it. Well, not everybody. There were a couple of white tourists who had about as much rhythm as a body lying in state....and much to Tony and Sugar's amusement. They laughed their asses off at the awkward, offbeat movements of the white folks who looked like the Walkers on The Walking Dead.

The next day, Tony and Sugar went on a tour of the landmarks around the capital, Monrovia, and the African art stores before taking a trip to neighboring Ghana. As they rode along what is called the *Slave Coast* near the Bight of Benign, they saw the slave ports that their ancestors made their final voyage from to North America, never to return home. Just to witness a place that served as the staging area for the greatest crime against humanity produced an eerie feeling in both Tony and Sugar, while the guide explained the history.

Not long after the tour ended, they caught a quick flight to Accra, Ghana where they had an authentic West African dinner at an upscale restaurant frequented by people of damn near every ethnic background. There were even a couple of celebrities from

America present. Morgan Freeman, who was there to shoot some new movie he starred in, was there with John Amos, who'd played James Evans from Goodtimes, who lived in Liberia nine months out of the year. There a couple of tables away, two well-known iconic African American actors sitting there dining as big as day with an entourage of Africans around them was a sight to see, to say the least. Following dinner, Tony and Sugar stepped to another part of the restaurant thinking they could mellow out, but to their surprise it was a colossal, full blown club packed with patrons.

"I'm going to run to the potty," Sugar said, before placing a kiss on Tony's lips.

"Okay, Baby Girl." After Tony sat down at the bar, a tall African who looked like the cat who played Shaka's character in the movie *Shaka Zulu*, came and sat down a few seats down from him. At first Tony didn't pay the man any attention, even when he noticed a few stares at him. Little did this man know, however, he was being sized up due to Tony recalling the tour guide's admonitions of roving gangs who preyed on tourists inside and outside the city. Finally, the man came and sat next to Tony who was now on heightened alert.

"You're an American, aren't you?" the man asked, smiling.

"Yes," Tony replied, staring him directly into his eyes with a serious look. "Why?"

"You have the look," he said, still smiling.

"And you look like an African," Tony replied. The man laughed. Tony didn't.

"Yep. There you have me. I am an African," he said, before downing his drink. "You're also a Marine." Tony looked at the tat on his forearm and realized it gave him away.

"My markings gave me a way, aye?" Tony grinned, but he was still wary. He didn't quite know what to make of this cat or his intentions, if any. He continued to keep an eye on him and one eye out for Sugar who was known to go on extended stays in the lady's room.

"Yep. But only a man who is a fellow Marine would know that to know what your markings mean."

"This is true. Were you in the Corp?"

"Yes. But the British version. The Royal Marines. Did five years with two tours in Afghanistan before making my quick exit to pursue bigger and better things in life than fighting people who had every right to kill us."

"Bigger and better things here in Africa?"

"Yep. You would be surprised of the things Africa has to offer. But I know. I know. Living in America, you are trained to believe we are all a bunch of jungle bunnies running around in the jungle with bones in our noses." Tony laughed.

"Well, to be honest with you, if I hadn't been in this neck of the woods before on tour to know better, I would probably be inclined to believe some ignorant shit like that," Tony said with a chuckle.

"I'm Ike," the tall African said, extending his hand.

"I'm Tony." The two engaged in a firm manly handshake staring into one another's eyes without blinking - the kind of handshake where men tested each other's strength and weakness. It's an alpha male thing. Seconds later Sugar returned.

"So is this the Queen?" Ike asked as he stood back to his feet to show his respect.

"Yes," Tony replied guardedly. "This is the Queen, alright. Baby Girl, this is Ike. Ike this is my wife, Constance."

"Well, hello. Are you from Africa?"

"No. I'm from Orlando, Florida," Sugar quipped. Ike laughed.

"Disney World, aye? Or the land of the sunshine. You sure look African to me, however. I guess that is a testament to the strong genes of our ancestors." Sugar smiled.

"Something like that. And yeah, we all have roots somewhere here in Africa," Sugar said, before she sat down.

"And you look like your ancestors came from West Africa."

"You know, my grandmother once mentioned to me that is where our relatives came from."

"Is that right? That really isn't surprising since most of the slaves who made the unfortunate voyage to America came from this region. Speaking of slavery, did you guys tour the coast?"

"Yes, we did," Tony said, "And it was the most eerie, uneasy feeling I ever experienced and I've been to damn near every country and landmark in the world, even those places where mass murders took place."

"Yes. And that uneasy feeling came from the spirit of our restless ancestors haunting that coast. So, what are you two here on, business, pleasure or both? Oh wait! Before you answer that. Can I buy you two a drink?"

"No, I'm good," Tony replied. "Baby Girl, you want a drink?"

"Sure."

"Waiter, can we get some service, please, sir?" Ike demanded. "This young lady needs a drink."

"I'll take a Hennessy on the rocks, please," Sugar said.

"And I will take a White Russian, sir. Okay, I was saying?"

"What was our business here," Tony answered.

"Oh yeah. So it is business or pleasure or both?"

"Pleasure, but I'm always looking for a business opportunity."

"Yes. And you are in the right place. Liberia is bustling with promising business opportunities with that American trained female dog in office."

"Wow. Why does she have to be a bitch?" Sugar asked.

"Well, let's just say I have my personal reasons. But I hope I didn't offend you," he said, touching Sugar's hand.

50

"No. I'm not offended. I'm sure you have your reasons."

"Yes. I have my reasons. Let's just say, she's made things a little difficult for my business interests. So difficult, I may have to ponder relocating from this area."

"Well, nothing good lasts forever," Tony said from experience. "You have to get shit while you can before it runs its course."

"Yes. You are correct. That reminds me of the African proverb: *Even the sun sets on the wayfarer in its appointed time.*"

"If you don't mind me asking, what is your business?" Tony asked.

"A little bit of this. A little bit of that. But mostly diamonds."

"Really?"

"Yep."

"You mean like blood diamonds?" Ike laughed.

"I think you've been watching one too many movies, Tony."

"Well, okay. Conflict diamonds." Ike laughed again, this time even louder.

"Again, you have watched one too many movies, my brother. Right now there is no conflict of any kind. In fact, presently, things are relatively peaceful here in the Motherland, for now anyway. I have positioned myself to take full advantage of an opportunity I was given while serving the great nation of Britain. For centuries, the Europeans have come here with their exploitation bullshit and cornered the market on the diamonds. In fact, they've done this for centuries. Over in the Congo, where my product comes from, millions of Africans died harvesting those diamonds at the hands of the Dutch. Millions more had their hands chopped off with machetes for not working fast enough. But, the new era of political change in this part of the world has presented the African with opportunities they did not have in times gone by. I guess you can say I was born in the right place at the right time," Ike said before downing his drink.

"So this business is lucrative, I take it," Tony asked.

"Is it lucrative?" Ike asked in an animated tone, before ordering another White Russian. "Let me ask you this. What is said to be a girl's best friend, in America?"

"Oh I can answer that," Sugar interjected. "A diamond." She showed off the one Tony bought her for her birthday. Ike and Tony laughed.

"Okay. And how many American women, like your Queen, have their best friends on their fingers? Not just in America, but in Europe and anywhere else there are white people. They love the stones. Get my point?"

"So, you are making a mint over here on diamonds?" Tony asked.

"No. Not over here. In the good old US of A. I only acquire them here and ship them out to America where they will end up in jewelry stores near you. They don't hold much value here unless you can ship them abroad."

"That easy, aye?" Tony asked.

"Well, I didn't say that," Ike said, laughing. "But easy enough. And well worth it. But hey, enough of this talk about diamonds and money. You guys are here to have fun. What are you doing tomorrow?"

"We will stay the night and head back to Liberia some time tomorrow."

"Why are you leaving so soon? There isn't shit in Liberia. Ghana is the place you want to be."

"We have a room there and we kinda like it," Tony said.

"Okay. Can I convince you guys to stay at least one more day in Ghana? I promise you it will be well worth it." Tony looked at Sugar to get her input.

"Well, sweetie? It's up to you."

"Sure. I'm fine with that, Bae."

"Okay. It's settled!" Ike said, excitedly. "There is a fantastic party I'm throwing in my home tomorrow evening that you must not miss. We are turning up Nigerian style," he said, before downing his drink. "Here is my business card. You can reach me on this number. Make sure you call me tomorrow morning so me and my woman, Samira, can take you on a little tour."

"Okay. Cool," Tony said.

"It was nice talking with you two. I'm going to have to return for the evening. See you tomorrow, bright and early," he said, before walking away.

Early the next morning, Tony placed a call to Ike who was already downstairs in the hotel's lobby.

"Hello, my brother. Are you and your Queen ready?" Ike asked.

"Yeah, bruh, we are ready. Give me five minutes. The Queen is kinda slow, you know." Ike laughed.

"Yes. That's not just your Queen, if that gives you some solace. That's in their nature," Ike said, looking over at his wife who looked like the lighter version of the African supermodel, Iman.

"Well, I'm glad to hear that I'm not the only cat in the world who has to deal with this," he said smiling. Ike laughed. He, like Tony, truly didn't mind the process because they knew when their women emerged from their mirrors and extended grooming, they were going to be immaculate. "We will be down in a minute, bruh. At least that's the plan," Tony said before hanging up. "Baby Girl, Ike is downstairs. How much longer you gone be?"

"Oh chill out, Bae. I'm coming. Ike will just have to wait a little bit longer," she said, as she put the finishing touches on her hair. A few minutes later, she and Tony walked downstairs where Ike and his woman were waiting in the lobby.

"Tony, Constance, this is my wife, Samira. Samira, this is Tony and Constance - the people I was telling you about last night."

"Hello. So nice to meet you!" Samira said.

"Nice to meet you too," Sugar replied.

"So have you been shopping yet?" Samira asked, excitedly.

"Well, not quite." Sugar looked over at Tony. "But I plan to real soon." Sugar chuckled.

"Really? Well, you will love the shops here in Ghana. We have stores here that can put shops in Paris to shame!"

"Awww damn!" Tony said. "She's found herself a shopping buddy." Ike laughed.

"My sentiments exactly," Ike replied. "That could be good for us, however. Let them shop while we take a tour of the city. Samira, you two go do all the shopping you want, while Tony and I go do some male bonding. And honey, take the bodyguards with you."

"Why don't you take them with you," Samira quipped. "You need them more than we do. We are covered," she said revealing a sub machine gun pistol in her purse.

"Samira, I think we're going to get along just fine," Sugar said, smiling.

"Precious! Don't be difficult here," Ike said giving her that look.

"Oooo-Kaaay. But you warn them to keep up and not to be waiting around for us to rush our shopping."

"Tell me if they do this and I will cut their heads off and feed them to the hyenas," Ike said jokingly, before placing a kiss on her cheek.

"No! You mean I will cut off their heads and feed them to the hyenas myself," she said before she and Sugar walked away.

"Be nice, woman," Ike jokingly yelled as they exited the lobby.

"Ike, I have a question. Why is your woman walking around with a fully automatic HKK in her purse?" Tony asked with a raised eyebrow. Ike laughed.

"It is a long story, my brother. I will tell you all about it soon."

"But they are not in any danger, are they?"

"No. No, of course not. They are fine. You would have to know about Samira's background to understand why she's armed like that. Again, we will talk. But I can assure you, your wife is safe with my Samira."

After the limo driver did a tour through town, he took Ike and Tony to a small airstrip where a helicopter was waiting.

"Now for the best part of the tour of the Motherland," Ike said, smiling. "I have something I want you to see, my brother."

"Okay. But do we have to fly?" Tony asked with a slight frown.

"Yes. Where we are going, it is not accessible to automobiles. Besides, it would take us over 11 hours by car. What's wrong, Tony? You dislike flying?"

"Dislike is an understatement. I detest flying." Ike laughed.

"That's interesting."

"Why is that interesting?" Tony asked.

"It's interesting that a Jarhead would hate flying," Ike said with a chuckle.

"Well us Jarheads didn't have to fly a whole lot. At least not my unit which is why I bypassed the army and the air force." Ike laughed as they stepped on board the chopper.

"I can assure you, my brother. You are in good hands with Ike Quartier," Ike said as the blades of the helicopter began swirling before taking flight.

As the chopper came into full view of the activity below, the armed soldiers could be seen scurrying about in position, and the workers pushing wheelbarrows went about their business as if they didn't see the descending helicopter.

"Welcome to my diamond factory or as the street hustlers in America would say, my diamond trap," Ike said smiling. "Well, at least part of it. This is just the distribution point. The minds are in the Congo where I am banned for now." He grinned.

"Wow!" Tony sat in the chopper and scanned the area. From the ground, one would never think this place was tucked off in the cut. The vegetation that surrounded it was so dense the factory couldn't be seen unless it was by air.

"Now you see why we had to access it by air. In this business we have to use extreme caution. Right now there are people here in Africa and elsewhere who would like nothing better than to find this location. This is part of the risk," Ike said as he motioned for the pilot to turn off the chopper. "Let's exit, my brother, and take a tour."

As he and Tony exited the helicopter, the armed guards dressed in fatigues flanked them and stood stoned-faced with their watchful eyes surveying the jungle backdrop. Walking through the huge warehouse that looked more like a Sam's Club Store, Tony noticed bricks of what looked like coke lined up on crates with a forklift sitting nearby. On the other side of the room there were crates with assault rifles, hand grenades, ammo, and other munitions ready for shipment. In another part of the room there were flat screen TVs, computers, laptops, other appliances and all-terrain vehicles ready to go on the black market.

After Ike spoke with a man dressed in a white lab coat, holding a pen and a clipboard, he and Tony walked into another part of the warehouse. When Tony walked in he saw wheelbarrows filled with diamonds and some with gold bullion. While Ike spoke with another professorial looking cat, who wore and dressed in a white lab coat as well, Tony walked over to get a closer look at the precious stones and metals. He wore the same look of amazement on his face touring Ike's factory as when he toured Armando's coke factories in Bogota and Mexicali. It must have been over 50 million dollars' worth of diamonds in the wheelbarrows. *This man definitely has his hands in a lot of shit,* Tony thought.

"My brother," Ike called out to Tony. "Come." Tony wandered on over to Ike and the factory manager. "I want to introduce you to my uncle. Uncle Yahya, this is my friend, Tony."

"Nice to meet you, Tony," the older distinguished looking African said before shaking Tony's hand.

"So what do you think, my brother?" Ike asked.

"What do I think? I'm thinking I have never seen this many diamonds in my life. Not even in a movie," Tony said, looking at the precious stones in amazement. Ike laughed.

"Trust me. There are many more where these came from. Now do you see why we must take all precautions? I know people who would kill each and every one of us just to get their hands on the stones in here. Particularly a Russian asshole I know named Lavrov."

"I'm sure," Tony said. "I've known people back in Brooklyn, who would kill for far less. Now did you just say a Russian named Lavrov?"

"Yes. Yuri Lavrov. Nicknamed the Reaper. Have you heard of him before?"

"Yeah, I think I have. I think I heard of a Russian mafia cat based in New York by that name. I heard the Italians mention him. Is he giving you some grief?"

"Yes. Giving me grief is an understatement," Ike said with a chuckle. Tony could see the discomfort on his face at the mention of this Russian's name and he wondered why would that be the case for a powerful man like Ike. "But we will discuss that later," Ike continued. "We have a party to get ready for. And not just any party. A Nigerian party! Let us go, my brother. Uncle, I'm going to go now. We will talk later. Don't forget to come to the party tonight although I know you won't stay for long." Ike then embraced his uncle before he and Tony exited the factory to head back to the city.

Chapter 5
Diamonds Are a Gangster's Best Friend

The ballroom of Ike's mansion was decorated with expensive African art. The ribbons, balloons and ornaments were the colors of Africa: red, black, green, and yellow, giving the room a beautiful spectacle. The buffet table contained a mixture of West African cuisine and American. There was the African dish, Jalloh rice, Groundnut stew, samosas, spring rolls, barbequed Goat, meat kabobs, meat pies made with wild game, and various exotic fruits. On the American side there were burger sliders, chicken tenders, fried chicken, hot wings, deviled eggs, tuna and chicken salads, and pizza. The female wait staff and greeters all looked like they belonged in a supermodel magazine. They were all beautiful.

While the chefs stood around the buffet table giving a last minute examination of their culinary artwork, the security were pacing about the room as if they were going over mental notes of tonight's detail in their minds. The distinguished guests began to trickle in one by one until the ballroom was filled to capacity. Soon the crowd's overflow extended out to the back patio deck that surrounded a huge Olympic-size pool. When the party's host walked in with his lovely wife, accompanied by his new friends, Tony and his Queen, who were equally stunning, all eyes were trained on them.

"Ladies and gentlemen, and distinguished guests. May I have your attention please," Ike said as his deep thunderous voice silenced the room. "I want to introduce you to my guests and new friends from America. Tony and his lovely Queen, Constance. Come and give them a warm African greeting!" One by one the partygoers all came to personally meet and greet Tony and Sugar, which was something they were not used to in a party setting. Typically, in America, when people are introduced, the most one may get from them is a hello before they go back to what they were doing. But this was the African's demeanor. They were friendly, personable, warm, and patient.

"Constance, you look stunning tonight," Samira smiled and said. "Those new clothes you purchased from the bizarre fit you very well."

"Why thank you, Samira. And you look absolutely gorgeous yourself, honey." Sugar saw a lot of herself in Samira. They both had powerful men who were shot callers in their own realm. And they both possessed a ruthless side.

"Come. Let's go out where the women are congregating," Samira said, before she grabbed Sugar by her arm. It wasn't hard to see that Samira was a domineering woman. She didn't take no for an answer and there was an air of ruthlessness in her that someone like Sugar, who was no doubt ruthless herself, could pick up on.

There was more to Samira than met the eye. She was definitely a story untold. Her story started during the Liberian civil war in which Charles Taylor, Prince Johnson, and Samuel Doe were all locked in a violent power struggle. After Samira was taken captive by a gang of Samuel Doe's loyalists, she was raped for days on end. When she escaped, she became a fierce resistance fighter on the side of Charles Taylor, and later battling against him after he betrayed the revolution. She was so fierce and vicious in battle and struck such terror in her adversaries, she was given the nickname the Liberian Lioness.

She killed so many of Doe's men, and sometimes in the most heinous of ways, that for the duration of the war there was a million dollar bounty on her head. When the war was over, she would eventually take part in a resistance against Taylor who, in her eyes and many others, had betrayed the revolution. During an ambush in which she was the target, out of ammo, and the last survivor, she concluded she would kill herself rather than be taken captive. Ike, who was sent in on a covert mission by the

British government to help take down Taylor, killed the ten of Taylor's soldiers and rescued her. From that day, she and Ike were inseparable, pretty much like Sugar and Tony.

"Tony, come with me. I want to talk with you," Ike said before he led Tony to a huge VIP room that only had a few people inside who were government officials of Ghana, Liberia, Sierra Leone, and Nigeria, Ike's home country.

"Gentlemen, how are you all doing?" Ike asked as he embraced each of them. "I hope you are enjoying the festivities. I would like you all to meet my friend, Tony from America." After they all gave Tony a warm reception, Ike took him to the balcony with a beautiful ocean view in the background.

"So, how are you liking this Nigerian shindig as you say in America, my brother?"

"Oh it's like that, Ike!" he said, looking up at the starry African sky. "You put on one helluva party, bruh."

"Why thank you, sir. Glad you and Constance are enjoying yourselves. Now let me get straight to the point of why I brought you out here," he said before motioning the waitress over. "Honey, can you retrieve my friend and I a drink? I will take a white Russian and my friend here…"

"I will just take a non-alcoholic drink. Something sweet and fruity please." After the waitress walked off to grab their drinks, Ike continued.

"Okay. Now to the point. How would you like to go into the diamond business?"

"Me? The diamond business?" The question somewhat caught Tony off guard. The way his mind worked, he automatically assumed there was an angle of some kind.

"Yes. You," Ike said smiling.

"Well, sure. But that depends."

"Depends on what?"

"It depends on what kinda catch there is."

"Catch? There is no catch. I don't deal in catches. What you see with me is what you get. So again, there aren't any catches. Just a few caveats."

"Okay. And what are the caveats?" Ike paused as the waitress returned with their drinks. "Thank you, beautiful."

"Okay. The caveats are in this business people play for keeps. You recall me mentioning a Russian named Lavrov earlier today?"

"Yeah. I recall."

"Lavrov is the caveat. In fact, he is the only caveat to be concerned over at this time.

"Okay. So what would my role be?"

"Your role would be my role. I'm going to hand this business over to you lock, stock and barrel."

"Wait a minute. You mean to tell me that you will just hand this lucrative business over to me, just like that? I don't mean to be disrespectful in anyway, but what is your angle here, Ike?" Tony had been in the underworld too long to know that when a gangster gives another an offer that is seemingly too good to be true, it usually is. There was almost always an angle.

"I have no angle other than self-preservation. See, my brother, I am a billionaire who has his hands into all kinds of shit as you witnessed with your own eyes earlier today. I'm not hurting for anything. If I wanted to, I could walk away from everything tonight and never make another dime again in life and I will be fine, as well as all my descendants. This diamond business is lucrative, there is no question. But this Lavrov who just intercepted a shipment and slaughtered my couriers, I would rather give that business away than to let that muddafucking Devil from Europe take it. And this is why I am making you such an offer. If you don't accept, I understand."

"Okay. I see," Tony said. "You want me to be the straw owner?"

"Well, that is a way to look at it. But the difference is, this will be your business from the day you accept terms along with most of the profits. I will only take a small percentage….sort of like an investor. I have a couple of conditions, however. The people who I have employed, allow them to maintain their jobs and positions, including my uncle. The other term is to keep the operation here in Ghana."

"Okay, so let me get one final understanding. Upon my acceptance of terms, I just come into this business as the new owner and you as the CEO become retired upstairs?"

"Yes!" Ike said before he downed his drink."

"And the reason why you are doing this is because of self-preservation?"

"That is partly the reason. Sure enough I do not want some fucking piece of shit, unprincipled Russian who has no morals taking some shit I and other Africans built," Ike said with a righteous indignation. "These diamonds are a gift from the Creator, and it wouldn't be right for those whom he blessed to be the overseers to allow some Devil from Europe to take it over. See, unbeknown to many, Russia is one of the biggest diamond producers in the world, although the diamonds found there aren't of the same quality as the diamonds here in the Motherland. Lavrov, who is a greedy bastard, has set his sights on the stones my nation was blessed with, and I cannot allow him to prevail. So, I would rather hand this over to someone I like and above all trust, than to let him take it, which is what will eventually happen if I fail to follow through with a contingency plan. I know I hold power here. In fact, I hold more power than most of the western wanna be Presidents here on this continent. However, that power does not extend to America. At least not right now, but I'm working on it. You are my hope, Tony."

CATO

"But how do you know that you can trust me? We just met two days ago." Ike laughed and downed his drink before ordering another one.

"Well, I know I can trust you for three reasons. One, you are a fellow Jarhead. Two, I have an old wise lady here whom the spirits of my ancestors speak to, to confirm that you are trustworthy. Three, I did my homework on you last night. Your name is Antonio Stallworth and you are out of Brooklyn. You are a gangster and major cocaine kingpin who has a distribution network that stretches from the east coast all the way into California and on down into Florida. You were recently in Riker's Island jail for the murder of Nathan Ward, who headed a black syndicate in the five boroughs of Brooklyn. Shall I go on?"

"No," Tony said smiling. "It appears you really have done your homework. But I guess your source didn't tell you that I am no longer in that business?"

"No. That part they didn't divulge to me. But what I heard was enough to know that I have the right man for this business. You are like me in the sense that you are the consummate businessman who doesn't leave loose ends or take any shit. This is what will be needed to deal with the caveat I spoke about earlier. Do we have terms? Are you in?"

"Yes, tentatively. But before I am all the way in, tell me what else would be required of me."

"Okay. In the beginning, you will have to constantly travel here, which means it would be wise to purchase a home or a villa. The reason why you would have to travel here often is to make your presence known, and to make sure the business is running smoothly. You may even have to travel to the Congo in the future where the diamond mines are located. Recall earlier I told you I was banned from entering its borders?"

"Yes. And why is that?" Tony asked.

"Well, the President and I are former friends and business partners. That was before I started courting his oldest daughter who was crowned Miss Africa and is a well-known actress throughout the continent." Tony laughed.

"So you jeopardized a lucrative business and friendship over some ass? Typical." Ike laughed out loud.

"No. It's not what you think. I would never jeopardize my hard work over some ass, especially when there is too much here and elsewhere around the world. She and I were actually in love. The only reason why I'm not with her now is because she thought it was more important to obey her father's blessings than to live happily-ever-after with the love of her life, and that I understood. See, in Africa, family ties are strong and the children are beholding to their parents until death. We follow the blessings and admonitions of our parents even into adulthood, and she was no different."

"Oh. I see. Well, I'm puzzled on something, Ike. If these diamond mines are located in a nation you can no longer step foot in, why doesn't the President just take the shit over himself and cut you all the way out? Like, why does he need you in the picture anymore?"

"Good question, Stallworth. I like that. That means you are paying attention to know all angles here. Two reasons. The international community has put pressure on him not to centralize the diamonds after a U.N. agreement was reached following what you westerners called "the blood diamond" wars. Therefore, based on this agreement, he cannot profit from them or else there will be huge divestment of his nation. Two, I have some things on him that if it ever got out, he will be sitting next to Charles Taylor in a prison cell in the Hague as a war criminal ."

"Okay. I understand. So regarding this offer, with having me as the new owner and CEO, you want both President Kabila and Lavrov to think you bowed out?"

"Yes! Exactly," Ike said before downing the rest of his drink. "Now let me warn you, Tony. At first, Lavrov may be thrown off the scent trail, but he will recover quickly and get back on it. And what he's tried to do to me, he will no doubt do the same to you. However, the dangers for you will be higher being that you reside in the same city that he's based in. But I understand that you are a man who can handle himself well, so that I'm not worried about. But nonetheless, you would still have to take all precautions."

Tony stared off into space momentarily as the ominous signs of the gangsta shyt entered his mind. He knew that it was one thing in dealing with the Italian mafia, who other than some unannounced resentment of being subordinate to a moolie, the relationship was civil because their number one goal was making money. However, the Russians were different. Known for their penchant for brutality, they were on a whole nother level. Facing off with them, particularly this cat Lavrov, nicknamed the Reaper, Tony knew that it was a strong possibility that he would have to revert back to his own brutal past. In considering Ike's offer and the caveats involved, he also took into consideration his promise to Sugar that he would step down from his drug empire. However, Sugar knew better than anyone that he wouldn't remain idle and live the square life. She even urged him to find something to stimulate him just as much as the dope business did. But all that aside, Tony lived by a rule his o.g. uncle Walt once taught him. *Never let your woman keep you from making money.*

"One more question for you, Ike."

"Okay. shoot."

"How did Lavrov know your distribution points in the states, where the shipment was coming, and who the couriers would be?"

"See! This is what I like about you, my brother! You ask questions....the right questions which I have asked myself. As of right now, I'm not at all sure. After the last shipment was hijacked, I looked deeply into this matter to see who the traitor was in my ranks."

"So you have no clue as to who it is?"

"No. Not the slightest." Tony thought to himself. He knew that before he totally committed, or at the very least shortly thereafter, he would have to find out right away the identity of the rat.

"Okay, Ike. I accept your offer."

"Welcome aboard, my brother," he said, giving Tony a firm handshake. "I can assure you that this will be your last business venture, because soon you will have enough money to move to Africa with your Queen and never have to worry about anything else again in life other than the place and time the next party will be."

"That sounds like my kinda living. On straight baller status for life." Tony smiled.

"Congrats, my brother. I promise you. You have made the right choice. Now let's go back and join the party and have some fun before people start missing us."

Tens of thousands of miles away, in what was only supposed to be a vacation, Tony had found a replacement for his illicit hustle from the most unlikely of sources, in the most unlikely of places: in Africa, the cradle of civilization. Going back to his roots proved to be more than just reconnecting with something innate and deep down inside of him. It proved to be something that would give him a new sense of purpose, but this time minus the exploitation and degradation that came with his former hustle. However, some of the same rules that applied to that hustle applied to the current one he was set to go into. With something as international as the diamond trade and the many players and villains involved, the stakes were much higher now than they were when he flooded the streets of New York and beyond with his high quality coke. This time he would have an inevitable clash with men from a part of the world where life was cheap and death and brutality was the order of the day. This inevitable clash with the Russians would be the catalysts for some gangsta shyt.

In the wee hours of the morning, after the party was over and everyone returned to the homes and hotel rooms, Tony and Sugar laid across their hotel bed rehashing the party like no other they had just experienced a couple hours earlier. Sugar, who was feeling the effects of the many shots of hen and coke she imbibed, happily expressed how appreciative she was about the trip and even mentioned relocating to Ghana. It was then Tony broke the news to her about the business venture he had just officially entered into with Ike.

"I'm glad that you are enjoying yourself and ecstatic that you even wanna relocate here one day, because I have some good news that I'm sure you will have no issues with."

"Ummmm okay. I'm listening," she said as she began to monitor him closely.

"First of all, what kind of vibe did you get from Ike and his wife?"

"I get a good vibe from them. They're genuine. Samira is a little rough around the edges and I detect that comes from some shit she's been through, but all in all I really like them both. Why what's up?"

"Good. Ike gave me an offer tonight that I just could not refuse."

"And what's that?" she asked, still monitoring him closely.

"He handed over his diamond business to me. I'm talking the entire business."

"Ummm Ooooooo-Kay. But what strings are attached, Bae?"

"There aren't any."

"Wait a minute. He just met you a couple days ago and he just hands over a diamond business that I'm sure is worth hundreds of millions of dollars, and there aren't any strings attached?" Sugar's body language displayed a slight uneasiness. The news kind of caught her off guard as it did Tony when he first received the offer.

"Well, let me put it this way. I wouldn't necessarily call them strings. Just a caveat or two as he called it."

"Okay. Then what are the caveats?" Sugar continued to monitor him carefully.

"There's a powerful crime boss based in the states who's been trying to muscle in on his shit. So with himself out of the equation, he believes this will save the business and the wealth of Africa."

"Okay. But still. Why you? He couldn't just kill this muthafucka and be done with it to save his own shit? We are talking about major loot here with these diamonds. This crime boss who's been trying to Deebow his business, he will be trying to do the same to you once he find out you are Ike's stand-in, would he not?" Tony recognized the apprehension in her voice.

"Baby Girl, if it was that simple, I'm sure Ike would have done it already. This crime boss is connected with the Russian mafia. Besides all that, for Ike it isn't just about the money. If you noticed, Ike is more concerned with the preservation of his culture than anything else. A man like Ike could have moved to America or somewhere in Europe a long time ago, and left Africa a memory with the type of loot he's got. He has his hands in damn near everything, and is the boss of bosses here on this continent. Again, it's not all about the money to him. He sees the diamonds and the other mineral wealth here as a blessing from the Creator and that it would be a sin if he didn't use his wits, his wealth, power and influence to keep it out of the hands of Devils, as he termed it."

"Okay. I understand that, Bae. I'm just concerned about the risks for you. You just walked away from a business that was filled with risks, but at least you and I both knew all too well what they were. Remember the incident on the beach? I'm sure with an international hustle like these diamonds, there are unforeseen risks or at least some you are not used to."

"Baby Girl, how can I ever forget what happened on the beach?" he asked he as rolled over and kissed her. "But risks are risks in my book. Furthermore, I am not a newcomer on the international scene. Nor is this my first rodeo. I understand risks better than anyone and they are all the same. The consequences just have different levels of severity. The people who prevail are the ones who prepare for them the best."

"Yes, but the best way to prepare for them is to avoid the ones that are unnecessary, right?"

"This is true. That's if a person wants to live their life like that. I'm not that person. Everything we do or want in life has some risks involved. This diamond business I'm about to go off into, I can see Ike's vision. He is trying to protect and preserve something that transcends money and profits. Now there is nothing wrong with making money in the process and I would be lying to you if I told you that it wasn't a motivator, but there is something bigger at play here than just lining my pockets. I wanna do something that has a greater purpose than what I have done before. Fighting for a nation and killing people who never called me a nigger, let alone treated me like one, was not only the biggest mistake of my life, but it lacked purpose for me. This is an opportunity to make amends for that and to give my life a greater meaning."

"Okay Bae. This is partly why I love you. I'm with you till the end. Till they lower us into the ground." Deep down inside Sugar knew she would be at Tony's side no matter what he did to make money. She knew what and who she married: a gangster. And one she adored more than anything in the world.

"Thank you, Baby Girl. I knew you would have my back no matter what," he said before they kissed. Not long after their conversation about tonight, Tony and Sugar eventually fell asleep in each other's arms.

Early the next morning, Tony and Sugar met up with Ike and Samira for breakfast at their mansion before catching a quick flight back to Liberia. Today was the last day of their trip before they headed back to the crib. The trip to the Motherland produced more than Tony had bargained for. The opportunity that Ike extended to him was not only an opportunity of a lifetime, it was the answer to the boredom he discovered after handing over the crown to his underboss, Genie. However, little did Tony know, this new hustle wouldn't be too far off from his old one. It was still illegal and still had its share of haters who wanted what he had and would stop at nothing to take it, and that would serve as the catalyst for some gangsta shyt.

Chapter 6
First Order of Business: Finding a Rat

After the plane touched down at JFK airport, and finally came to a stop, sending Tony's heart rate back down to normal, he and Sugar grabbed their bags and were scooped up by their limo driver, Stanley. When Tony got back to Brooklyn, he found out that his issues with *perro loco* was one for the record books. Macky Boy had taken care of that business like the young prodigy professional that he was. What he did for Tony and Genie, had only added to the respect that they already had for him. He became an instant hero throughout the organization who would be next in line for the crown in the event Genie stepped down or suffered an untimely death.

The first thing Tony did regarding his new business was to make inquiries into Yuri Lavrov. Once he found out who some of Lavrov's business associates and underlings were, he had them trailed. He was hell bent on keeping this shit as clean and untangled as possible since something like this could become blown totally out of control, which was the last thing he wanted. The next order of business was to make plans to go back to Africa. It was time to smoke the rat out of its hole, and that needed to be done before a shipment could reach the shores of this country. After settling in with Sugar, Tony met up with Genie to explain to him what was about to take place and that he would need Macky Boy to travel to Africa with him.

"What's good, bruh?"

"Oh nothing, but selling this good coke," Genie quipped. Tony laughed and sat down at the bar. The empty club's jukebox played.

"So how was Africa?"

"Africa was like that, my brother. We really had a nice time. In fact, I'm going back the first of next week."

"Oh yeah? Must be a business opportunity there or sumpin,'" Genie said with a chuckle.

"Yep! A business opportunity like you wouldn't believe, bruh."

"Real talk?"

"Real talk. Try diamonds."

"Diamonds?"

"Yeah. Diamonds. A broad's best friend."

"How did you come across some shit like that, T? You were only there for a few days."

"I'm not exactly sure. But if you are a believer in fate, or even spirits, it was no accident. I was just in the right place, the right country, at the right time."

"So fill me in on the specifics."

"Well, I ran into this Nigerian gangster who gave me an offer I couldn't refuse. This man has his hands into everything imaginable. He did his homework on me and came to me with an offer to take over his diamond trade to keep this Russian mafia cat from taking it."

"A Russian mafia cat? What's his name?"

"His name is Lavrov. Yuri Lavrov. They call him the Reaper. Does that name ring a bell?"

"I've heard of him, T. He's a heavy hitter. Do you want me to put Macky Boy on it to find out more about him?"

"Yes. In fact, I was going to ask you for permission to let Macky travel to Africa with me when I go back. We have a rat we need to flush out. Some muthafucka is on Lavrov's payroll."

"No problem, T. But you don't have to get permission, bruh," Genie said, laughing before he downed his drink.

"No. Of course I do, bruh. This is your organization now."

"I know it's my organization, bruh. But this is your family. We are all family. This new venture you are about to go off into,

I am here to help you in any way I can. This family, including the muscle, is here at your disposal."

"I appreciate that, bruh. Much respect." Tony stood up and embraced his best friend. "I will get at you later, bruh."

"Okay. Bet."

***

When the plane touched down on the runway, a limo was there to pick he and Macky Boy up.

"How are you gentlemen doing this evening?" the limo driver said in a thick African accent.

"We're good," Tony answered.

"I was sent here on Mr. Quartier's orders to pick you up and take you to the villa he rented for you. Is there anywhere you would like to stop en route?"

"No. We are good. We would like to go straight to the villa, and get a shower and some rest after that flight." The limo driver nodded his head.

"I completely understand, sir," he said before pulling away. Within a half hour Tony and Macky Boy arrived at the villa. When they walked into their rooms, which were joined together, there was fruit, a full juice bar, and finger food all laid out in a manner that was totally Ike Quartier. A few minutes later, to their pleasant surprise, four beautiful African girls walked in.

"We are here to give you a sponge bath," one of them said in a soft sweet voice. Tony and Macky Boy looked at each other momentarily before Tony responded.

"That won't be necessary for me," he replied. "Macky Boy?"

"Uhh sure," he said before following them into the hot tub room. Tony walked into his room and hit a shower before collapsing into his bed.

The next day, Tony was awakened by a phone call.

"Hello."

"My brother, good morning."

"Morning, Ike."

"Let's go for a workout," Ike said as he tied his sneakers.

"Sure," Tony said as he looked at the clock which showed 5:30 am.

"Okay. I will be there at a quarter till to pick you up." Tony rolled over and laid there to gather his thoughts. The jet lag had his body totally thrown off. After a couple of minutes however, he hopped in the shower and then dressed in his workout clothes. At exactly a quarter till, Ike pulled up to the front of the villa and scooped he and Macky Boy up.

"My brother, good morning!" he said with excitement.

"Morning bruh."

"Are you enjoying this fresh air?"

"I always do. But I just have a little jet lag from the flight here."

"And that will soon pass once we get into this workout." When Ike pulled into his backyard, Tony was surprised to see how enormous it was. It looked like the African outback, only it was fully equipped with an obstacle course, pull-up bars, weights and a shooting range, similar to his own back home. After exiting Ike's ride, they did some stretching, then a jog before hitting the obstacle course. They went from the pull-up bars, to the weights, to a track with hurdles. Tony had finally found a cat who could keep up with him in a workout. Ike who was ten years Tony's senior, was in tremendous physical condition, which was a testament to his clean living, hardcore workouts and a strict vegan diet. Although he was 44 years old, he looked like he was 24. The only thing that slightly gave his age away was his battle-hardened face.

"Great workout aye, my brother?" a sweaty Ike asked, breathing slightly heavy.

"Yeah, bruh. I'm surprised I was able to keep up with you. I haven't worked out in a few days until now which is why I'm kinda breathing heavy here," Tony said with a chuckle.

"Well, I certainly could not tell. You worked out like a beast, my brother. I'm going to have to take you hunting out in the bush the next time we go out," Ike said smiling.

"Okay. I look forward to it, Ike," Tony replied with an apprehensive look on his face.

When the chopper touched down on the landing pad a few feet from the thick brush near the factory, Ike, Tony, and Macky Boy were met by the armed guards as they exited the aircraft.

"Hello, Mr. Quartier," a senior guard said.

"Hello, Colonel. How's everything?" Ike asked before shaking his hand.

"All is well, sir. The latest shipment arrived this morning."

"Okay, great. I want to introduce you to my friend and new business partner, Tony. Tony this is Colonel Kobani."

"Good to meet you, sir," the stocky colonel said as he shook Tony's hand.

"Likewise."

"Colonel this is the man you and the others will answer to from this day forward."

"Yes sir," Kobani said, looking at Tony as if to size him up.

"Okay, Tony, let's go inside to introduce you to the others." As they headed to the factory, Macky Boy quickly surveyed the area. He also kept a watchful eye on the guards and their commander who was hanging in behind them. Though Macky Boy was young, he had a gift for peeping out shit that others failed to pick up on, which is why Tony brought him along. Tony totally trusted the youngster's judgment. There was something telling Macky Boy that the Colonel was suspect and perhaps even the guards, but that was just his nature. He only trusted his instincts. When Ike informed the Colonel that he would have to answer to

Tony from now on, the expression on his face spoke what he would not dare to verbalize. The look reminded Macky of the look on the Professor's face when Sugar made the announcement that she was taking over in Tony's absence. It was the unmistakable look of envy and jealousy that typically had treachery hidden deeply away until it was time to rear its ugly head at the most opportune moment. Once inside the factory, Ike began introducing the others to Tony.

"Uncle, how are you today, sir?"

"I'm blessed, Ike."

"Great, uncle. Do you remember my friend Tony from America?"

"Yes, I do remember the fellow," he said smiling.

"Okay, good. From this day forward everyone will answer to him. He is my new business partner in charge of all aspects of the operation."

"Is that right?" the uncle said, smiling.

"Yes and I expect everyone to be totally subordinate to him. I trust his judgment and leadership."

"Oh yes. Of course, my nephew," he said with a smile. Congratulations, Mr. Tony." Tony smiled and nodded.

"Okay. Great," Ike said. "Is there anything else you would like to add, my brother?"

"No. I think you covered everything," Tony said. "But Mack and me would like to take a quick look around, if it's cool."

"Oh sure, Tony. This is your factory now. Do your thing." Tony and Macky Boy began touring the facility while Ike spoke privately with his uncle.

"Okay, Youngster, I want everything bugged. Every place tucked away out of sight, every crack and crevice and hiding spot, I want them bugged," Tony said as they walked around inspecting. "I even want the bathrooms bugged. If a mouse farts up in this bitch, I wanna hear how long and how often."

"Yes sir. Consider it done." Macky took a small pouch from his pocket that contained a box. Inside the box were small electronic bugs powerful enough that they could pick up conversations all the way in America. After planting the bugs in the places Tony had mentioned, Macky and Tony went back out to join Ike.

"Did you get acquainted with the place, Tony?"

"Yes."

"Okay. Well, is there's nothing else, let's get back to the city," Ike said before they departed the factory.

When they passed by the guard's post, Macky casually stuck a bug inside the crack of a board without them noticing it. As they boarded the chopper, and it lifted off the ground and into the air, the colonel stood there waving goodbye.

Back in the city, Ike treated Tony and Macky to dinner.

"So how are you feeling about this new business venture, my brother?"

"I'm excited, Ike," Tony responded while the waitress poured their drinks.

"I'm delighted to hear that. So what do you think of the people at the factory? What kind of vibe do you get from them?"

"To keep it real with you, I don't think they took the news that I was the new boss too well." Ike laughed before he took a sip of his lemonade.

"Of course. You're an American. But don't let that discourage you. Over time, they will get used to it."

"I hope so, Ike."

"What about my uncle? How do you feel about him?"

"I think your uncle will be cool no matter what. He strikes me as the loyal type. Death before dishonor."

"And you are right. My uncle is a war vet. He fought in Zimbabwe against the Europeans and their African puppets. To know his story would give you some insight on how far he's come. When he returned home he needed intensive therapy. Being out in the bush fighting in some of the most intense battles, turned him into something we were not expecting when came home. Uncle was a cold-blooded killer who was known for not taking any prisoners. By the grace of Allah and our efforts, he is now a mild-mannered, soft-spoken man who I have yet to see become angry in the 30 plus years since the war ended."

As Tony listened to Ike's uncle's struggles with readjusting to society after returning from war, he thought about his own ordeal after coming back from Afghanistan and Iraq. Those memories of having death all around, was one that the strongest minds could never completely shake. The best that one could hope for after experiencing it, rather than going on the psyche meds, was to learn how to cope with it. The human mind, though it is a remarkable organ capable of doing almost anything, it is not made to fully deal with all the blood, guts, dismembered, broken bodies, and dead children that comes with war and conflict. Perhaps the reason Tony was able to adjust to society better than anyone in his unit was because he never really stopped killing. When he came home, the skills he learned over there were still relevant and useful.

"My brother, are you with us?" Ike asked, looking him in his eyes.

"Yeah, I'm here," Tony responded. Ike smiled.

"You drifted back, didn't you?"

"Yeah, Ike, I do that from time to time."

"I understand. I too have my moments." Ike took a sip from his drink. "So what are you and Macky's plans for the evening, my brother?"

"Oh, I have no plans, Ike. I guess I will play it by ear."

"Okay, good. I have somewhere I would like to take you and the youngster."

"That's what's up. What time?"

"It will be a little later this evening. Perhaps 7 ish?"

"Okay. Bet."

Later that evening around 7, Ike had his chauffeur to scoop Tony and Macky up and take them to a remote location down a long, winding dirt road surrounded by jungle vegetation. As soon as the limo pulled up to this building, they could hear screams and yelling coming from inside. When Tony and Macky walked in, there was Ike, a couple of his soldiers, and Colonel Kobani standing in front of a man named Jalloh, who was hanging upside down with his feet and arms tied behind his back over a pit with Cobras coiled underneath him. He was bloody, sweaty and his eyes displayed pure terror as Tony and Macky looked on stoically without even making a facial expression.

"My brother, how are you tonight? Glad you could make it," Ike said, smiling. "This is not what I had in mind for us tonight, but it was some last minute business that required my immediate attention. This won't take long," he said before training his attention back on the man in chains. "Okay, mudderfucka, I'm going to give you an opportunity to do something important for the first time in your insignificant existence. I'm going to allow you to save your own life here tonight. Where are my muddafuckin' stones? And who was the white man you were speaking with in town?"

"I swear on my life, sir! I don't have any stones in my possession! The white man whom I met in town was a tourist asking questions regarding directions! It was just a friendly, but harmless, exchange between he and I! I swear, Mr. Quartier! I don't know him and I never took any stones, sir!"

"Liar!" Colonel Kobani yelled. "One of my soldiers saw you take some stones and then head back into town to meet with this white devil!"

"No! No! Your soldier did not see me take anything of the kind!"

"We suspect that this man who worked in the factory took some stones and passed them off to a buyer," Ike said to Tony. "We also suspect that he is a spy for Lavrov." Tony nodded his head as he noticed he had started to piss on himself.

"May I try something, Ike?" Tony asked.

"Sure." Tony walked and looked down at the pit of the angry Cobras who were moving about in a frenzy. They were poised to strike the first thing that moved within their striking range and envenom it perhaps with a full dose of deadly neuro/hemotoxic poison.

"Sir, look. We don't want to kill you here tonight. We want to work with you to resolve this situation," Tony said to the man calmly. "Do you have a family?"

"Yes! Yes! I have two kids and a wife!" he answered frantically.

"Okay, good. I have a wife also. But I don't have any kids. Not yet anyway. However, if I did and was in your shoes, I would come clean. I am in charge of this operation now and therefore I call the shots. However, your life is in your own hands. Those Cobras won't be as forgiving as I am." The man looked down at the agitated snakes who moved about below ready to strike anything that moved. "Tell us what you did with the stones and the identity of the man who you spoke with in town and you will go back home to your family, safe and in one piece."

"Sir, I did not take any stones I tell you!" he yelled. "Nor did I meet with any white man! I am not a thief and I don't know of any white man!" he said forcefully. "If I thought it could save my life to tell you, then that is just what I would. But I am being truthful!" Tony turned and looked at Macky and Ike.

"This man is telling the truth,'" Tony said, stepping away from him.

"Liar!" Colonel Kobani said before swinging a machete that severed the rope that suspended the man in the air away from the deadly serpents. Before Jalloh could hit the ground he was struck several times. His high pitched screams could be heard all over the building. But it did not deter the Cobras who continued to peck him over and over with such force, it sounded like he was being punched by grown men. Even after he ceased all movement from the paralysis and shock that had set in, and foaming from the mouth, they were still striking him continuously without pause.

"What was the hurry?" Tony asked the Colonel.

"He was a fucking liar!" the Colonel shot back.

"I don't think he was a liar, Colonel. And we will never know that for sure, now will we? But listen here! From here on out, you don't do shit until I tell you! Is this understood?" Tony said, looking him in his eyes with a no nonsense look on his face.

"Yes. Understood," Kobani said, reluctantly. Tony looked over at Macky as if they were communicating through mental telepathy. Macky then cut his eyes over at Kobani and gave him a cold look. If looks could kill.

"Well, I guess we are finished here," Ike said. He then turned to Kobani. "Kobani, I want this man's family compensated from the fund. Is this understood?"

"Yes sir."

"What is the fund?" Tony asked.

"It is a trust that we have for our people's families just in case something happens to them," Ike replied.

"Take it out of the Colonel's pay."

"Huh?" Ike asked with a bewildered look on his face. The Colonel too had the same look on his face.

"This is my show now, right?" Tony said, pointing to himself.

"Yes, my brother, it is your show now."

"Well, okay. The compensation will come out of the Colonel's pay."

"Okay. It is settled," Ike said. "You heard him, Kobani. You will compensate this man's family from your own trust."

"But sir."

"But nothing, Kobani! The matter is settled!"

"Yes, sir," he said, looking at Tony with a look of resentment. However, he dared not say anything out of the way. Little did he know, Tony had visions of throwing him in that pit alongside the man he just killed. But he resisted the urge because his instincts told him there was a reason why Kobani wanted to silence this man and he needed to keep him alive long enough to find out.

"My brother, I hope you didn't feel I was stepping on your toes back there," Ike said as the female waitress brought him a drink.

"No, not at all. I'm just curious as to why Kobani was in such a rush to kill the dude."

"Weren't you going to kill him anyway?" Ike smiled and asked with a raised eyebrow.

"No, I was going to let him go. But I was going to keep an eye on him. Now I'm going to keep an eye on the man who was in a rush to kill him. Or silence him."

"Really? You were going to let him go?"

"Yes. He wasn't lying. A man who was lying would have eventually cracked and come clean especially with a pit full of Cobras directly up under him. He was telling the truth."

"But you could be wrong," Ike said, smiling."

"About dude or Kobani?"

"Both."

"This is true. But I don't think I'm wrong on either."

"Were you willing to take a chance on being wrong about Jalloh, the dead man?"

"Yes," Tony replied. "I don't think the consequences would have been high if my judgment was wrong about him. Not nearly as high if you are wrong about the Colonel. Sooner or later we would have found out what we wanted to know about Jalloh. Now we will have to find out what we need to know about the Colonel."

"We will see," Ike said. "I think Kobani is a man of integrity. But who knows. It wouldn't be the first time my judgment was flawed. So on a much lighter note, do have you any prospects on a home here in Ghana yet, my brother?" Ike asked before downing his cognac and Goat milk chaser.

"Not at all. I was hoping you would help me out on that. But hold up. I do recall a nice crib I saw on the outskirts of town earlier today."

"I think I know exactly which one you are speaking of. It has the Spanish style rooftop, right?" Ike asked smiling.

"Yes! That is the one. Is it empty?"

"No. Empty as in is anyone staying there?"

"Yes."

"No, but it will be tomorrow."

"No, Ike. If there is someone already staying in it…"

"No. It is settled. The house is yours."

"Well, out of curiosity, who does it belong to?" Ike grinned and sipped his drink before answering.

"It belongs to me, but Kobani is living there for free. I have another home for him. One that is more suitable for a man like him." Tony chuckled and did not go any further with it. He knew Kobani would be pissed, but he didn't give a fuck.

Early the next morning Tony, Macky, and Ike worked out. After lunch, Tony sat in his room listening to the goings on inside the factory. The bugs Macky planted were working like a charm. Tony could hear everything going on clearly as if he was standing right there. Kobani could be heard levying profanities about Tony being in charge and it was much to Tony's amusement.

Kobani reminded him of a drill sergeant during boot camp on Parris Island. The recruits called him ole Iron Ass because he had shrapnel lodged in his ass from Vietnam that was never removed. When he walked through metal detectors he would set them off. The one thing everyone knew about ole Iron Ass was he was one mean muthafucka whose breath smelled like shit. Kobani was his clone. After listening to the activity a few more minutes, which seemed relatively harmless, Tony turned off the listening device and put it on record before placing a call to his boo who he had begun to miss something serious.

"Hey Bae!" Sugar said into the phone.

"Hey Boo!" Tony said smiling. 'What are you doing?"

"I'm about to get my hair done. And you?"

"All is well. Just getting some things taken care of before I leave for home. Later today, Ike is going to give me a tour of a crib I saw that I like."

"Oh yeah."

"Yeah, sweetie."

"How does it look?"

"From the outside it looks nice. That's all I saw. But it does have a huge Olympic-sized pool."

"Oh ok. Make sure you send me some pics."

"Okay, Baby Girl. So is everything else alright?"

"Yeah. Everything is fine. My brother will be getting out in a couple of weeks and I'm kinda worried about him once he's in the free world."

"Oh yeah? That's what's up."

"Tony, I wanna make sure he is on the right track when he gets out. You think we have something for him to do so he can get on his feet?"

"Yeah, Baby Girl, I'm sure we have something for him."

"Okay, Bae. Thanks. I really want him to leave Orlando. Better yet, I want him to leave Florida, period. He won't ever be able to get on his feet there with his record. Those Crackers there are notorious for holding a black man's past against him for life."

"Yeah, I know. We got him though, sweetie. That's if you can convince him to leave Florida and come this way."

"Yeah, I know. He's never been out of Florida before, except when he traveled to see his girl."

"Alright Boo. I gotta go get dressed. Ike will be here in a few minutes."

"Okay, Bae. I'll talk to you later. Don't forget to send the pics of the house now. You know I gotta give my input." Tony smiled.

"Okay, baby, I won't. Talk to you later."

Chapter 7
The Lavrov Connection

Tony hung up and headed to the closet to retrieve some clothes, he looked out of the window and noticed a white man walking across the street and into the hotel's bar. This was the same white man who he'd seen at least twice since he arrived. *I wonder is that the same white man that Kobani claimed one of his men saw Jalloh speaking with,* Tony thought to himself.

After quickly putting on his clothes, Tony decided to go to the hotel bar to investigate further. Once he made it downstairs, he saw the tall imposing white man, with slicked back hair and a ponytail, sitting at the bar drinking by himself. He had the look of someone who was trying to pass himself off as a tourist, but his body language spoke otherwise. This man looked almost as if he was home. Tony watched him carefully, then walked over to the bar and sat down a few seats away from him as the man spoke with someone on his phone. When he noticed Tony sitting next to him, he told the person he was talking to that he would get back with them later. After ordering another drink he downed it then ordered another one. When the bartender passed him his drink he pretended as if he didn't see Tony sitting there. Tony knew he saw him, but he too continued to play as if he wasn't there either. When the man downed his drink and ordered another one, a tall white female who looked like Brigitte Nielsen, who played the wife of the Russian boxer Ivan Drago in the movie *Rocky IV*, walked in and sat down up under him. Although she was dressed in business attire, she still had that high dollar prostitute aura about her. After he handed her some money and said something to her that Tony could not quite make out, the tall Amazon kissed him on his cheek and walked back out.

After a few more minutes of pretending he didn't see the only person in the bar sitting next to him, the man finally broke his silence.

"Good morning, sir," he said in a European accent.

"Morning."

"An American." The man smiled .

"A European," Tony quipped. The man smiled and downed his drink.

"So how long have you been here?" he asked.

"Probably about as long as you been here," Tony replied. The man laughed again before ordering another drink.

"I bet you're a New Yorker."

"And I bet you're a Russian," Tony said with a slight grin.

"Hmmm. Did my accent give me away?"

"No. The hammer and cycle." The man glanced at his tattoo on his forearm and smiled.

"So are you enjoying your stay here in Ghana?"

"I better. I paid a handsome ransom for a villa," Tony said.

"Oh, so you're an implant. Okay. I love this place, but not enough to move here. They haven't gotten their shit together here yet," he said before motioning for the bartender. "So how long have you lived here?"

"I never said I lived here."

"Oh okay. Of course you didn't. My apologies. How long have you been visiting here?"

"Long enough to know it's hot as hell here."

"Oh okay. So you just arrived here. I knew it was hot when the plane entered the Ghanaian airspace," he said with a chuckle. "So don't tell me. You retired and moved abroad. Is that the case?"

"Something like that," Tony said guardedly. Recognizing the seemingly harmless, probing nature of his questions, he didn't want to give him much.

"Well, I don't mean any offense, but you look a little too young to be on a permanent fishing trip," the Russian said smiling.

"No offense taken. Let's just say I made a few sound investments here and there."

"Oh really? Do tell. I have yet to make a sound investment that will send me on a permanent vacation. What's your formula?" he asked. Tony's mind drifted back to how he used to get it how he lived. Images of the many dead bodies of the marks and his rivals flashed in his mind.

"My formula was leave no stones unturned, no loose ends untied by handling my business."

"Hmmm. That sounds like a winning formula."

"It worked for me. Tried and tested. So now that you know why I'm here. What brings you here to Africa?"

"I'm in the import/export business. I work for a diamond dealer in the states."

"Oh okay. So you are into diamonds."

"Yes. A woman's best friend," he said, just as his Amazon broad walked in.

"So what does that entail? I mean, do you buy or distribute?"

"I do both," he said as his girl sat on his knee, looking Tony up and down."

"Sunshine, this is…"

"I'm Antonio," Tony interjected.

"Nice to meet you," she said, shaking his hand. Tony looked down at her hand which was smothered in diamonds. The Russian saw Tony's reaction to them.

"Pretty, aren't they?" He smiled again. Tony nodded. "I told you diamonds are a girl's best friend," he said before downing his final drink and standing up. "Well, friend, good meeting you. I have to go now. I have a meeting with a broker here shortly." His girl stood up with her eyes still on Tony.

"Good meeting you too." Tony shook his hand. Before walking out of the bar, the Russian turned back to Tony.

"Here is my card. Whenever you are back in the states, look me up. Maybe we can grab a drink or two together," he said before he and his broad walked out of the bar. Tony looked at the card and saw the name Vladimir. Stuffing the business card into his wallet, he thought to himself, *Vladimir. You're in the diamond business too, aye?*

Ike and Tony pulled up to the Spanish-style house that had been lived in by Colonel Kobani, which was now Tony's new crib. Kobani was there to remove the last of his belongings on to a moving truck. As Tony walked passed him, Kobani gave him a look that would have killed if it had been a bullet.

"Hello, Colonel. Good morning," Ike said.

"Good morning, sir," Kobani said, as the two movers placed a huge dresser into the back of the moving truck.

"Damn!" Tony said looking around in amazement. "This crib looks 100% better than it does from the outside."

"You mean you don't like the way the exterior looks?" Ike asked.

"No. I like it, bruh. It just looks so much better inside. Surprisingly better," Tony said as he walked around inspecting.

"Yes. It's a nice villa," Ike said smiling. "My Samira designed it herself, believe it or not. This was our first home."

"Yeah, well she knew what she was doing. My Sugar is going to really dig this spot," Tony replied before he pulled out his phone and started taking pictures. "Got a question for you, Ike."

"And what's that, my brother?"

"Not that I really give a shit, but where is Kobani going to stay now? I recall you saying he will stay in his rightful place. What did you mean by that?"

"He will stay with Jalloh's widow and family. Not in the same house, of course. That would be disrespectful to his memory, but in a loft connected to the house.

"No shit?" Tony said, looking at Ike with smiling.

"No shit." Ike's expression was serious. "Jalloh and Kobani are from the same tribe. Their customs calls for this. And sadly, I had to enforce it. When it comes to their customs, however, Kobani is a deviant, though a good man."

"Okay. It all makes sense. He kills the bread winner of the family unjustifiably, now he has to stand in for him."

"Yes. That is the logic. Even if it wasn't the custom, I would have forced him to do it anyway. It is only right. Hopefully, Jalloh's boys don't kill his ass," Ike said. "So, my brother, what do you think? Are you going to take it?"

"No doubt. I want it."

"Okay then. It's yours. You are now a resident of Ghana." Ike shook his hand.

On the ride back to the hotel, Tony couldn't take his eyes off Vladimir's card.

"Is there something on your mind, my brother?" Ike asked.

"Yeah. Earlier I met a Russian in the bar at the hotel and he gave me this business card."

"Oh yeah? Did you speak with him?"

"Yes. He told me his business was diamonds."

"Did he now?"

"Yes. When I first saw him, I recalled what Kobani said about Jalloh meeting with some white man in town."

"What did he look like?" Ike asked as his eyes switched between Tony and the road.

"He was tall and had his hair slicked back in a ponytail. He also had a hammer and cycle tat on his forearm."

"Hmmm. Russian," Ike said, almost to himself. "And he said he was in the diamond business you say?"

"Yes. A buyer and distributor."

"I'm wondering who this man is, because no business is done here without my knowledge or blessing. This man, did he say where he was staying?"

"No, but I already have my man, Macky, tailing him. There was just something about him that I needed to know more about," Tony said as the limo pulled into the hotel's parking lot.

Sitting at the window inside his hotel room looking through a pair of binoculars, Macky's eyes were trained on the entrance-way of the sister hotel across the street, which was the last whereabouts of Vladimir. After sitting there for about half an hour of constant vigil at the window, Macky decided to take a quick break. After retrieving some fresh African brewed coffee and tea cakes that room service had brought him, he went back to the window to resume his surveillance. As he sat there sipping on the strong, steaming hot coffee and taking small nibbles from the cake he held in his off hand, he steadily peered through the binoculars. After an alert came across the computer monitor connected to a GPS tracking system, Macky sat still like a predator in wait, bracing for the arrival of one of the cars he stuck a tracking device on at the diamond factory. According to the monitor, the vehicle was about 3 miles out and approaching in the direction of the hotel.

Five minutes after the monitor alerted Macky of the incoming vehicle, the Euro Mercedes Benz pulled up in front of the hotel. After it came to a stop, the driver, wearing a derby on his head and dressed in a suit, quickly stepped out of the vehicle and handed a valet the keys and rushed inside the hotel. This man who moved with a slight limp, walked inside the hotel so fast, Macky couldn't quite make him out. And the way he acted, that was his goal. For several minutes, Macky sat there patiently with his eyes still peeled through the binoculars and sipping on the coffee which had now become lukewarm.

A few minutes later, there was movement. A tall white man with a ponytail walked out with the mystery person talking and laughing. The mystery person who wore the dark shades and the old man derby pulled down on his head, Macky still couldn't quite make out. Somewhat frustrated that he couldn't make this cat out, Macky threw his binoculars down on the bed and rushed down to the lobby to perhaps get a better look at who this man was. When he exited the elevator and walked to the lobby's exit, the man was gone, and the white man whom he spoke with stood outside smoking a cigarette.

"Fuck!" Macky said under his breath. He then walked quietly back inside the lobby so as not to give himself away to the Russian.

This time, the mystery man had evaded detection. The fact that he went through the pains of hiding his identity, Macky's instincts told him that there was definitely a Lavrov connection and he was hell bent on finding out the extent of it and who the players were.

Chapter 8
The First Shipment: Tony's Show Now

Early the next morning, as a new shipment of diamonds arrived, a phalanx of armed men waited on the airstrip. Once the carts containing the precious cargo were removed from the plane and transferred inside the factory, the plane fueled up before taking off. The armed men walked around outside of the factory like soldier ants guarding the nest and their Queen.

Inside the factory, Tony stood with Ike's uncle as he oversaw the workers begin the painstaking process of examining the stones to make sure they were all real. The diamonds numbered about a couple hundred thousand, worth about $20 million wholesale. After a tedious and thorough examination, the diamonds would be put on a FedEx plane and shipped to the states. Ike had a serious system going. All of the FedEx pilots were on the take. On one shipment alone they made twice their yearly salary. Once the diamonds arrived in the states, Ike had men on the ground who intercepted them and took them to one of many stash houses overseen by a Nigerian cousin named Peter.

The last shipment that was hijacked had made it off the plane and was on its way to one of the stash houses when the courier's van was run off the road and they were subsequently killed. Ike suffered a $10 million loss. Tony made a few changes, however. Ike's men on the ground were replaced with his own. After this shipment, Ike's cousin, Peter, would be dismissed. The only people Tony would retain were the FedEx pilots. He was going to make sure that this first shipment and every other shipment thereafter was going to go off without a hitch. No one was going to just take some shit away from him, even if that meant he had to fly back to the states with it.

When the FedEx plane's tires touched down on the runway, Tony's heart rate returned to normal. The pilot was given an extra stack to allow Tony to fly along with the shipment. Outside the airport, Genie's muscle armed with assault rifles, waiting in their vehicles, scanned the area from east to west, with a careful eye. As the snow began to fall, the three men on the ground, dressed in bomber jackets, placed the huge cylindrical containers of diamonds on the back of the waiting truck. Before Tony climbed in, he handed the men their pay before the driver drove away.

While the truck carrying the precious cargo traveled up the highway, the song *Diamonds* by Rihanna played appropriately from the speakers. Two of the four SUV caravan, led by Cassadine, the new head of the muscle, followed close in behind them. There were two more truckloads of men in front. Tony surveyed the area as the talkative driver rattled on about the weather. His instincts told him that there wasn't going to be an attempt on this shipment, but he nonetheless remained vigilant. If there was going to be an attempt, the only other logical place would either be at the stash house or near it. If, when or wherever, Tony concluded that those muthafuckas had better come with their A game this time, because unlike Ike, he was prepared for whatever.

Once the truck's GPS indicated that they were less than a mile from the stash house, Tony radioed Cassadine and reminded him to keep his eyes peeled. After going about a mile down the winding dirt road, the stash house, a white compound that looked more like one of those buildings you would see near an airport hangar, came into full view.

"Make a pass and come back through," Tony told the driver after seeing a black Hummer sitting about 400 yards away on the side of the road. Feeling some kind of way about it, Tony hit Cassadine up on the radio again.

"Hey Cassadine, we're going to go to the end of the block. I just saw a vehicle a few hundred yards up the road backed in. If you aren't looking you will miss it. Did you see it?" Tony asked as he turned around in his seat to see if it was following.

"Yeah, I saw it just as we passed it. I'm going to go check it out. Hey make a u-turn and check that vehicle out," Cassadine said to his driver. Before they could make it to the Hummer it sped off. Cassadine then radioed back to Tony.

"Hey, Mr. Stallworth, the Hummer tore out on us. Should we follow it?"

"No, absolutely not. Did you get the license plate?"

"Yes. I got it."

"Okay. Don't pursue it. Let it go and get back here."

"Yes sir." He told the driver, "Alright. You heard him. Head back to the stash house."

When the truck Tony was riding in pulled into the compound, leaving his men parked outside on full alert, one of the men inside pulled down the compound's door. When Tony stepped out of the truck he was greeted by Ike's cousin, Peter.

"Mr. Stallworth?"

"Yes, I am he," Tony said as the tall man with wide shoulders shook his hand and embraced him."

"Everything went smoothly this time," Peter said. "Did my cousin inform you what happened to the last shipment?"

"Yes, he told me which is why I made sure I took extra precautions this time to ensure it didn't happen again."

"Yes, I saw the men in the vehicles. For a minute there I thought they were here to steal the shipment.

"Yeah well, sorry I didn't give you a head's up, but I don't take chances and neither do I broadcast my moves."

"I understand, my brother."

"Did you happen to notice the other vehicle? The black Hummer?" Tony asked.

"Yes, I did happen to see it. It circled the block a couple of times before it finally parked. I passed it off as one of yours after you arrived."

"No, it wasn't one of mine. When my men went to check it out, it took off."

"Well, I am certainly glad you arrived prepared. I can only imagine what would have happened if you hadn't," Peter said, looking all wide eyed. He was definitely not the gangster type.

"No doubt. What I suspect as I did before, there is someone on the inside tipping the hijackers off. The last shipment was hit not long after it left the airport. This time they waited for it to come all the way to the stash house as if they were changing up tactics."

"You think so?" Peter asked with surprise.

"I don't think so. I know so. How did they know to come here? There is a rat in your cousin's organization."

"You mean there is a rat in your organization," Peter said. "And you must find it sooner rather than later." Tony nodded his head in agreement.

Chapter 9
Baby Girl, I'm Home

Later that night, Tony walked into the bedroom of his crib to find Sugar asleep. He didn't tell her he was coming to the crib, so as not to tip anyone off about the arrival of the shipment. After taking off his clothes, he kissed his wife on her forehead causing her to turn over on her right side. Still asleep, he smiled and kissed her on her lips. She wiped the kiss off her lips and turned over on her left side.

Tony then said to her, "Oh so you gone just wipe my sweet kisses off your lips, woman?"

Sugar then opened her eyes and smiled. "That's what you get for sneaking up on me." He collapsed on to the bed beside her. "You lucky I didn't spark your ass," she said as she sat up in the bed.

"Ohhhhhh, so you knew that was me kissing on you, huh?" he said as he started tickling her sides which was something that made her laugh uncontrollably. "And you were going to shoot me too, huh?" he said as he kept tickling her.

"Yes! I knew it was your ass!" she said as the room filled with laughter. "And no, I wasn't going to shoot you. Why would I shoot the man I love?"

Soon the tickles graduated into kisses then the kisses graduated into something much more passionate that transferred into the bathroom where Sugar ran a hot bubble bath. Afterwards they slipped out of their clothes and slid down in the foamy bubbles. With their legs intertwined, they held each other tightly while they kissed and stared into each other's eyes as if they hadn't seen one another in a lifetime. Eventually Sugar inched closer to Tony as her sweetness began to grip him like a suction cup. Its warmth, along with the oily bubble bath in the water, struck the pleasure centers of Tony's brain, causing his eyes to turn into small slits.

With each slow and steady movement of her hips, their hearts fluttered in sync.

The chemistry and the adrenaline that flowed between them could be seen in every movement of their muscles as if they shared one body. Their eyes told a love story to one another without the agency of speech. Other than the occasional sounds of soft moans, heavy breathing and the sloshing of water caused by Sugar's gentle, but steady gyrations, the dark candlelit bathroom was eerily silent as if they were the only two people on planet earth. And as far as they were concerned, on this night and in this moment in time, they were earth's only two inhabitants, nothing else and no one else mattered. Not even Tony's phone that started ringing the moment he and Sugar started their night of passion.

When the water had become lukewarm, this was their cue to take this important matter to the bed. After they stepped out of the bathtub with foamy soap suds slowly streaming down their chiseled bodies, Tony faced his woman and began caressing her lips and tongue with his. Their tongues looked like two Dolphins involved in a hypnotic underwater mating ritual, intertwined, infused, moving back and forth and pulsating in circular movements. After Tony lifted her up from the floor, and cradled her into his arms, they continued to kiss slowly as he carried his Queen to their bed where he laid her down gently. There he continued kissing and licking her softly on her neck, followed by her beautiful, firm hand-sized breasts.

From there, he slowly and methodically made his way downward to her thighs. Instinctively, her legs slowly parted open. Looking down, Tony could clearly see her moisture which added to his own excitement. As he slid his tongue softly over her inner and outer sugar walls, her feet balled up and her toes curled. When he found her outer spot, her entire body tensed up, and her well-defined, six-pack of muscles tightened as if she was doing sit ups. Her low pitched gasps, followed by moaning and whimpering, encouraged him to lick more. As his tongue continued to move in and around her sweetness, ever so softly like a feather, the look in her eyes which were fixated on him and his tongue, let him know that she was about to release her heavy burdens. When she grabbed his head, her body bridged up, as he took all of her into his mouth and held it while his tongue moved ever so slightly. Watching her stomach and the glazed look in her eyes, he knew it was time. Just before the shriek, her eyes looked at him endearingly.

"I love you," she said softly as a tear rolled down her beautiful face. After a few thrusts to completely release her first batch of pure nectar, Tony eased his manhood deep inside of her while kissing her wildly all over her chin, neck and ears, while the song *One Plus One by* Beyonce played softly in the background. Every thrust forward, Tony found her spot. And soon thereafter she would release another load, one after the other. Then came the inevitable switching of positions with soft passionate kisses in between. After a couple of hours of reaffirming their undying, everlasting love, they both finally collapsed in each other's arms from near exhaustion.

CATO

Chapter 10
The Reaper

That next afternoon, after waking up to the smell of an aroma coming from the kitchen, Tony checked his phone and saw that Genie had left him several messages for him to get in touch with him ASAP.

"Hey, Bae, brunch is done, so get your ass up outta that bed," Sugar said over the intercom. "Be up there in a minute."

"Okay, sweetie, I'm already up," he smiled and said before returning Genie's call. "What's up, Genie? I saw where I missed ya calls. My phone was on silent."

"Yeah, bruh, we got a situation!" Genie said before downing a stiff drink.

"What's up?" Tony said as he sat up in the bed.

"One of my stash houses got hit and was burned to the fucking ground. And it wasn't no accident either."

"Real talk?"

"Yeah, real talk. And two of the guards got murked. Their throats were slit from ear to ear."

"Okay. Give me an hour and I will be there," Tony said before hanging up his cell phone.

After throwing the cell phone across the room, a naked Genie reached over to the nightstand and poured another drink, as his woman, Sissy, who was also naked, rubbed his back in an attempt to comfort him.

When Tony arrived at one of the many dope stash houses that belonged to Genie, he was met by Cassadine and the muscle, armed with fully automatic assault rifles. A clearly upset Genie was smoking and pacing back and forth outside of his canary yellow and black convertible mustang as the song *Somebody Gotta Die* by Biggie Smalls played from the car's speakers. When Tony saw Genie puffing on a black and mild, who had given up smoking a couple years ago, he knew something was seriously wrong.

"Damn!" Tony said under his breath as he surveyed the destruction of the burned out barn. "Have you inspected it yet, Genie?" he asked as he peered at the still smoldering rubble.

"No, I was too fucking pissed to do anything but look at this shit. By the time I got word, it was already burned to the fucking ground."

"Where are the men's bodies?" Tony asked.

"They're over there about 50 yards off in the bushes. Cassadine and the muscle got here before the fire department and moved them so the police wouldn't be called." Tony, Genie and Cassadine walked over to the bushes where they saw the bodies of the men, stiff with rigor mortis, whose throats were slit.

"Whoever did this was a professional. Look at that cut to the carotid artery. It's a perfect incision as if a surgeon did it," Tony said as he examined the wounds. "Did y'all find anything else that stuck out?

"One of the men found this doll here stuck in one of my men's mouth," Cassadine said as he handed it to Tony.

"It's a Grim Reaper doll," Tony said under his breath. He recalled Ike mentioning the same kind of doll that was left on his wife's car.

"What the fuck is that? Some Voodoo shit or sumpin'?" Genie asked.

"No. It's a calling card," Tony said as he stared at the blood stained doll.

"A calling card?" Genie asked with a wrinkle in his forehead and right eyebrow raised.

"Yeah," Tony said before heading to the burned out barn. "What kind of loss did you take on this one, Genie?"

"A small one. There was only about five bricks inside. Luckily, most of the shit was already on the street. We were at the tail end of this package."

"It appears they took the shit. They didn't burn it," Tony said as he examined the ashes.

"How you know, bruh?" Genie asked.

"There's no smell. Do you smell any coke?" Genie sniffed the air.

"No. No I don't."

"Me either. Besides, we would see some small rocks if it was burned. Whoever did this, took the stash, killed the men and burned the barn down," Tony said as he looked around to survey the area. "Where are the dogs?"

"They're inside their kennels. The men always locked them up when they are here," Cassadine said.

"Fatal mistake," Tony said, shaking his head. "They must have been afraid of them or something."

"Yeah," Cassadine said. Tony shook his head again.

"If those dogs were running loose on this property, those scary muthafuckas might still be alive," he said angrily. "Okay, Genie, let's go."

"Hey, Cassadine, get some people out here to clean this shit up ASAP," Genie said. "But before you do, get those fucking bodies out of here."

"Yes, sir. Consider it done."

As Tony and Genie walked away from the smoldering barn, Genie continued to look at the blood-stained doll in his hand with a curiosity.

"T, what's up with this fucking doll?" Genie asked as he and Tony walked to Tony's ride. "I noticed the look on your face when you saw it."

"I didn't wanna say anything in front of Cassadine and the men. That doll is the calling card of that Russian muthafucka,

Lavrov. This was his way of letting me know that he knows I've taken over Ike's diamond trade."

"Okay. Well, we'll get up the muscle and we'll hit the muthafucka with everything we got right away then."

"No, bruh, we have to show some restraint right now."

"Restraint? What the fuck we have to show restraint for? We ain't never showed restraint before. Give me one good reason."

"Bruh, this isn't like the Natty Boy thing. This is the Russian Mafia we are talking about here. That doll he left behind, he wanted us to know he was here. Think, bruh! Think! Do you think someone who broadcast that they just walked in, took your shit and murked your men ain't prepared for a response? No! He wants a response. He want us to go charging in, bruh. We have to play this thing smart. We play chess, not checkers. He knew to connect you and me and knew where at least one of the stash houses was at. Doesn't that give you some kinda pause here, my nigga?" Tony's words seemed to have an effect on Genie. He stood there in deep thought before he responded.

"Okay bruh. I feel what you are saying. But you know as well as I do, we can't let this ride."

"Fuck no! We can't let it ride. And we're not going to let it ride. We just have to use our wits on this one. We can't go full guerilla on this like we did with them syndicate niggas. What we are going to have to do is be surgical. We may even have to use some diplomacy, because this thing can get real political real quick being that this muthafucka is connected, you feel me?"

"Yeah, I feel what you're saying," Genie said, just before Tony pulled off in his Challenger. Genie then shifted his eyes to what was left of the smoldering barn. Although he wasn't as calculated as Tony, he was smart enough to know he had to think differently now that he was in charge. He had to transform himself into a calculated thinker, just like his mentor, in order to have the same successes as that mentor. He knew the days were gone where he was the reactionary, impulsive hardcore street cat who once used strong arm guerilla tactics to respond to any and all offenses. Things were different now. He was now a boss.

CATO

Chapter 11
So, We Play Chess

The next evening Tony flew back to Africa. After an overnight stay in Liberia to rest from the grueling 23 hour flight, early the following morning he caught a private plane to Ghana where Macky and Ike were waiting on him in a limo.

"My brother, how was your trip?" Ike asked.

"Bittersweet," Tony replied as climbed in the limo and he sat down.

"Meaning?"

"The shipment arrived to its destination without incident. But two of my brother's men were murdered and his stash house was hit."

"Oh no! Any clues who did it?" Tony pulled out the grim reaper doll and handed it to Ike.

"Lavrov!" Ike said. Macky looked at Tony.

"Mr. Stallworth, do you need me back home?" Macky asked.

"Not just yet. Your man, Cassadine, got things held down back at the crib. I need you here so we can find out who the fucking rat is on this end like before I leave. If Lavrov knew to tie me and Genie together, there's no telling what else and who else he will tie me to. This shit has gotten real. And we have to deal with it fast."

"My brother, I will assist you in any way that I can." Ike said, with his hand on Tony's shoulder.

"I know. The way you can help me is to help me flush out the traitor."

"I should just have everyone killed and be done with it," Ike said, looking out of the window at the fast moving countryside with a frustrated look on his face. "This is how I would normally handle this."

"No. We wait. We must have the traitor lead us to Lavrov. The best way to catch a rat is to set a good trap and then be patient."

Later that evening, Tony and Ike stood on Ike's balcony looking up at the beautiful African sky.

"Ike, I need to know everything about Lavrov." Tony said. "Who he does business with. What type of rackets he's into. What kinda women he fucks with. What's his drug of choice, if he indulges. Whether he's gay. I need to know everything about this man." Ike smiled as he continued to lean over the balcony and stare up at the starry sky.

"You know, my father once told me that the stars you see in the sky are our ancestors guarding and protecting us. I used to actually believe that shit until my dear mother was killed, and all those people who died in the war, including many in my Samira's family. What do you think, my brother?" Ike turned to Tony and asked, "You believe in guardian protectors?"

"Yes I do," Tony said showing his two gold-plated .45 pistols sitting in their holsters. Ike smiled.

"I'm talking beyond that. By the time you have to use those, it's already too late. I'm talking about the guardian protectors who are always there preventing us from harm before danger materializes."

"Yes, Ike, I do. We are the guardian protectors. You and me. You are protecting the wealth of Africa from vultures who could care less about anything other than money and power. They don't care about heritage. They don't care about culture. They don't even care about human life. All they do is what vultures do which is to feed on the weak and infirmed. Back home I am the guardian protector of my family, friends and organization. This is why I need to know everything about this Russian, so I can better protect them." Ike smiled and turned back to the sky to stare at the stars.

"Lavrov deals with the Mexican Cartel. His main business is cocaine which he distributes in Europe and in America. He occasionally deals heroin also. He has a son and a daughter who are estranged from him. He also has a brother who has sickle cell and a heroin addiction, who is closely connected with his business. I'm not sure of his brother's identity, however. Although Lavrov is known to deal with a few women on rare occasions, there are two main women who are black who very seldom leave his side. Identical twins sisters, one dark as me, and the other with a light complexion, who are his own personal attack dogs that he trained. He seems to have a fetish for black whores."

"So he's a trick?" Tony asked.

"No, he's more than that. He's perverted. And so are those two she devil bed wenches of his who very seldom leave his side. This, and a few other things, has caused some issues with the Russian Mafia. They only tolerate him because of his penchant for brutality, which is something seen as a huge plus in their world." Tony listened intently as to find some sort of weakness or angle in which he could use to his advantage. Every man had one. "He is also related to the top boss, Konstantin Antonov, his uncle. Lavrov's mother is the boss' sister. The word is Konstantin hates him, but won't rid the earth of him for the reasons I mentioned. Konstantin and his sister are extremely close. They are the last surviving siblings of eight children."

"I see you've done your homework, Ike."

"Yes. I was forced to. This is an extremely dangerous, unpredictable man that you must learn. Besides, he once threatened the life of my Samira. He left his calling card on the hood of a rental car she drove while in the states a year ago. My brother, we must deal with this man. Your wife and your friends back home are not safe as long as he lives. But you do understand the delicate political nature of this regarding his Mafia connections?"

"Yes. So, we play chess," Tony said as the limo pulled into Ike's garage.

*****

When the black SUV pulled into the produce bazaar, the Russian, Vladimir exited with his Amazon broad. As he and his woman walked slowly down the aisles handling and picking out fruit, Macky watched from a distance through his binoculars. Nothing seemed out of the ordinary. That was until the same Euro Benz appeared that Macky saw back at the hotel a couple of days ago. The same stocky man wearing the same dark shades and old man derby climbed out of the vehicle and casually made his way through the bazaar. He didn't stop to talk with anyone or peruse the aisles. He went straight over to the Russian and his girl who peeled off to shop while the two men talked.

At first they all stood there looking over the fruit as if they didn't know each other as Macky stood on the corner of the building talking to himself as he peered through the binoculars.

"Come on. Turn around so I can be in on your conversation. Come on. Turn around."

Seconds later, Macky got what he wanted. The Russian and the stocky mystery man turned around as the tall Amazon continued to browse and pick out fruit. As the two spoke to one another, Macky who was an expert lip reader, a skill he picked up from his father whose mother was deaf, began reading their lips. After the brief conversation of small talk, the Russian handed the stocky man an envelope before he walked back to the Benz and pulled away. Macky watched the vehicle as it made its way to the traffic light. After the broad made her purchases, she and the Russian left soon thereafter.

As the black Benz with the mystery man inside turned left onto the intersection, Macky lagged in behind it. The GPS he placed on the car must have fallen off, because it was no longer tracking the vehicle's movements. This time, however, GPS or not, Macky was determined to find out who this dude was.

When the Benz reached its destination in a huge, affluent subdivision, Macky peeled off on a side street to keep from being detected. After locking his car doors, he traveled on foot to where the Benz had parked. When he spotted it, the mystery man was removing a box from the trunk. After closing the trunk shut, he walked over and checked the mailbox before aimlessly walking into his crib as he read a piece of mail, while Macky stood off a distance steadily snapping pictures of him and the apartment flat he walked into. Before leaving, Macky slid under the Benz to see if the GPS was still there and to his surprise it was.

Figuring it had malfunctioned, he removed it so it wouldn't be detected. He didn't bother to replace it with another one because now he knew the exact location where this mystery man resided. After throwing the malfunctioned GPS in a nearby canal, Macky got in his car and drove off. He had everything he needed now to I.D. this man once and for all. The association between this mystery man and the Russian definitely had a Lavrov connection. In the coming days all matters concerning this Lavrov mystery would be revealed in such a way that some of the parties involved would not be ready for it.

Chapter 12
A Matter of Life and Death

Later that evening, Ike hosted a party at his mansion that included wealthy African businessmen and women and some politicians and foreign dignitaries. There was one surprise guest that Ike wouldn't have expected in a thousand years to crash his party. It was his ex, Enid Kabila, the daughter of President Kabila of the Congo. Her beauty was breathtaking. When she walked through the door, everyone inside took notice of her, including the women who were hissing like cats, while the men all gawked like birds of prey. When Ike's wife, Samira, walked in and saw her, she lost her damn mind. She went straight to Ike who stood out on the balcony with Tony, Macky and a Russian ally of Ike's, Mikhail Chernoff, who was a mutual enemy of Lavrov.

"Ike! What the fuck is that bitch doing here?" Samira screamed as she walked onto the balcony. "Either you remove her peacefully from my home or I will remove her by force!"

"Who Samira? Remove who?" Ike said holding her shoulders.

"That bitch, Enid! Your ex-whore!" An amused Tony smiled and turned away. He realized that the African women could get just as turned up as their sisters back in the states.

"Enid is here? Here in this house, right now?" he said with surprise.

"Yes!"

"Where?"

"Here in our home! Don't play games with me, Ike! You had to have known that bitch was coming here! How else would she be so bold as to come here?"

"Sweetheart, I swear on my ancestors I had no knowledge of her visit!"

"Yeah, okay. If you don't want you and *her* to join your ancestors, you had better get her the fuck out of my home!" she yelled.

"Okay, my Queen! Hold on! I will take care of it!" He turned to Tony and the Russian. "I will return shortly," he said in a hurried voice. Tony and Chernoff laughed.

"Handle your business," Tony said under his breath mockingly before Ike rushed off to the guest room with his Queen behind him, mean mugging.

"Whew!" the Russian said as he turned to Tony. "Talk about a woman scorned." He chuckled.

"Yeah, she is hot as fish grease right about now," Tony said smiling. "I had to make sure she didn't have a weapon in her hand after she walked in. Nothing like a black woman scorned." Tony laughed. Macky smiled, but elected not to say anything, as usual.

"Yes, especially that black woman," the Russian said. "Do you know her history?"

"No, Ike never divulged that to me." Tony replied.

"Well, let's put it this way. As you African Americans say, she's nothing to be fucked with. Like, really. That is all I will say on that," Chernoff said before downing his Vodka. Tony smiled and thought about his own woman back at the crib who also was someone you didn't wanna be fucked up with. But he could look at Samira and tell she was a different kinda dangerous, especially when he first saw her toting that fully automatic HKK like it was a part of her hand. There was no doubt in his mind that this drop dead gorgeous African sister, who had a hardness to her, was once a soldier. Perhaps even a mercenary. Little did Tony know, he was right, but there was much more to this strong-willed sister's story that he, or no one else for that matter, other than she and Ike, could ever imagine.

When Ike spotted Enid, she was surrounded by five gloating cats who were sweating her for an autograph.

"Okay. Okay. This is not a groupie setting," Ike said sternly. "I need you gentlemen to rejoin the other guests and cut this out." He looked at Enid. Samira stood a few feet away, arms folded, and her feet tapping against the floor like a Rattler's tail with her eyes trained on her old rival, Enid. Enid's two colossal body-guards stood nearby looking on intently, but with a slight nerv-ousness. They had hoped to God nothing popped off, because the last thing they wanted to do was get into some shit with an inter-national gangster like Ike who was without a doubt, one of the most powerful men on the continent.

"Enid! Why did you come here?" Ike asked sharply.

"Isaac, how are you?" she said, smiling as she tried to kiss him on the cheek. Ike nudged her away and looked at Samira, knowing if he didn't she would explode on them both.

"I'm fine. Again, why did you come here?" he again asked sharply. Deep down inside Ike was still in madly in love with this woman, but had to play the part in front of the boss standing be-hind him.

"I came here for a legitimate reason. I wouldn't dare disre-spect you and…your wifey," she said smiling. The wifey com-ment and the smile, further incensed Samira. Viewing it as a slight, she stepped forward aggressively to check her, but Ike held her back. Being two former rivals, Samira and Enid had some history between each other.

"Couldn't you have called, sent an email, a text, or maybe even a Facebook inbox? Anything would have sufficed rather than coming into me and my wife's home." Ike's face showed frustration.

"I know. I know," she said with her head down. "But my rea-son for coming here was far too important to do over a phone call or email. It is a matter of life and death. Can I please speak with you in private on this matter?" she said to Ike, looking at Samira who was about to explode. "I promise you, Samira. I don't mean any disrespect to you in your home."

"Hell no!" Samira yelled. "You asking for privacy in my home?" Again, Ike had to hold her back. By this time some of the guests started peeking around the corner to see what the commotion was about.

"Hold on, Enid," Ike said as he gently grabbed Samira by her arm and led her a few feet away.

"My Queen, listen to me," he said holding her face. "I understand your anger, but I detect there is an extremely important reason as to why Enid would travel all the way here to see me personally, knowing that her father would sternly forbid it. I suggest you allow me to speak with her and see what is going on. Then afterwards, I will make her leave the premises. You have my word." This seemed to slightly calm Samira down.

"Okay," she said in a low voice. "But after she explains herself to you and the reason for her visit, that bitch leaves!" she said looking over at Enid. Enid smiled mischievously and turned away.

"Okay, sweetheart. Can you please go back in and entertain our guests? You know how I deplore public spectacles." Samira looked at him, gave one last dirty look at Enid, and stormed off to the guest room.

"Okay, Enid. Let's speak in private," Ike said sternly. Part of him was happy to see the woman whom he was once madly in love just a few years ago. Then again, another part of him was pained to see her. She was the one woman who broke his heart. As they walked away together to the balcony Ike admonished her. "You really shouldn't have come here," he said to her as they made it out on the balcony. "Hey, my brothers, I'm going to need some privacy to speak with this woman."

"Okay," Tony said before whispering in Ike's ear. "For a minute I thought you would be yelling for help." The two chuckled before Tony, the Russian, and Macky left Ike and Enid alone to have their conversation.

"Okay, now what is it? Why did you come here?"

"First of all, don't pretend you aren't happy to see me as much as I am happy to see you," she said smiling as if her presence would be a welcomed surprise.

"Actually, seeing you has resurrected the grief I had long since buried. So I'm not at all happy that you have come to my home. Neither is my wife. But what does me being happy to see you have to do with your visit?" Enid laughed, leaned over the balcony and looked up at the starry sky.

"You know, all this time I felt we could mend our differences to at least be friends. Honestly, I wanted to reunite with you. I have never loved a man before you, and have not loved one since I lost you."

"Look, Enid…"

"Are you in love with her?" she interrupted.

"What?" he said with surprise. The question caught him totally off guard.

"You heard me, Isaac. Are you in love with her?" she asked as she moved closer to him.

"Enid, I know damn well this is not your purpose for coming here? If it is, this is most disrespectful to me and my wife!" he replied angrily.

"No, it is not my reason for coming here, but I have to admit, I planned on taking full advantage of this opportunity to ask you this question that has burned in my mind for years. Now I would like to know. Are you in love with her?" she asked looking him directly into his eyes.

"Yes! I am in love with her! Now what is your purpose for coming here this evening?"

"My father needs you!" she blurted out. "There is going to be a coup in which he will be taken into custody and killed immediately." Ike saw the look of anguish on her over her father's plight and let out a wicked laughed.

"So he sends the very woman here to ask for assistance of the man he forbade her to never see again? Get the fuck out of here!" he said as he darted to the balcony and looked out into the horizon.

"No! You are wrong!" she yelled. "He doesn't know I'm here. I came under my own volition to ask for your help."

"What makes you think I would ever help your father after he tried to ruin my life and on a couple of occasions tried to have men take it?"

"My father never tried to have your life taken. And he didn't try to ruin your life either. I made the decision to break off our engagement. Not him."

"You broke it off because of him. And he did try to have my life taken on at least two occasions. I know this for a fact!" he yelled.

"Okay. I didn't come here to argue with you on my father's treachery....real and imagined. I came here to ask you to help save his life."

"So, if I save his life, emphasis on if, what is in it for me? I mean, any gesture or favor from me will come at a hefty price."

"Well, I'm sure he would appreciate you for saving his life and his presidency. Something like that wouldn't go unrewarded."

"Yeah, whatever. I need something in stone on that," he said walking back off to the balcony. "Your father's word is meaningless to me. A baboon's word holds more weight than your father's. Besides, I may not be able to prevent the inevitable. Your father has made many enemies. Which one is seeking to exact some revenge on him?"

122

"The guerrilla leader, Laurent Mbembe," she said.

"Hahahahaha! Mbembe. Yet another former business partner of your father's turned enemy. Enid, has your father made out his last will and testament? I sure hope so."

"I did not come here to be ridiculed and have my father insulted! I came here to seek your help! You know better than anyone how these things end up. Everyone dies! Me. Our son!" she said before she held her mouth. Her emotions got the best of her. Although she wanted Ike to know about their son, she didn't mean for him to find out this way. She had planned on telling him, but not like this.

"*Our son*? Did you say *our son*?" Ike said approaching her.

"Yes," she said turning away.

"Is this some sort of sick trick or something? How could you have a son from me?"

"No. It is not a trick. We have a son. He's six years old. I was never supposed to tell you about him. My father forbade me from ever telling you." Ike looked as if all the wind in his sails had been deflated.

"You have a son from me?" he said under his breath as he paced around like a man disoriented. He didn't know whether to cry with joy or combust with anger. At this point he didn't know what to think with the plethora of thoughts and emotions going through his mind. "This is all the more reason why I should not help your father. I should let Mbembe do what he has set out to do to him."

"Yes. Maybe you should, Isaac. My father has certainly earned your wrath. But Enoch hasn't. I don't have to tell you that Mbembe will not leave any loose ends behind." Ike sunk down in a chair and put his hands over his head.

"Why is she still in my home?" Samira yelled, standing at the entrance.

"I'm leaving now," Enid said as a stunned Ike continued to sit there without moving a muscle and with his head in his hands.

"Yes! I know you are leaving now! I came to make sure of it this time!" Samira said.

"No need to. I said what I came here to say. Now everything else is left up to your husband," Enid said, looking down at Ike before walking away.

"What is left up to you, Isaac?" Samira demanded, standing over him. "Did you hear me, Issac? What is left up to, you?" Ike didn't say a word. He just continued to sit there still stunned with his head tilted down to the ground. He didn't see anything at this point, nor did he hear anything. Not even the wife standing over him yelling to the top of her lungs. *I have a son!* he kept saying over and over in his mind.

The next morning, Tony, Ike and Macky put in a vigorous work out on Ike's obstacle course. Afterwards, they went to breakfast where Ike mentioned Enid's dilemma.

"My brother, last night at the party the woman you saw was my ex who came to me with a plea to save her father's life. As you already know, her father is President of the Congo, Joseph Kabila, my former friend and business partner. There will be a coup attempt and if it is successful which more than likely it will be, he will be killed immediately afterwards. Now under any other circumstances I could give a chimpanzee's left nut what happens to him, but there are others I'm concerned about. Enid broke the news to me that we have a son, who will more than likely be killed right along with she and her father. This is how these things usually end here on the continent, similar to the new lion that takes over a pride. All the cubs that belong to the defeated patriarch are killed. I cannot allow that to happen to my son and his mother. He is my only child. And she is his mother whom I still love." Tony looked at him and clutched his shoulder.

"Okay, my brother, what do you need me to do? How can we help?"

CATO

Chapter 13
A Reunion Between Old Friends and Foes

Laurent Mbembe was a battle hardened rebel leader who had spent most of his years on this earth as a mercenary. At the tender age of 12 when he should have been having dreams of being a professional soccer player like most kids in his village, he was an assassin and enforcer for local warlord and militia men. After losing his left eye and almost his life on a mission in Liberia a few years back, he developed greater ambitions like taking over an entire nation and becoming its dictator.

After being resettled in the Congo by President Kabila and made a business partner to show his gratitude for his service to Africa's freedom struggles, Mbembe became restless. He just could not adjust to the civilian business world shit. Many say it was because he had been out in the bush for far too long and what little humanity he had, he left it there. Others say it's because he is a man possessed by a jinn, an evil spirit. Whatever the case may be, the plan he set into motion was a classic case of biting the hand that fed him. When Kabila found out Mbembe's ambitions, he jailed him, but soon thereafter he escaped and became the leader of a growing rebel faction who had been using blood diamonds and heroin to fund their insurgency.

Before Mbembe joined the rebels and brought his organizational skills, his larger than life reputation and his guerilla slash mercenary experience, the men were nothing more than a roving band of young criminals and marauders. Now they were a serious, disciplined force to be reckoned with who could plunge the nation back into instability. The one weakness they had was without Mbembe, they weren't shit. They would become splintered and unstable if anything ever happened to him.

After the first supply truck rolled into the camp bringing in food, booze, bottled water, clothing, medicine, boots and other much needed supplies in the jungle outback, Mbembe, his young lieutenant and protégé, and 4 other underlings all sat inside a tent to discuss the plan to attack the capital next month. At this time, most of the men were out on patrol and conducting attacks on inept, poorly trained government troops. The government soldiers were afraid of the rebels who showed no fear in battle because of a weed that contained a narcotic like substance they chewed that made them feel invincible.

There were stories of young rebels walking into bullets and laughing as they were mowed down, and many say that it was because of the weed they chewed just before going into battle. There were other stories of them running into tanks and armored personnel carriers with explosives strapped to their bodies and blowing themselves up. During their rigorous training, they would ingest this hallucinogenic weed and were sent walking out into a Lion Pride or into the Silverback Guerillas lair. The men who came back alive and unscathed, they became fearless and almost worshipped as Gods. This is partly why one of Mbembe's rebels was said to be equal to five government soldiers. In fact, in one firefight that took place in a nearby town, five of Mbembe's men took on forty government troops. When the gun smoke cleared and the dust settled, thirty-five of the government troops lay dead and the other five had thrown down their weapons and run off into the bush. Only one of Mbembe's men died. After this battle, there were widespread reports that government troops retreated in the face of the rebels advance. So this was definitely cause for concern for President Kabila. The fear was, if and when the capital was attacked by Mbembe, his men were subject to tear out and abandon him to his fate.

While the plan of attack on the capital was being discussed inside the tent, Mbembe and his men were totally unaware what was unfolding outside. Two of the guards jugular veins exploded as the sharp combat knives simultaneously cut through their necks like soft butter. The hands that tightly covered their mouths that muffled their screams, slowly loosened their grip as the men's limp bodies sunk to the ground. As they lay there taking their last breaths, with both shock and resignation in their bulging eyes, two of the three men dragged their bodies into the nearby bush out of sight. The next two men on the west side of the camp, met with the same fate. Their bodies too were dragged into the bush out of sight. With the camp now rendered totally unguarded and defenseless, the three men advanced on to the tent where the general and his underlings were plotting, while the other two served as east and west look-outs.

As the three men dressed in dark clothing stood in stealth right outside the tent blending in with the surrounding darkness, the men inside continued to discuss their plans with an occasional laughter. Mbembe could be heard talking about his plans for Enid once he took her into his custody. Mbembe had a notorious reputation as a rapist of women, preferably young girls. Though Enid was older, she was nonetheless considered to be the Congo's most prized jewel. Very few women in the world could match her beauty. So in his mind, he had to have her as a final rebuke to her father. He would probably rape her right in front of him before he slit his throat. One of the masked men who stood there seemingly incensed at what he was hearing, decided it was time for them to make their move. Hand signaling to the others, one of the masked men, accompanied by another who crouched just behind him, held up three fingers. When the third finger went up, the three men simultaneously rushed inside the tent and the only thing that could be heard was the deadly whispers of the silencers, grunts, and the thudding sounds of bodies hitting the dirt floor. Everyone was killed immediately with the exception of Mbembe. He was hit in the back of the dome with a rifle butt before two of the men dragged him outside. After gagging and hogtying him like a game animal, the five men departed the camp with their quarry without further incident. The attack was surgical, quiet and swift. When they reached the waiting helicopter and threw Mbembe onboard, he was just beginning to wake up. After the chopper took flight, the five men unmasked. Ike, Tony, Macky, Kobani, and Kobani's right hand man, Ali, sat there stone-faced staring at Mbembe when he began gaining consciousness and trying to levy his protestations. After a few seconds of watching him struggle to speak, Ike removed the gag from his mouth to hear what he had to say.

"What the fuck is this? And where the fuck are you taking me?" Mbembe asked in a strong Nigerian accent as he laid there tied up like a helpless animal that was ready for the roasting spit.

"What the fuck does it look like and where the fuck do you think you're going?" Ike asked. "You have been taken captive and your monkey ass is being handed over to President Kabila." Mbembe let out a loud wicked laugh.

"Who the fuck are you to be taking me into custody?" he said with contempt. "I am a freedom fighter trying to liberate this fucking continent from that jackal." Ike let out his own wicked laugh.

"Freedom fighter? You are a fucking mercenary who sells out to the highest bidder. You are no more a freedom fighter than I am," Ike said as the chopper shook from the turbulence.

"I asked, who the fuck are you?" Mbembe demanded.

"Okay. If you must know, I will give you a hint who I am. Nine years ago in Liberia out on the beach, just after you and your men executed ten young boys and girls who dared to defend their nation from you and Mr. Taylor. I am the reason you're missing that eye."

"Ahhhhh. But you did nothing about it except take a shot at me from behind a bush, huh?"

"No, I arrived there just after they were slaughtered. Besides, I was there on assignment that had nothing to do with dealing with a petty criminal like you."

"Okay. So what assignment are you on now?" he asked sarcastically.

"I'm on assignment to save my son. My original intent was to kill you and leave you for the hyenas and other scavengers out in the bush. I don't normally take captives. But while en route to pay you a visit, I changed my mind." Mbembe laughed mockingly.

"And why the change of heart?"

"I didn't say I had a change of heart. I had a change of mind."

"Well, okay. Why the change of mind, asshole?"

"Because you are more valuable to me alive than dead. You are going to help me get back in the good graces with an old friend."

"Hahahaha! If you are talking about Kabila, he's nobody's friend. He is just like any other western puppet. He is a lap dog opportunist who would stab you in the back just as soon as look at you. If you were on fire he wouldn't piss on you to put out the flames."

"And you are right. He is a snake. A venomous one at that. But who isn't? Besides, I wasn't motivated to come see you because of my love for Kabila or his love for me. I was motivated by the love of my son. Preventing more unnecessary strife and bloodshed in this land was an added motivation. It's bad for the continent. It's bad for the people, and it's also bad for my fucking business. Now, our little conversation is over," Ike said as he reached down and placed the gag back over Mbembe's mouth.

When the chopper landed outside Kabila's Presidential palace, about 50 soldiers rushed out and surrounded it with their guns pointed. Moments later President Kabila, accompanied by his daughter and the Vice President, walked out of the palace balcony to see what the commotion was. Kabila approached the chopper surrounded by his men.

"Mr. Quartier, it's been a long time. Why have you made this grand entrance on my lawn? I thought I told you never to step foot back into the Congo? Give me one reason why I should not have you shot?" Kabila said with a stern face.

"Yes, it has been a long time," Ike said, looking at him with hostility in his ebony black eyes. "Having me shot was the last thing you said to me 6 years ago." He stood in the door of the chopper as the soldiers kept their weapons trained on him.

"Okay and nothing about that threat has changed. You had better hurry up and give me a good reason for being here," the President said. Ike stared at him momentarily with an obvious disdain. He then turned around and grabbed the rope that bound Mbembe's feet and dragged him off the chopper onto the ground in front of Kabila. His body made a thudding sound when it hit the ground. He let out a grunt and winced in pain after the wind was nearly knocked out of him. He levied profanities underneath the gag at the soldiers who looked down at him. Realizing who he was, they took a couple steps back. Although he was tied up, gagged and rendered harmless, they nonetheless still feared this man.

Kabila stood there as if he was in shock. Right on the ground was the mighty Mbembe who was the stuff African legend was made of, hog tied like a wild beast and looking most undignified. Ike stood there staring at the President as if he awaited his next move. Suddenly, Kabila recovered from his shock.

"Mr. Mbembe, welcome to the capital. Delighted to have you with us. We are going to put you on display like a zoo animal in a cage, followed by a first class trial, quickly followed by a first class firing squad. But don't piss me off, because I may conjure up a much more interesting end to your miserable life." Kabila then motioned for the soldiers to lower their guns. "Take this piece of elephant dung into custody," he said to the soldiers. Four soldiers followed his orders and immediately grabbed Mbembe and carried him away while he continued to muffle insults.

"I want you to know that I am deeply indebted to you for bringing in that animal," Kabila said to Ike. "With that criminal eliminated, this nation and the entire continent will be a more peaceful, stable place. I also want you to know that on this day ends all of our differences." He extended his hand to Ike. Ike looked at it momentarily before deciding to shake it, followed by a tight embrace.

"I'm going to be brutally honest here, I didn't do this to renew our friendship. I did this for my son and his mother. Now if you don't mind, I would like to see my boy," he said looking past Kabila.

"Sure. Sure." Kabila turned and nodded at Enid who was still standing on the palace's steps at a safe distance. She then turned and rushed inside excitedly. Ike handed Kabila the coordinates of Mbembe's base camp.

"I think this will be helpful to you and your nation," Ike said with his eyes still trained on the entranceway of the Presidential palace for any signs of his son. Immediately, Kabila recognized the gift that he was just given being a former air force pilot.

"Thank you!" Kabila said in a rushed tone before quickly turning to his general. "This is the base camp where those monkeys are hiding out. Take care of them tonight! Immediately!"

"Yes sir!" the general said before rushing away with his men.

Ike introduced Tony, Macky, Kobani and Ali. "I wouldn't have been able to pull this off without my friends," Ike said to Kabila before turning his attention back on the Presidential palace waiting for his son to show himself. "This is Tony Stallworth, his right hand man, Macky, Colonel Kobani and his man, Ali,"

Ike said as he again looked towards the palace anxiously. Kabila shook their hands and gave each of them a tight embrace.

"Now they are my friends and the friends of the Congo, forever," Kabila said proudly. "You men saved my nation and perhaps even my life and the lives of my family. For this, I am forever indebted to you. Anything you need businesswise or personal here in the Congo, just ask it of me and you will have it."

"Thank you, Mr. President," Tony said. "I may have a couple things in mind." They all laughed out loud as he and Kabila again, embraced tightly. At this time Enid returned with a young boy wearing glasses, dressed in a school uniform with a bowtie. Ike could barely contain himself he was so excited.

"Isaac, meet your son. Isaac, meet your father," Enid said as Ike eyes welled up with tears. He picked the young boy up, held him in the air and looked him over as if he was inspecting him.

"You gave him his father's name?" Ike asked. "I thought you said his name was Enoch?

"Enoch is his nickname. Isaac is his birth name, just like his father," she said smiling. Tony, Macky, and the President all looked on with smiles. Even the hardcore Kobani who was as sullen as a Silverback gorilla, managed to produce a smile as did his protégé Ali who was his clone.

"And yes, he is you reincarnated. I figure that a male child who looks so much like his father, must carry his name."

"He does look like his father," Ike said proudly.

"And he has his father's intelligence. He already speaks three languages," Enid said proudly.

"Wow! Six years old and you already know three languages? You are much smarter than your father could ever be," Ike said as he placed the young lad back to earth. The young boy smiled shyly before he spoke.

"I am also good at football," he said seriously. Everyone laughed.

"Is that right?" Ike asked. "Well, you are going to be good at everything. We have a lot to catch up on, my son."

"Okay, I think it is time to take this reunion inside," Kabila said. "This is a festive night and cause for celebration," he said before they all headed to the palace.

Chapter 14
Mystery Man Revealed

The next evening, Tony, Macky, Kobani and his man, Ali, flew back to Ghana, leaving Ike behind to spend time with his son. After Tony and Macky went to Tony's new villa to get some much needed rest, a few hours later they went to the factory. While en route, Macky briefed Tony on the mystery man and the Russian. He would have mentioned it to him earlier, but he was under strict instructions from Tony not to divulge any information regarding the investigation into leaks in the organization in front of anyone, not even Ike. It wasn't that Tony distrusted Ike. He just thought it was best that only he and Macky knew what was going on regarding the progress of the investigation.

Once they arrived at the factory, Ike's uncle, wearing his customary white laboratory jacket, greeted them as they walked in the door.

"Mr. Stallworth! How are you men doing today?" he asked, shaking Tony's hand before shaking Macky's.

"We're good. How are you, sir?"

"All is fantastic. We received a partial shipment today as you already know. The other half of the shipment should be in shortly. I was in the process of inspecting them before we conduct our analysis.

"Yes and that is why I'm here. Where is Kobani today?" Tony asked, looking around the factory. "I didn't see him outside with his men."

"He went to pick up my son from his home. He should arrive here any minute, now."

"Okay. I'm going to my office. Carry on with what you were doing, sir."

"Yes, Mr. Stallworth," he said before walking back over to the team of men and women who were counting and inspecting the diamonds.

"Okay, Macky, we need to make sure the bugs are still in place."

"Yes, sir," he said before he went straight away and checked every crack, nook and cranny where a bug was placed. After a few minutes of checking and inspecting the bugs, he returned.

"They are all still in place and working, sir," he said to Tony.

"Okay. Tonight, I want you to listen to every word said on them, even if it takes you all night. I want that fucking rat found once and for all."

"Consider it done, sir."

When Tony and Macky were about to pull off, Kobani pulled up with a gentleman sitting in the back seat. As Kobani stepped out of the sedan he nodded his head to Tony who gave him a half smile and a nod back. Though Kobani had come to terms with being subordinate to Tony and had thus softened his position on him, especially after the Mbembe mission, he was still feeling some kind of way since Tony had put him in his place early on. As soon as the man in the back seat stepped out of the car, Macky's eyes zeroed in on him like an eagle who had locked in on its prey. Tony noticed it.

"What's up, youngster?"

"The cat there with the Colonel, he's the mystery man who been meeting with the Russian in town."

"Are you sure about this, Macky?" Tony asked as he watched the stocky man, intently.

"I'm positive. Same build. Same old man hat. Same shades. Same slight limp. I literally followed him to his front door. It's him. I put that on everything," Macky said confidently.

"That's Ike's uncle's son. And he's our rat," Tony said as his green eyes turned to small slits. Initially, Tony along with Macky had suspected Kobani. But all this time it was Ike's cousin who only played a minor role in the operation. He had remained out of sight perhaps purposely, but now he shows up on the day of the new shipment. To Tony, this was no coincidence. He was scouting. He was Lavrov's plant. This situation had just gotten real as the proverbial plot had just thickened. In America, it is said that blood is thicker than water. Whether or not this held true for Africa, Tony was about to find out. As the rat walked into the factory and embraced his father at the front entrance, Tony stared at him with a deadly gaze. That familiar, unmistakable look of death was back in his eyes again.

CATO

Chapter 15
In Comes the Two Sisters

Yuri Lavrov was just like any other heterosexual man. He loved beautiful women and pussy. His taste in women was unusual for a man who grew up in Eastern Europe. He loved black women, particularly African American women. There were two identical twin orphaned girls who he kept with him at all times. These two sisters, Angel and Blaze, who he trained in the deadly skills of the Spetsnaz, the Russian Special Forces, they were totally loyal and submissive to him like two trained attack dogs.

For years, they served as both his bodyguards and his freak bitch sex toys. They did anything and everything he told them to do without a second thought. If he told them to fuck some random person's brains out right there in front of him, they did it without hesitation and with a perverted satisfaction, which is how many of his rivals were lured in. As the rivals busted their last nuts, their throats were slit.

If he told them to blow someone's brains out, they did it with the same zeal and perverted satisfaction. Their weapons of choice, however, were knives as sharp as surgeon's scalpels. Their preferred method of killing was up close and personal. The ambush would be quick and vicious from each side, like the Velociraptors on the movie *Jurassic Park*. Before their hapless victim realized what was taking place, he was too weak from the blood loss to fight them off. If he managed enough strength to run, they would pursue him like two determined sister lionesses who tasted blood and locked in on their kill. When they caught up with their victim, he would die from a thousand cuts.

They were Lavrov's own personal Black Widows, hence their nicknames. Angel was dark as night and Blaze was light-skinned. Imposing figures like their old man, Lavrov, they stood at 6'3." Their bodies were chiseled with maybe five percent body fat.

They were drop dead beautiful, cunning, intelligent, educated, articulate, multilingual, charming, vicious, and above all, deadly. And they were almost as feared as their master, Lavrov.

When the tall, long blonde haired man wearing dark shades walked into the backroom of an Asian bar with the two beautiful black women close at his side, like he owned the joint, there were four older Asian men sitting at a table eating noodle soup and playing cards, while two younger guards dressed in suits stood erect at the door. Their lean physiques and stone cold sculptured faces were reminiscent of the disciplined, no nonsense Red Army Chinese soldiers. A younger, slim Chinese cat in his mid-thirties dressed in dark blue slacks and a white collared dress shirt and tie, leaned with his back against the bar sipping on a drink, looking on at the card game like an uninterested spectator.

"How are you gentlemen doing today?" Lavrov asked as he pulled up a chair and boldly sat down next to the old men. The old men sitting at the table didn't even bother to look at him. Ignoring him, they just continued their poker game and slurped down the noodles in their soups with the chopsticks. Finally, the younger Chinese cat standing at the bar, spoke up.

"Mr. Lavrov! It is good custom to make an appointment. My uncles hate spontaneous visits. And more than that, they hate rudeness. Coming here unannounced disturbing their card game, this they consider to be rude. Even if they entertained your visit here today, they are unaccustomed to women being present while talking business," he said, looking over at the widows with a contemptuous look.

Lavrov's face wrinkled, looking over at Angel and Blaze as if he was trying to figure what the old men saw wrong with them. They showed zero emotions to the slight from the skinny man who they would eat for breakfast, if unleashed. They just stood there looking straight ahead as if they didn't hear what was said.

"So with that said," the nephew continued. "Why don't you get up from this table, put that chair back where you got it, leave here and take those black whores with you."

Lavrov smiled as he cut his eyes over at the widows who were still looking straight ahead like mannequins with zero emotions, with not so much as a blink.

"Now, Mr. Bobby Chan. Is that any way to talk to a man you guys owe a great bit of money to? I have yet to get a refund on that bad batch of heroin you guys sold me last month. Besides that, I mean, you guys have become kind of wealthy and fat off me since you arrived here. Your uncles here are eating big bowls of noodle soup, blowing their money on young whores and poker games while I'm being deprived of what's owed me. Seems like you would be just a little nicer to me and show some respect," he said in a slight Russian accent. Lavrov was educated in America and spoke perfect English. His Spetsnaz training involved learning how to speak English with a classic American accent so he could infiltrate the American soldiers in the event of a war.

"The respect cuts both ways," Chan said. "We have our customs and just because we are in America and have taken full advantage of everything it has to offer, doesn't mean we forget them. Now again, I demand that you leave *now!*" he said in a stern voice. "Next time, contact us and set up an appointment before you decide to waltz in here." One of the older men frowned, shook his head and said something in Mandarin without looking up.

"My uncle just instructed me that you are not to contact us. We will contact you. Goodbye, Mr. Lavrov!"

Lavrov smiled and looked down at the floor as if he was trying to restrain himself. As he stood up, towering above the four uncles, he picked up one of the old men's cards up and turned them over. It was a royal flush. The soldiers at the door turned to face Lavrov like trained attack dogs as the widows in turn, faced them in their own attack mode. Just like that, the situation had become tense. Not wanting an escalation, the nephew waved the soldiers off.

"Looks like it's your lucky day," Lavrov said to the old man, grinning and looking at the flush. "See ya later, Mr. Bobby Chan." Lavrov stormed out of the room with the two widows behind him in lock step.

Every Friday evening Bobby Chan's Chinese Mafia uncles, aka the four uncles, frequented a high priced whorehouse, Madam X, in Greenwich Village that had a spa, a bar, a huge Olympic-size pool, and a bathhouse. Being the consummate creatures of habit, the four uncles were very particular about who they cavorted with, even when it came down to getting their rocks off. Their routine was to first get a deep tissue massage followed by acupuncture. Afterwards, they would get into the pool with the high dollar whores to have cocktails and be dirty old men. This gave them time for the Viagra to kick in before they got their freak on in a larger room equipped with beds where all the fucking took place. Everything from role playing to S and M to receiving golden showers was on their list of fetishes. Looking at these elderly men one would confuse them for Tibetan Monks. Behind closed doors, inside their whorehouse retreat, however, they were anything but men of piety and righteousness.

After the four uncles received their deep tissue massage, it was time for them to receive their acupuncture. As they laid there on their stomachs, their muscles completely relaxed from the deep tissue massage, they carried on a jovial conversation in Mandarin as four women walked in and began the acupuncture procedure, while soft Asian instrumental mood music played in the background. After the ladies placed the acupuncture needles in the appropriate pressure points, they walked out of the room momentarily. A few minutes later they returned to remove the needles.

When the uncles stood up, they moved their arms around and about in the air as if they were new men, rejuvenated by the ancient Asian procedure. Outside, two of their bodyguards laid back in their seats inside the Jaguar with their throats slit from ear to ear while the car remained running and the Asian techno music played from the car's speakers. Their lifeless wide stretched eyes displayed both shock and anguish. Whoever was responsible for the savagery, moved swiftly, silently, decisively, and deadly. This was the work of professionals who took pride in their work. The men's carotid arteries were cut with the precision of a surgeon. At the most, they felt a slight stinging sensation followed by immobility and blackout. Although the inside of the car was a gruesome scene, their deaths were nonetheless humane. Much more humane than the fate that awaited their bosses who were inside the whorehouse about to get their old men freak on.

When the four uncles stepped down into the pool butt ass naked, a naked waitress came by with a serving tray that contained alcoholic drinks and a mixture of red, black and green grapes. After serving them, she walked away giggling after one of the uncles smacked her on her ass and made a dirty old man comment to her. A few minutes later, four sexy young girls, two Asian and two white, walked in, in bathrobes as the old men's eyes were trained on them. Standing there at the edge of the pool, the young whores smiled and dropped their robes at the same time, revealing smooth, young, pristine bodies. These girls could have been no more than 16 years old, just as the old men had requested. Once inside the huge Olympic-sized pool, each girl was paired off with one of these men who were old enough to be their great grandfathers. The men laughed and talked in Mandarin as the girls flirted with them and fed them grapes as if they were Kings.

As all involved continued to have a blast in the dimly lit swimming pool enclosure, there was a slight, calm ripple on top of the water on the opposite end of the huge pool, followed by something swimming gracefully below the surface towards them. The underwater movements of these objects were smooth, serene and peaceful as none of the pool's occupants noticed it. The four uncles were preoccupied with the young tender things in front of them, as the Viagra had begun to kick in. And the young girls were preoccupied in doing what prostitutes do….making old men feel young and virile again. And they seemed to being doing a damn good job of it as they should. They were paid well. The house got a stack a piece, while the girls received the same amount, plus tips for any extracurricular freaky shit. To these men, the fee was akin to a tip at a low scale restaurant. These crime bosses were so wealthy, they made Bill Gates look like a welfare case.

When one of the uncles looked down at the water he noticed a red fluid oozing up to the surface.

"Shénme tā mā de," he said in Mandarin. What the fuck?! The red fluid also caught the attention of one of his brothers who also noticed it. Almost simultaneously, the brother who stood on the far end let out a yelp and pushed one of the young girl's away from him. She fell back in the water as he held his crotch. At this point, two shadows underneath the water's surface quickly rose up in front of the men like attack submarines. One of them held a knife between her teeth as she held up a severed penis still attached to its balls in her right hand. She grinned as she displayed it to the poor fellow it once belonged to.

"I think you lost something, daddy?" she said in a sensual voice. When he reached down to make sure he still had his goods, he pulled up his hands and screamed. His goods were gone. The pool turned red with blood as he struggled to get on to the dry landing. Another uncle let out a yelp as well. His body bristled as if a jolt of electricity surged through it. When he looked down, he saw something that resembled a snake. He clutched his stomach as the pain hit him. He was horrified when he realized it was

146

his long intestine snaking out of his abdominal cavity and floating up to the surface of the water. He was cut from his dick all the way up to his chest cavity. The incision was clean and straight.

The young girls were slow to react due to the several shots of alcohol and the zanny bars they took prior to coming out so they could stomach dealing with these dirty old men. Once the sight of the bloody penis and intestines finally registered in their brains, they screamed at the top of their lungs as they frantically leaped from the pool and fled, leaving the old men to fend for themselves. The other two brothers who were standing in the middle during the initial attack, once they realized what was taking place, it was too late for them. The bloodletting was already well underway and at a point of no return.

The widows were unmerciful and relentless in their attack. Their swift and constant slashing techniques with short combat knives in both hands, unleashing in a deadly rhythm, was medieval and brutal. It was reminiscent of that brutal scene in the movie *Patriots* when Mel Gibson's character was giving the British soldier the business with the two tomahawks, in what would be one of the most graphic movie scenes ever. One of the brothers managed to muster enough strength to get out of the pool, although he suffered massive blood loss. Perhaps he was operating on pure adrenaline produced by his body going in fight or flight mode. Blaze, was undeterred as she pursued him relentlessly. She was locked in on him like a predator on wounded prey, and there was no way he was going to escape her wrath this day. When she caught up with the slow moving and defenseless old man, he resigned himself to fight rather than flee. The fright in his eyes told the story. *Fight or die!*

As she hovered over him like an ominous storm cloud that blighted out the sun, with a crazed smile on her face, he turned over on his back in the dying cockroach position and made a pathetic attempt to fight her off, but this only seemed to increase her blood frenzy. Like a wild beast with claws slashing, she was all over his ass. The lightning fast movement of those short combat knives in Blaze's hands were like a blur worthy of a slow motion replay for the spectator to fully appreciate the speed. She made quick work of him. The masterful way in which she used those knives, it was as if they were a part of her hands, which was a testament to Lavrov's training. Within seconds, the old man's entire body was a bloody mess with cuts from his head to his toes. Throughout the entire ordeal, the Chinese mobster who for over half a century had many men killed on his orders, screamed and screeched in pain like a bitch until his tormenter made the humane decision to end his suffering with a final coup de gras to the jugular vein, nearly decapitating him. The force of her slash, coupled with the sharp razor edges of the knife, made with the same carbon steel, cut clean through his vertebrae with ease. His dangling head was held on to his neck by a strand of skin and cartilage.

As the other three uncles floated face down in the pool that had now become colored red with their lifeblood, as if someone dumped red dye in the water, Angel realized her work was done and pulled herself out of the water onto the deck. As her tall muscular, but shapely, frame moved stoically alongside the edge of the pool like a supermodel on the runway, showing no emotions, she looked down at the tray that still had the refreshments sitting on top of a serving stand and smiled. She grabbed a handful of the grapes and began eating them.

"Hmmmmm. These are soooooooo sweet," she said as her sister walked up to her and invited herself to a couple of them. After popping the grapes into her mouth, she chomped down on them. Her eyes lit up as she looked around surveying and gloating over the human carnage.

"They sure are sweet." She smiled. Before shedding their blood soaked wetsuits and dropping them into the pool, they collected some souvenirs from the bodies of the old men and walked away from the macabre crime scene enjoying the grapes as if it was just another day at the office.

That evening Bobby Chan got a ring at his door. When he opened it, no one was there. *I could have sworn I heard the doorbell ring,* he thought himself. Looking around from side to side cautiously, he scanned the streets and didn't see anyone. Before he closed his door something told him to look down. Directly at his feet, there was a package with a UPS sticker addressed to him. Somewhat apprehensive, he hesitantly picked up the package and walked back inside his house staring at it. With the package still in hand, and his eyes scanning it from corner to corner, he sat down at his kitchen table. After a few seconds of contemplating whether he should open it or not, his curiosity got the best of him. When he cut open the box, he saw two bundles wrapped in bubble wrap. He opened one of them to find a doll. Bewildered by this strange looking doll, he held it in his hand and analyzed it as his wife walked into the kitchen and smiled at the sight of the doll. After kissing him on the cheek she went to the refrigerator, grabbed some orange juice and sat back down at the table next to him.

"What is it, dear?" she asked, before taking a sip of the juice.

"It's a freaking doll. What does it look like?" he shot back sarcastically.

"Yes, I see that it's a doll. What kind of doll is it? It sure looks creepy."

"It looks like the Grim Reaper."

"Grim Reaper? What is that?" she asked before taking another drink of her o.j.

"A Grim Reaper symbolizes the bringer of death and the taker of the souls of those who died," he said, still analyzing the doll.

"That's spooky," she said with her face wrinkled up. "Who in the world would send you something like that?"

"I'm not sure. And there is no return address."

After losing curiosity in the doll, Chan placed it down on the table, and trained his attention on the second wrapped package. Pausing for a second to analyze it in an investigative manner, he began to open it. Once he removed the bubble wrap he found a 4 by 4 gift box wrapped in cotton. After removing the cotton followed by the box's top, he pulled back another layer of cotton to see four fortune cookies attached to four severed penis stained with dried coagulated blood. Bobby Chan and his wife let out blood curdling, high pitched screams that could be heard throughout their upscale, gated neighborhood.

Chapter 16
A Woman Scorned

Two days after Tony found out the identity of the rat, he and Macky were set to meet up with Ike at his crib to break the news to him. When Ike had decided to remain behind to spend some time with his son in the Congo, he hadn't sat down to explain to his wife the bombshell Enid dropped on him of a long lost son. Ike confided to Tony that he was trying to figure out how he would break it to Samira, who wasn't the easiest person in the world to reason with. She was a hot-tempered, strong-willed black woman who was use to calling shots and getting her way. The only way Ike was going to overcome her undying jealousy for Enid was to unleash the alpha male and calm her ass down. Even with that last line of defense every real nigga had in his arsenal, there was still a good chance she would go the fuck off anyway.

One week later, when Tony and Macky arrived at Ike's crib, they saw two of the maids, a butler and two members of Ike's security standing outside with startled looks on their faces. Inside Ike's crib, the unmistakable sound of domestic drama was taking place. The sounds of broken glass, screams and curses could be heard. Each time a glass broke after coming in contact with the wall and floor, the maids and butler would react to it by hunching their shoulders and ducking their heads as it was being hurled at them. Ike's guards, however, tried to remain stoic in front of Tony and Macky.

"I don't think it would be wise to go in there, sir," the wide-eyed butler said to Tony who was just about to grab the knob to the front door. Tony smiled.

"Somebody has to go in. If not, you are going to have a dead boss on your hands." When Tony and Macky walked inside, an expensive looking piece of porcelain flew passed them and hit the wall next to the front door. It broke into a hundred pieces. Luckily for them they ducked in the nick of time. Ike could be heard inside the bathroom where he was barricaded in.

"My Queen! Must I remind you that is your shit you are breaking. Not mine!" he yelled.

"I don't give a fuck! Whatever I break, it is mine to break you no good motherfucker!" she screamed from the top of her lungs. Tony and Macky stood there seemingly lost on what to say or do. Tony was somewhat amused at the situation as Samira dared Ike to come out and face her like a real man.

"Come out of there and face a real woman, motherfucker!" she yelled. "That is your problem. You are not used to dealing with a real woman! You are only used to associating with bush bitches and whores!" When Tony and Macky entered the huge hallway leading to the bathroom Ike was held up in, they saw Samira pacing back and forth in front of the door looking like a hungry animal waiting for its dinner to come out of its hiding place. When she saw them she started protesting even harder.

"I see that your friend has come to save your miserable life! You are going to need him and the Ghanaian army when I'm done!" she yelled to the door.

"Tony! Is that you?" Ike yelled with his ear to the door.

"Yes, it's me. Should I come back?" Tony asked with a light-hearted laugh.

"No! No! No! Whatever you do, do not leave me in my time of need, my brother." Tony and Macky chuckled.

"You will have to come out of that fucking bathroom sooner or later, you coward!" she screamed at the door.

"I don't know, my Queen. It's pretty roomy and comfortable in here. And there is a nice big screen television in here too with all my favorite channels. A man can stay in here for days." Tony grinned, but quickly erased the smile when Samira turned to him with seething anger. Her eyes showed something in them at that point that said shit had just escalated to another level.

"Okay motherfucker! Okay! I have something that will make you come out of there and face me much sooner than you think!" she yelled before storming away.

"Tony! Did she leave out?" Ike asked with his ear to the door.

"Yep."

"Where did she go?"

"If I had to guess, she's going to get some fire."

"When you say fire, you mean a gun?" he asked with his ear still up to the door and a concerned look on his face.

"Yeah, bruh," Tony said with a grin. "She's not really going to shoot you though, is she?"

"I'm not sure this time. She now knows about my son," Ike yelled as he tried to listen out for her footsteps. Moments later Samira came rushing around the corner chambering a 7.62 bullet into an AK.

"If you don't want to get shot, you had better get the fuck behind me!" she yelled to Tony and Macky.

"My Queen! Whatever you are about to do, don't do it, dear. You have to allow me to explain." When she took aim at the door, Tony realized she was serious and quickly snatched the gun out of her hands. Almost as soon as he took the chopper from her, her right hand was coming out of her boot with a knife. Before she could swing it, Macky grabbed her hand and restrained her. Samira was dangerous. She seemed to revert back to her days of fighting in the Liberian civil war.

"I think you ought to come out now, bruh," Tony said in a serious tone as he held the chopper in his hands.

"Are you sure? She's no longer armed?"

"I'm sure. She's not armed anymore."

"Let my arm go, motherfucker!" she demanded with her bloodshot red eyes looking up at Macky. When Ike exited the bathroom, Macky let her go, and she immediately pounced on Ike like a wild animal.

"You no good motherfucker! It took your friends to save you!" she said as he fended off her hard punches and kicks. Tony had to grab her.

"My Queen. Calm down! Now!" he said in a stern voice, but to no avail. She landed a kick to his chest that upended him over a chair. He popped up angry. When he rushed her, she punched at him while Tony held her with a firm grip. It took all he had to restrain her. Samira wasn't the average female. She was 6"1 and was 175 pounds of muscle. She was also a martial arts expert and trained to kill with anything she got her hands on. On top of that, she was as strong as the average man.

At this point, Ike seemed to have had enough. He snatched her away from Tony and manhandled her into the living room.

"You are going to finish hearing me out if I have to kill you!" he said to her in a deadly serious voice.

"And that is just what you will have to do, motherfucker," she said with a crazed look in her eyes.

"No! I want you to calm down and hear me out!" he said as Tony and Macky looked on. This was no laughing matter anymore. If Tony and Macky had not been there, someone might have died this evening. This was the reason for the concerned looks on the faces of the hired help who were standing outside where it was safe.

"Are you going to calm down or am I going to have to leave until you do?" he said as he held her tightly.

"So you are going to be with that whore, aye? Go ahead and join her then, motherfucker!"

"I'm not going to be with any whore. But I will not stay here with you acting like some, some, some, hood rat!" Tony nearly collapsed to the floor. To hear an African call someone a hood rat shocked and amused him.

"Hey, Ike, I think we should come back later, bruh," Tony said as he tried to contain his laughter.

"I think that would be a good idea too, my brother. I tell you what. Even better. I will come to your villa as soon as I am in control of this crisis," he said as he continued to hold his wild cat wife at bay.

"Control? You need to control your worthless dick and keep it in your trousers!" she said mockingly.

"Okay, my brother. See you later," Tony said before he and Macky exited Ike's crib. As they walked to the car, the hired help was still posted up outside in the same spot looking crazy. In a weird way, the drama Ike was going through made Tony think about his own Queen back at home who he hadn't had one argument with the entire time they'd been together, not even a sharp disagreement. The one thing that was mandatory in Tony's personal life was peace in the home. It was the one thing that his father and uncle instilled in him. *Never have a broad who won't give you that peace that every man needs,* they would often tell him.

Chapter 17
Thicker Than Blood Relations

Lying in bed at his new villa, Tony placed a call to Sugar, and before the second ring, she picked up.

"Hey, Bae!" she said excitedly.

"Hey, Baby Girl! What you up to?"

"I'm just chilling and going over the store's books. What are you doing?" she asked before entering some data on the online spreadsheet.

"I'm here at the villa missing me some you sumpin' serious."

"Oh really?" she asked smiling. "How much?"

"So much so, I called you. Words can't adequately express how much I'm missing the love of my life right now."

"That's still not telling me how much. Express it to me in classic Tony Stallworth terms." She stopped typing, sipped her Hennessy and listened intently.

"Okay, I can see where this is going. You want me to talk nasty to you because you're horny, right?" Tony said with a chuckle.

"Sho' you right. You already know. I stay horny," she said as she got up from the computer desk and walked to their bedroom and lay down across the bed. *This is just what I needed,* she thought to herself and smiled as she opened her nightstand drawer and looked at her toy.

"Hmmmm. Okay. What are you wearing right now?" he asked in a sexy voice.

"Nothing. Only a robe. You already know."

"Hmmmm. Is my pussy getting wet already?"

"You already know that too. It's always wet, especially the minute I hear your voice."

"Mmmmm. I see. Where are your hands, right now?"

"I have one holding the phone and the other on her," she said smiling. Her eyes began to narrow from the pleasure she was beginning to feel from rubbing on her sweetness.

"Mmmmmm. So, is my moist, wet tongue down there yet, softly licking on it?"

"Yeeeesss!" she said as she reached over and took her toy out of the nightstand.

"Mmmmmm. Are you holding my hands and watching me as I lick it good, baby?"

"Yesssss! I am!" she said as she put him on speaker phone before rubbing on her sweetness began to pick up the pace.

"Mmmmmmmm. Have I climbed on you and start fucking that pussy good yet?"

"Oooooooh yeeeesss, Bae!" she said as her hand had begun to pick up speed while pushing the toy in and out of her with a slow, steady, methodical rhythm.

"Mmmmm. Am I hitting it from the back now, baby? Is your face down on our bed, and your ass up into my chest while you feeling this dick deep inside you?

"Oooooh yeeeeessssss!" she said as her hand now moved rapidly over her clit that had now swollen to its full capacity from the excitement. Her toy traversed her walls, as she pushed it in and out with each quick movement of her wrist. Her legs began to shake and wobble as they weakened from the pleasure. The moment she closed her eyes to visualize riding Tony, she pulled the toy out of her and squirted her warm juices all over the towel that was settled under her ass. She panted and moaned as the juices continued to flow freely.

"Mmmmmmmm baby. Did you just cum for me and leave a puddle in the bed?" Tony knew his woman.

"Yeeesss, Bae!" she replied in a low exasperated voice. "Did I? Damn, Bae, I reeeaaalllly needed that!" she said as she continue to rub her cat slowly as if to calm it down. "When are you coming home, now?" she asked. Tony laughed.

"I will be home soon, baby."

"Okay. I hope it's like real soon. And stay away from those pretty African girls. I heard those bitches put spells on men to keep them from ever leaving." Tony laughed out loud.

"That, you don't have to ever worry about and you know that. There isn't a spell powerful enough to keep me away from you."

"Better not be. I would hate to superglue your dick to your leg while you sleep," she said in a serious voice. Again, Tony laughed out loud.

"Oh no! That is exactly why I'm going to behave myself. I need my dick free and hanging."

"Ummmmm. Hanging, you say? Talking like that make me wanna have another session," she said as she continued to rub her cat.

"Nah, baby. We gone have to stop at one session tonight. Ike should be here any moment. If he ain't dead," he joked.

"Huh?" Sugar asked with a confused look on her face.

"I will tell you about it later." He chuckled. There was a ring at the door followed by the sound of Ike's distinct voice.

"Hey, Baby Girl. Speaking of the devil. Ike just walked in. I will get at you later, okay?"

"Alright, Bae. I'm going to keep this pussy warm for you."

"You do that, Baby Girl. You do that." he smiled.

"Muah!" she said with her lips making a kissing gesture.

"Muah!" Tony replied before hanging up the phone and walking into the living room.

"My brother, I see that you are still alive and in one piece," Tony said laughing.

"Yes, my brother. But barely. I do think if I was as light as you are, by tomorrow, I would have a black eye for all to see," he said, holding his eye. "Damn! My queen sure can pack a punch!"

"Well, my brother, if you think she hits hard, what I'm about to tell you will floor you. Sit down," Tony said as he sat on a barstool, at which time Macky walked in and sat down beside him.

"What is this news that I have to take a seat?" Ike asked with a wrinkle in his forehead.

"Since I decided to take over your operation, Macky and I have been trying to find that rat in your organization. We have placed bugs in the factory, placed GPS's on cars at the factory and have tracked those coming and going. The same rat who's been informing that Russian about the shipments, we tracked him also. The same rat who got your shipment intercepted and the couriers killed. This rat is your cousin. Your uncle's son." Ike immediately shot to his feet and shook his head.

"What?" he said in total disbelief. "Which one? There are two."

"The cousin here in Ghana. Macky was finally able to track him to his home the other day after he had met again with the Russian in town at a produce market."

"You mean Ezekiel. Are you sure that this is true, my brother? I don't need any room for error on this." Tony looked at Macky and nodded his head for him to speak.

"Yes. I am 100% sure he is the man who's been meeting with the Russian," Macky said. "I'm 98% sure he is the rat."

"And that 2% possibility that he isn't the rat is what makes me hesitant to buy into this." Ike shot back. "I need to know for sure. I need 100%. Not 98%. Not 99%. I need 100% proof." Tony looked at Macky. He knew the minute they I.D.'d the rat that this was going to be a trying situation. However, whether Ike came to terms with it or not, this was now his show and that rat had to be dealt with, even if he had to take care of it himself. Or have Macky to do it.

"Well, my brother, I understand your dilemma, but I totally trust Macky's judgment," Tony said. "However, if you need more proof to be 100% sure there are ways we can find out."

"Like what?" Ike asked with a cynical look on his face.

"Leave that to us. We will find out," Tony said.

"Okay. Do whatever it is you have to do, but don't touch my blood. Leave that to me. If he is the traitor he is mine to deal with."

"Okay. Cool. But he must be dealt with if he's the rat," Tony said with a serious look on his face.

"That goes without saying, my brother,." Ike said as he headed to the door. "I'm like you. I never leave loose ends either. Even if those loose ends are my blood. You do whatever you have to do to prove your case," he said before walking out. Ike didn't want to accept that his blood was the traitor. The very charge actually angered him. Macky looked over at Tony.

"Do you want me to handle it?"

"No. At least not yet," Tony said as he stared out of the window watching Ike get into his ride. He now questioned his decision to tell Ike that his cousin was the rat. It was beginning to look like blood is thicker than water in Africa like it is in America, after all.

The next day there was a gathering at Ike's crib. The usual dignitaries, politicians and wealthy business people were all present. If one wasn't invited to one of Ike's gatherings he was a nobody. It was the one event that people inside and outside of Ghana was never a no-show to, if invited. It was akin to receiving a Presidential invite. The kind that very few people turned down unless they were some racist Tea Party asshole who would rather be shot in the head 20 times than to be seen smiling and kicking it with the "colored guy." When Tony and Macky walked in, they were greeted by Samira. She acted as though nothing happened the day before. It was as if it she was a totally different person.

"Hello there, Tony!" she said as she hugged him.

"Everything's good, First Lady," he said smiling. "How are you? You taking care of my man?"

"Yes. All is well. And I am taking care of your man as long as he continues to take care of me," she said donning a diamond ring so big, that it made the rock of Gibraltar look like a $2 hit of crack.

"Oooo-Kaaay. I see that he is doing what he supposed to be doing."

"Yes, he is. And he means the world to me," she said enthusiastically. "Now how is your wife?"

"She's fine. Just talked to her yesterday."

"Good. You need to be there with her, her every waking moment."

"Are you kidding?" he said jokingly. "She would grow tired of me in less than a week." Samira laughed.

"Okay. Understood. But don't be away from her too long. We Queens need our Kings by our sides to rule the kingdom."

"No doubt," Tony said just as Ike walked in.

"My brother! How are you and Macky?" he asked with his hand extended.

"All is well, my brother. We decided to come hang out with you for a little while."

"Good! I want you to come with me for a minute. I have someone I want you to meet. Baby, we will be back in a moment," he said as he placed a kiss on her cheek.

"Okay, my King. I'm going to entertain our guests before they consider us bad hosts."

"Okay, Queen. See you shortly." As Ike, Tony and Macky walked through the hallways, the speakers played soft music amid the laughter and chatter of the guests in the banquet room.

"Okay. What did you do to her?" Tony asked smiling.

"Who me?" Ike asked, pointing at himself.

"To Samira. She's like a little pussy cat right now."

"Oh. I did nothing other than tell her the truth."

"So you telling me that a woman who was about to hit you off with an AK, was calmed down by you coming clean? I don't believe it." Ike laughed as they stepped onto the elevator.

"Well, when I first broke the news about my son, she didn't give me time to explain. She went ballistic as soon as I sat her down and told her. After she calmed down long enough for me to tell her the entire story that my son wasn't conceived during the time she and I were together, all was well."

"Okay. But how did you calm her down to even explain that much to her? The woman I left you with was out of her mind and passed the point of explanations." Ike chuckled.

"I fucked her good," he said as the elevator door opened up. "Works every time like a charm for me with these African women," he said smiling.

When Ike, Tony and Macky walked into this dark, dimly lit room, Tony and Macky saw what looked like an elderly lady far back in the corner of the room in a chair watching one of those Nigerian versions of the soap operas, which were very popular throughout all of Africa. Ike walked up to her and kissed her on the cheek and forehead.

"Hello, grandmother," he said before whispering something in her ear. The elderly lady just continued to look straight ahead without even acknowledging the two strangers in her huge bedroom. Ike looked over at Macky.

"Hey Youngster, come sit here," he said, pulling out a chair. Macky walked up somewhat reluctantly and sat down in the chair in front of the elderly lady who looked like she was in her 50s. Her silver hair was dreaded up neatly. Her eyes were a light brown and her skin tone was immaculate. She looked as if she stood nearly 7 ft tall, although it was hard to tell by her sitting down. When she grabbed Macky's hand, it was clearly twice the size of his. By all accounts this lady was a giant. Not saying a word, she smiled at him endearingly while caressing his hands. With a bewildered look on his face, Macky in turn managed to give her a half smile. This beautiful old lady sitting in front of him, he felt a strange kinship with, but questioned in his mind what her motives were. Though he was cautious and guarded as ever, he hadn't felt this type of motherly love since he was a small kid in Yonkers when his dear granny was alive, motherly love that he never received from his own heroin junky mother, who died from an overdose with a needle stuck in her arm. After about a minute she finally spoke.

"You have been on this earth for only 25 years, aye?" she asked. Her voice sounded exactly like Maya Angelou, but with a strong Nigerian accent.

"Yes, ma'am. I just turned 25," he said with an almost child-like smile.

"You are troubled in your soul due to your upbringing. You are missing something essential that every child must grow up with. Yet you are loyal. You have honor. You are a man of prin-ciple. You are also a killer of men," she said as the smile with-drew from her face and was replaced with a slight frown.

"But these men you have killed were bad men. Men with no earthly good in them. Men with no honor. In you, however, there is much earthly good. You are honest and there is much truth in you….something that the world has become void of." She looked over at Ike. "This young man speaks the truth. Believe everything that he has told you thus far and in the future," she said as she continued to hold Macky's hands tightly, and smiling at him endearingly as she would her own grandson. "I want you to take care of yourself and beware of your surroundings at all times, young man. Also beware of a pair of beautiful women you have yet to meet. Like you, they have killed many men."

Still smiling, Macky nodded his head at her. Before standing up he placed a kiss on her cheek, which surprised the hell out of Tony. He never saw that side of his number one killer, who was the exact carbon copy of himself. A young protégé, who he taught every deadly trick of his trade that he had stored in the dark recesses of his brain. There was much more to Macky's story that Tony wasn't aware of. He heard some things about his upbringing and after seeing the touching interaction between he and the old lady, he needed to know more about him. But that had to wait.

It was obvious why Ike brought them up there. This lady was what they called in the south a *root lady*. Meaning, she could tell fortunes and see into the hearts of men. Before they walked out, Ike walked up to her and kissed her once again on her cheek and forehead. The old lady then turned back around in her chair and resumed watching her soap opera.

After they all got onto the elevator, and the door shut, Ike said looking straight ahead, "That woman is my grandmother. She has the gift of my ancestors. She turned 105 today. The celebration downstairs is her birthday party." Tony and Macky looked at him in total disbelief regarding her age. Ike turned to Macky, looked him straight into his eyes and placed his hand on his shoulder. "Youngster, I want you to know I never doubted your judgment about my cousin. I just needed confirmation and I just got it. I want for my own sake one more thing done before I make my move. I need to make sure he is the only one in my family who sold me out to that Russian motherfucker." As soon as Ike said that, the elevator door opened and the three men walked back to join the festivities.

Not long after Tony, Macky and Ike joined the other guests, Ike's uncle walked in, much to Ike's surprise. His uncle, who was somewhat of a recluse, very seldom showed up to his events.

"Uncle!" Ike said excitedly with his outstretched arms. "I am delighted to see that you have finally graced my home with your presence. Everyone! This is my uncle," he said as his uncle looked at everyone shyly. The guests all stopped whatever they were doing and got up from their seats to greet him. For those who knew him, he was not only a national hero, he was a hero known throughout all of Africa. He was a freedom fighter and an oppressor's worst nightmare. His calm demeanor and shyness belied his reputation as a tenacious, anti-colonialist warrior. As the various people greeted him with handshakes and hugs, another man wearing an old man derby on his head walked in. At the sight of this man, Macky and Tony, who were sitting on the other side of the room being spectators , their eyes perked up. It was the rat. Standing right there in front of them as big as day rubbing elbows with the distinguished guests. After handing the butler his hat, the rat walked up to Ike and embraced him tightly. Ike stood back and smiled as if to get a better glance at him.

"My cousin! My favorite uncle's eldest son! How have you been? And what brings you here tonight? It's been a long time since you graced my home with your welcomed presence."

"Yes, my cousin. It has been some time. After taking that online job, I very seldom have much time to do anything anymore."

"An online job? What does it entail?" Ike asked as he led him to the guest room.

"It is a freight broker position. I move freight online."

"Is that right? That sounds like a very involved job."

"Yes. It involves moving freight air, land, and sea."

"Wonderful! As long as it keeps you busy and it's profitable. But you must get over here more often to see your cousin." Ike smiled and carried on as if everything was cool. The cousin had no idea that he had been I.D.'d as a traitor to not only to Ike's organization, but in Ike's mind, to the whole continent of Africa. Those diamonds were worth more than money. They represented the Creator's favor with the Motherland.

"When was the last time you've seen your grandmother?" Ike asked.

"I have not seen her since grandfather's passing."

"Wow! That was about five years ago, was it not?"

"Yes. Like I said. That job. It keeps me away from everything and everyone," he said with a nervous smile.

"Would you like to see her? She's upstairs," Ike said before he could refuse.

"Who, grandmother?"

"Yes."

"You mean, grandmother is upstairs? Here in this house?"

"Yes. She's been staying with me since grandfather passed on to our ancestors. Go on up and see her. I'm sure she would be most delighted to see you after all this time," Ike said as he grabbed his arm. "Do you still remember your way around the house?"

"Yes, I think so. But you know, Ike, Grandmother was never too fond of me. She once told me that she saw something foul in me. Who tells their own young grandchild this?" he said with a slight frown on his face.

"Nonsense! She loves you just as much as she loved me or any of her other many grandchildren. You were just a mischievous child at the time she said that. Now go on up there and see her. I insist. She would be happy, since it is her birthday party. I will escort you up there," Ike said as he pulled him towards the hallway leading to the elevator. Not once did he give him a chance to refuse. By this time, the rat knew he wasn't going to take no for answer. And there was no way he was going to leave that house without seeing his grandmother. Perhaps he was hesitant because he knew she could see through him. Or more importantly, in him. Once they reached her room, Ike spoke to her softly.

"Grandmother, I have someone who wants to see you. Someone you have not laid eyes on in some time now. Your other grandson, Ezekiel. " The rat approached smiling.

"Hello grandmother. How are you?" he said, smiling as he approached her with his arms outstretched. "It has been a long time." Granny didn't even bother to turn around or change the expression she had on her face. She just kept watching her Nigerian soap.

"I'm blessed," she finally answered, coldly. "Let me look at you in your eyes to see if you are the same rotten grandchild I've known all these years." He sat down in front of her with a shit eating grin on his face.

"He he he." He laughed halfheartedly. "I see you still say what comes to mind," he said as she looked at him in his eyes. After looking into him and studying him carefully for a few seconds without blinking, her eyes turned to small slits. He smiled at her as if he was trying to woo her. Suddenly, she turned away from him and resumed watching TV. "You have not changed. In fact, you are worse now as an adult than you were when you were a child. If I never saw you again it would do my heart and soul good." Ezekiel looked over at Ike who titled his head down to the floor in disappointment.

"I still love you, grandmother, no matter what you think of me," he said as he tried to grab her hand. When she jerked it away from him, he walked off with a defeated look on his face.

"I told you, didn't I?" he said to Ike before walking out of the room pass him. Ike looked over at his grandmother.

"You would do yourself a world of good if you cut ties with your cousin, son," she said with her eyes still glued on the TV.

She didn't even bother to look up. Ike put his head down and walked out of the room. Standing on the elevator, he was perplexed. A thousand and one emotions were going through his brain at one time. He knew that his cousin had to be dealt with and soon. But this wasn't just any cousin. He was more like a brother after Ike's parents took him in while his father was away fighting in the war. *Perhaps there is a way Ezekiel could redeem himself,* Ike thought as he watched Ezekiel walk back over and began interacting with his father and the other guests. But he knew better. There was no other way this thing could be handled any other way. Stallworth would lose all faith in his judgment if he failed or refused to.

Chapter 18
Judgment Day for Ezekiel

The streets in Ghana were relatively quiet as they normally were on Sunday mornings. The only people up moving around were the very few Christians who attended church services in a predominantly Muslim nation, where Mosques and other reminders of Ghana's Islamic past and present were everywhere. After the Russian and his girl pulled into the hotel's parking garage, the Russian hopped out of the Mercedes Benz, grabbed a suitcase from the trunk, before he and his broad proceeded into their hotel arm in arm. As they walked pass the only hotel clerk standing behind the service desk, he acted like he was reading. The bald ebony clerk cut his eyes from the papers in front of him, and looked over his glasses at them as they got onto the elevator.

When they reached their suite, his broad kissed him and proceeded into the bathroom to run some bath water. The Russian, tired from his girl's long drawn out shopping spree, the kind that every man dreads, placed the suitcase down inside the closet, kicked his shoes off and lay across the bed with the remote control in his hand. Lying there relaxed, he flicked the TV from channel to channel. After growing bored with the television selections, he tossed the remote on the nightstand and rolled over on his side.

Seconds after closing his eyes, a powerful hand holding a cloth violently covered his mouth. He tried in vain to struggle, but to no avail. The strong vapors from the chemical substance on the cloth began to overpower him. Moments later, the Russian was totally unconscious. The knock-out drug had hit its mark. Inside the bathroom, his broad had begun to undress. She was totally unaware that some masked intruder, for some unknown reason, had breached their room and just incapacitated her old man.

Once the intruder tied, bound and gagged the Russian, he turned his attention on the bathroom. The Russian's bitch was coming with him. When she opened the door and walked out to grab her toiletries, the same cloth covered hand draped her mouth. Her screams were muffled as she struggled to fight off her invisible attacker. As the vapors invaded her lungs, her once wide-stretched, fright-filled eyes that were trained on her old man laid across the bed hogtied, like one of those roasting pigs headed for the spit, began to roll in the back of her head as her struggling became more and more faint. Seconds later her body went completely limp, and the intruder laid her across the bed beside her old man.

After removing his mask, Macky placed a call. "Ok. The package is ready."

A couple of minutes later, Kobani and two of his men rushed into the room, grabbed the Russian and his girl onto their shoulders and took them away. As they passed through the lobby headed to the side exit, the hotel's clerk knelt down under the desk as if he was looking for something. Before walking out, Kobani smiled and placed a $100 bill down on the desk. When the men were out of sight, the clerk rose back up, cuffed his hush money, put it in his pocket and scanned the lobby to make sure no one was looking.

After throwing the Russian and his broad into the Range Rover, it pulled away with Macky trailing in a separate vehicle.

When the Russian regained consciousness, his eyes struggled to regain focus as the drugs began to wear off. At first the Russian didn't realize he was swinging upside down until the blood started rushing to his head, followed by sharp pain. Everything was upside down, including his girl who was over in the corner bound and gagged and her eyes displaying terror. As his eyes regained their full focus, he realized he was in a huge warehouse with two of three men he'd never seen before.

Tony, Ike and Macky stood in front of him with no nonsense looks on their faces. What he saw in their eyes was not good. It was at that point he attempted to plead his case in vain. But whoever gagged him, knew exactly what they were doing. The gag was on so tight he couldn't even move his lips to form a word. Being a mouth breather, he was struggling to breathe through his nose. He had no idea who these men were and why he was there. Whatever the reason, however, it obviously wasn't one that would end well, he guestimated.

"Hello, Vladimir," Tony said smiling. The Russian mumbled something as he recognized Tony as the man he conversed with at the bar.

"I'm sure by now you are wondering why we brought you here," Ike said. "Then again, I'm confident you know exactly why you are here." The Russian again mumbled something in vain, but the gag and masking tape over his mouth made it impossible for him to speak. When he got tired of trying to speak through his mouth, he attempted to speak with his eyes.

"Take the tape off his mouth, Kobani," Ike said. Kobani walked up to the Russian and viciously ripped the tape from his mouth with zero regard for his skin. Half of his mustache went with the tape.

"Fuck!" the Russian said with his mouth twisted from the pain of having the tape snatched off. "Now why the fuck did you bring me and my woman here? I demand some answers!"

"I was hoping you would tell me why you are here in Ghana," Ike said as he knelt down in front of him. 'But let's get something clear. You are obviously not in a position to demand anything. I will do the demanding."

"I'm a fucking tourist! Now what is the meaning of this?" Ike, Tony, Macky and Kobani just stood there looking at him and not saying a word. They were unmoved and undeterred by his evasiveness, like the feds in an interrogation.

"Go get him," Ike said to Kobani. Kobani followed his boss' instructions and stepped outside. Moments later he returned with two soldiers, one on each side of Ezekiel, whose hands were tied behind his back and his face sunk in from fear.

"Cousin," he said to Ike as he was about to begin pleading his own case. "What is the meaning of this?" Ike stood there shaking his head with a look of disgust on his face as the men hoisted Ezekiel up alongside the Russian suspending him in the air upside down.

"Do you know this man, Ezekiel?" Ike asked. Ezekiel hesitated and looked away. "Cousin! I think you know me well enough to understand how serious I am right now. I am in a very dangerous mood today and my patience has long run its course. Now I will ask you one more time, do you know this man?" Still defiant, Ezekiel didn't utter a word. "Okay. I see," Ike said with a wicked look on his face.

"Now I'm going to be fair and give you a chance to come clean, sir, since the cat seems to have my cousin's tongue." Ike said to the Russian. "Do you know this man next to you? If so, how?"

In his own show of defiance, the Russian gave his answer by spitting on the ground near Ike's feet. This infuriated Ike. He looked as if he was a man about to explode. For the time being, the two men refused to speak, but little did they know, somebody was going to talk.

"Bring them in!" Ike said to Kobani. "Someone is going to talk today! That, I can promise you!" Ike said as he stared the two men in their eyes.

"My cousin! Isaac! Can you tell me what is the meaning of this?"

"Shut up!" Ike said sharply. "Don't fucking 'cousin' me! You know damn well why we are here! You really disappointed me,

Ezekiel. You really, really disappointed me," Ike said, just as Kobani and his men returned with a huge cage on wheels, covered by a huge tarp that obviously contained animals inside. The unmistakable smell of wild animal musk invaded the closed in warehouse. The eyes of the two men began to bulge from fear and due to the blood rushing to their heads from hanging upside down. A smiling Kobani snatched the tarp from over the cage, revealing four hyenas that anxiously paced back and forth inside the cage. Their bone chilling laughter-like noises echoed off the walls of the warehouse. Their cold black eyes stared at the men as they licked their lips like predators do when dinner is served.

"Okay. Now who's going to talk first?" Ike asked as he looked back and forth between them.

"Cousin, I do not know this man!" Ezekiel said with his voice cracking from fear. Ike was unmoved by his words. He stared at him as if he was looking past him. As if he was history. Turning to Kobani, Ike nodded to him. Kobani then pulled up the door to the cage and released the hyenas into the pit below where the men were hanging from their feet. The four carnivores went straight to the men and began looking up at them as if they had already concluded they were dinner. To the hyenas, they were like the meat the African tribesmen hung from trees to prevent them from stealing it out in the wild.

When the men saw the hyenas approaching them, salivating and licking their tongues in and out of their mouths which meant they anticipated the taste of blood, shit got real. Their pleading increased twofold.

"Cousin! Isaac! My brother! For the love of our ancestors! Do not do this!" Ezekiel said desperately with his wide stretched eyes trained on the hyenas. The Russian too began pleading his case in English and in Russian. This seemed to amuse Kobani whose years of being a henchman for Charles Taylor in Liberia caused him to develop a sick enjoyment in seeing men suffer. But in Ike's business, Kobani was the man you wanted on your team. The was an old saying that "every tool box needed a hammer." Kobani was that hammer. Amid the begging and pleading, Ike, Tony, and Macky continued to stand there stone-faced.

"Lower them!" Ike said. The men screamed as Kobani smiled and began rolling the handle of the crank shaft that was attached to the chains that suspended the men in the air. Their screams and pleas could be heard in and around the warehouse. The soldiers who were posted up outside smoking and congregating, upon hearing the screams, all rushed to the glass windows to see what the commotion was inside. They knew when those hyenas were brought in, something gruesome was about to take place. The same primal curiosity in human beings in desiring to witness the proverbial train wreck, drove them to the window to witness a gory spectacle take place….men eaten alive by perhaps the most vicious carnivores in the wild. An animal whose bite radius ranked in the top ten, and whose jaws could crush elephant bones. As the men were lowered closer to the hungry hyenas, who were now standing on their hind legs in an attempt to steal their meal, the men's pleas and protestations persisted on.

"I'm going to ask you two one more time to tell me what I want to know," Ike said with an eerie calm in his voice. "The one who answers first, I will set you free." The men looked at each other as if they anticipated the other snitching the other out.

"Okay! Okay! Cousin. He is Yuri Lavrov's brother!" Ezekiel said. Tony and Macky looked on unmoved. They already knew there was a Lavrov connection, and they also knew that Ezekiel was the rat. Ike just needed to come to terms with it.

"He's Lavrov's brother, you say?" Ike said, looking over at the Russian. The hyenas by this time had now begun leaping to grab their meal. Luckily for them, hyenas are notoriously poor jumpers.

"Yes! He is Lavrov's brother!" Ezekiel said, looking at the Russian all wide-eyed and sweaty.

"Shut the fuck up!" the Russian said frowning. "You sniveling coward! My brother will have your tongue cut out and pulled through your neck for this!" Ike quickly turned and looked at the Russian angrily.

"How do you know he's Lavrov's brother, Ezekiel?" he asked with his eyes still trained on the Russian.

"I just know," he said looking down at the hyenas.

"Ezekiel! I love you. You are like a brother to me. But so help me, I will feed you to those hyenas, alive! Now I'm going to ask you one more time, how do you know this man is Lavrov's brother?"

"Okay. Okay. I spied for Lavrov. He paid me well. He just wanted to take over the diamonds and that was it. He said you were being unreasonable in his offers to you."

"I was being unreasonable in his offers to me? Do you know what his offers were? He killed two of my men just to steal a shipment!" Ike yelled. "So you say he paid you well, aye?" he said with a finality in his voice. "You betrayed me for money? You betrayed your nation and your ancestors for money? The two men who died at the hands of Lavrov, you delivered them to him! It's as if you killed them yourself! Those men had families! Now what do you think should happen to you, Ezekiel? I know what's going to happen to your friend here. And so do those hyenas. But you! What should I do with you? You have any suggestions on how your miserable life should end here today?" Tony stepped to Ike and whispered in his ear.

"I think we should keep Lavrov's brother alive, my brother. We can keep him as a bargaining chip." Ike looked down at the ground as if he was trying to gather his thoughts. He then nodded his head in agreement.

CATO

"Is there anything else you need to tell me, Ezekiel? You have placed me and my family in extreme jeopardy. You have placed us all in harm's way with your greed and treachery. I expect for you to finally do something honorable in your life."

Ezekiel's face said it all. He looked like a man who was standing before his Creator on judgment day having his earthly misdeeds read off to him. A calm seemed to come over his face. He was resigned to face the music.

"No. The betrayal started with me and it ends with me, cousin." At this point, Ike nodded his head as if to acknowledge Ezekiel's coming clean moment. He then took out his military issued .45 and pointed at his cousin's head.

"Our grandmother always maintained that you were a rotten child who would grow up into a man without honor," Ike said. "But I will tell her that you died an honorable man." Three explosions then rang out from the barrel of the pistol, and three bullets struck Ezekiel's head and chest. The blood streamed down into the pit staining the hyena's faces. As they licked themselves clean, the blood seemed to send them into a frenzy. Their laughter was now high pitched.

"Lower him into the pit," Ike said. Kobani followed his orders and lowered Ezekiel's body into the pit with the hungry carnivores. Before Ezekiel's corpse could hit the ground, the hyenas pulled it down and began feasting on it. The first place they started was his stomach, ripping out his intestines and entrails. The smell of the shit and digested food in Ezekiel's stomach fouled the air. The laughter coming from the hyenas was absolutely blood curdling. The flesh and sinew could be heard being ripped from the bones each time the hyenas pulled their heads back for better leverage to tear off chunks of meat.

The soldiers who were standing at the window looked on in horror. Their squeamish faces belied their reputation as violent

178

and brutal henchmen. This type of brutality, however, was different. There was something totally unnatural about seeing a man ripped to pieces and devoured by wild animals that made this totally outside of the realm of violence and brutality they were accustomed to. Although they lived in Africa all their lives, where the world's greatest carnivores ruled, they had never witnessed people being eaten by wild animals with their own eyes. Only heard of it.

As the Russian closed his eyes and screamed incessantly, and as his girl in the corner who had passed out twice, muffled out her screams from behind the gag, the hyenas continued to make short work of his partner in crime while Tony and Macky stood their chewing gum with the same stoic looks on their faces they had when the polar bears had Nathan Ward for a midnight snack. Ike's reasoning for allowing the hyenas to consume his cousin's body was so that there wouldn't be anything left of him to identify. And the hyenas who were voracious eaters were just the ones for the job. When they fed, they devoured bone and hair which is why they are considered Mother Nature's garbage disposals.

"You can open your eyes now, muddafucker!" Ike said to the Russian with disdain. "You can consider yourself lucky that you are not related to me. The blessing for you is, you happen to be related to Lavrov and therefore you will become a bargaining chip, but don't press your luck here today. I'm still thinking about giving these hyenas seconds. Perhaps one of your legs. Perhaps your cave bitch over there. So watch what you say to me!"

Kobani, who smiled and gloated over the hyenas feeding frenzy, seemed to be disappointed at hearing that he wouldn't be seeing them have the Russian for dessert.

After the soldiers took the Russian down, who had literally pissed and shitted in his pants, Ike, Tony, Macky and Kobani left the warehouse leaving the hyenas to consume the last remaining strands of meat from what was left of Ezekiel's gutted out carcass.

After the red Range Rover drove away from the secluded property which was the site of Ike's torture chamber, a tear rolled down Ike's face while he peered out of the window at the countryside, as his mind played back the fond childhood memories of his favorite cousin, Ezekiel.

Chapter 19
Tony's New Challenge

The next morning, the day of the second shipment under Tony's leadership, Tony and Macky went to the factory. As they did a walk through, the men and women worked feverishly to pack the diamonds in their crates. so they could be sent on their destinations throughout the states to be dispersed to every dealer, both legit and shady, in America. Like the last shipment, Tony was going to be there personally, every step of the way to ensure there weren't any hiccups. This time, however, Macky and two other guests were accompanying him: Lavrov's brother, Vladimir, and his woman.

Anticipating that Ezekiel had already informed Lavrov of the date of the shipment's arrival, Tony changed the game plan up some. The location of the safe house was changed to one of Genie's stash houses heavily guarded by the soldiers. The number of men in the escort at the airport was doubled. And the new landing spot was changed from JFK to La Guardia. There was no way this shipment, or any shipment thereafter, was going to be intercepted. Tony was going to put his reputation and life on it.

Not once during his reign over his illicit drug business were his shipments or stash houses hit by jackers. First of all, every jacker in the street worth the po hustling name and title knew not to. The risk was too high and the consequences were too great. What happened to Natty Boy Ward and the other syndicate cats served as a longstanding example of what could happen to any nigga who was foolish enough to cross Antonio Stallworth. The only time anyone dared to cross that line was the Professor and Chino Parsons. And the only reason they had enough nuts to do that was because they underestimated Sugar, who in the end, proved to everyone her ruthlessness. But this time there was no need for the Queen to show her power and authority. The King came home. Tony was back!

When the FedEx plane landed and came to a screeching halt, the waiting cargo vans back doors swung opened. Two men stepped out and posted up next to it and took a smoke. Outside the fence Tony could see Genie's soldiers posted up waiting and watching with a wary eye. As Tony climbed off of the plane, the two men mashed what was left of their cigarettes into the ground before the men on the tarmac took the cargo to the hangar. The two men standing near the van mashed what was left of their cigarettes into the ground and rushing up to the hangar to grab the precious cargo and loaded it into the van.

Just as the last crates were being loaded into the van, another van pulled up and parked a few feet away. Cassadine stepped out and fired up a Black and Mild while two of his men grabbed the blindfolded, bound and gagged Vladimir and his woman who were rolled up in a tarp and put them inside the van. After Cassadine received his orders from Tony, Tony and Macky climbed in the van with the diamonds before it pulled off. The van carrying Cassadine, his men and their captives, sped off in the same direction.

After the light turned green, the van carrying the precious cargo slowly crept onward to its destination followed by the phalanx of security behind them. The song *Hustle* by a local rap group, Trudrew DA Fam, played from the speakers. In the van trailing, Cassadine's head cautiously scanned back and forth at the passing cars as if it was on a swivel. As the lead van approached the intersection, which only had a few cars present, the light quickly turned red causing the van to come to a stop.

"Fuck!" Tony said. "Seems like every light in the fucking city is catching us." Tony's impatience was somewhat uncharacteristic. But there was something not quite right about tonight. He could feel it like he felt those Taliban ambushes back in Afghanistan. *I know it's coming, but where?* he thought as he looked from side to side. When the light turned green, the van's driver floored the vehicle. Just as he bolted through the intersection, a police car sped up and maneuvered around the soldier's vehicles and the van Cassadine was riding in and pulled in behind Tony's van.

"Hey, fallback!" Cassadine ordered the driver. He then looked back at Vladimir and his broad who bumped around in the back every time the vehicle made a sudden stop or erratic movement. The last thing he wanted to do was get pulled over with them hogtied in the back.

"Hey. Easy. Be easy," Tony told the driver as he peered back at the police car that was now following so closely in behind them it was nearly up on the van's back bumper. "And don't look behind you. Keep your eyes on the road and remain calm," Tony told him. For the next three miles the cop continued on following in behind them while Cassadine and the other vehicles hung back.

"Should I stay on the freeway?" the driver asked Tony with a nervousness in his voice.

"Yes," Tony said. "Just continue to drive until I tell you to turn and be cool. If that pig doesn't plan to pull us over, he should be turning off soon. By now he's already ran a check on the license plates."

After about another mile, Tony realized they needed to make some sort of move to see what was on the pig's mind.

"Go ahead and turn at the next exit," he told the driver. When the driver turned, the cop turned with him. At this time another police car had sped around Cassadine and pulled in behind the first squad car. Seeing this, Cassadine had his driver to peel off.

"Don't turn here," he said. "We will hit the next exit, circle around and catch up with them. Those crackers look like they are about to pull them over," he said before placing a call to his men who were trailing behind.

"Hey, I need y'all to keep in behind Tony. His van just turned off on the exit. We are going to get off on the next exit and circle around. Make sure you don't lose him. If those crackers pull him over, post up somewhere off a distance and keep your eyes on him at all times."

"Yes, sir," the cat on the other end of the phone said. Finally, the suspense was over. The lead squad car directly in behind Tony's van hit the lights.

"Shit!" the drive said as he looked nervously in the mirror.

"Be cool. Be cool," Tony said as the driver pulled off the side of the road. The other squad car quickly pulled around in front of the van and came to a stop. The police spotlight that shined directly on the back of the van was so bright it completely lit up the van's interior, so much so all four occupants could clearly be seen sitting there frozen in their seats. Macky eased his hand on his pistol as the officers exited their squad cars and approached the van in each direction. Cassadine's men drove by slowly looking on intently as they passed.

"Hey, Cassadine," one of the men said into the phone. "The pigs pulled them over."

"Shit!" Cassadine said, shaking his head "Okay. How far did they make it off the exit?"

"Probably about a half a mile."

"Alright. Go park somewhere off a safe distance and hang around, but don't let those pigs see you. Make sure you keep your eye on them at all times. Fuck!" he said before hanging up the phone. "Hurry up and get to them," Cassadine told the driver.

"Driver's license, insurance and registration," the cop told the nervous driver. His partner posted up at the passenger window and looked on with a wary eye with his hand placed on his gun. Shining the flashlight inside the van's interior, both pigs carefully studied each and every one of their faces and body movements while the driver gathered up the requested documents.

"Where are you guys headed?" the officer asked as he took the documents from the driver.

"We're headed to Flatbush," the driver said.

"Flatbush, huh?" the officer asked incredulously.

"Yes sir," the driver said.

"What are you carrying in the back?" the pig asked.

"Mail."

"Mail, huh?"

"Yes, sir."

"Mind if I take a look?" The driver rolled his eyes, exhaled and hesitated before answering.

"Yes, I mind if you take a look. Look man we are in a hurry. We have a delivery to make. And why did you stop us anyway?" the driver asked as his patience had begun to wear thin. "I wasn't speeding or driving recklessly." The officer's face wrinkled and one of his eyebrows raised.

"I conducted an investigative stop, what's called a *Terry Stop*. Is that okay with you?"

"Yeah. Well, it gotta be okay. You got the gun, the badge and the authority," he said combatively. "Now I gave you the documents you asked me for and you haven't even called anything in yet. What do you want? What's really going on? Are you harassing us?" he asked with his voice rising. Tony realized the driver was at his boiling point and nudged him in the back before he completely lost it. The last thing he needed to do was to piss this cracker off.

"Sir, I'm going to need you to step out of the van."

"What the fuck for?" the driver asked indignantly. "I didn't break the law! What the fuck is this?"

"Sir, step out of the vehicle sir. Now!" the officer commanded with base in his voice. His partner clutched his gun tightly at this point with his eyes locked on everyone inside the van. The situation had just gone to a place that Tony didn't want it to go to. The driver was hot headed and the cop was an asshole, which made for a volatile situation.

"I don't see why the fuck I gotta get out of the van," the driver said as he began to exit the ride.

"Keep your hands where I can see them and exit slowly!" the cop said as he took a few steps back with his hand on his Glock.

"Yeah okay, you scarey muthafucka," the driver said. By this time he was livid and totally out of control. He had had enough of the young cop.

"Just keep walking forward," the cop said. "Now put your hands on the back of your head!"

"Man, what the fuck for? I'm just saying, man. You got my insurance papers, the registration and the license. What more do you want? And you didn't even radio none of that in. Y'all muthafuckas must be hijackers or sumpin'. Where is y'alls backup? You done pulled four black men over in a van and no back up? By this time it's usually a hunard of y'all muthafuckas on the scene."

Tony looked around as the driver's words seemed to resonate. He was right. There was something funny about this stop. Where were the other pigs? Macky seemed to have read Tony's thoughts and eased his pistol off safety while the other officer watched the cat in the front passenger seat who was as still as a stiff in the morgue. His partner moved in on the driver, kicking his legs apart before he began searching him.

"Man, watch that shit!" the driver yelled. "Oh you like touching on dicks. You must be a faggot or sumpin'!"

"Shut the fuck up and keep your hands on top of your head where I can see them!" the cop yelled back as he continued frisking him.

"Man, what the fuck is this shit really about? Driving while black, muthafucka?"

"Yeah. I'm racially profiling you," the cop shot back sarcastically.

"Yeah, that ain't all you doing. This is a robbery," he said as the cop finished frisking him.

"You can turn around now," the cop said.

"Okay. Now does that mean we can go?" the driver asked.

"No. We are here to rob you, remember," the cop said, smiling as he looked at his partner who too was smiling. He then pulled out his Glock and immediately shot the driver twice in his chest. His partner stepped back and shot the cat in the passenger seat in the side of the head before Macky returned fire and shot him in the neck and chest. The bullet ripped through his carotid artery and blood sprung forth from his neck like a geyser. Losing the blood flow to his brain, he crumpled to the ground, holding his neck and died almost instantly. His partner returned fire into the van and ran to take cover behind his squad car. This is when four black SUVs suddenly appeared out of nowhere and began dumping automatic gunfire out of their windows into the van as Tony and Macky simultaneously flipped into the very back of the van and grabbed their pistols.

An imposing 6"8 Lavrov and the Black widows, who were wearing black leather jackets, quickly bailed out of the SUV and fearlessly began walking towards the van and firing through its windshield, which was now totally shredded by the flying lead. Fortunately for Tony and Macky, the van was armored plated. Otherwise they would probably be dead by now. When no one inside the shot up van returned fire, Lavrov signaled his masked men crouched down behind their trucks to approach the van.

Cautiously, they walked up to it, approaching it from each side with their assault rifles trained on it. When the first man peeked inside a shot rang out from the back of the van that exploded his head exploded like a watermelon. His limp body slumped to the ground. Seeing what happened to their comrade, the other men ran firing behind them before they took cover. Tony and Macky slid out of the back of the van with pistols in hand just before Lavrov and his men lit the van up with a deadly hail of lead. Everything on the van exploded including the tires causing the weight of the van to fall down on its rims. Broken glass and shards of metal flew everywhere as the bullets came into contact with the van.

Amid the constant deafening gunfire, Tony and Macky managed to slip into the bushes a few feet away, when suddenly, Cassadine and the muscle rushed to the scene with guns blazing from the vehicle's windows. When the tires of their SUVs and cargo van came to a screeching halt, the men quickly jumped out and began firing from behind their doors. One of Lavrov's SUVs exploded when a bullet penetrated the gas tank, and two of his men and the cop who had taken cover behind the exploded vehicle were set ablaze. As they flailed and ran wildly in an attempt to escape the flames that had totally engulfed their bodies, they let out faint screams. Running blindly in the line of fire they were mercifully cut down by a hail of bullets that ended their torment.

For miles around the gunfire and explosions could be heard echoing in the night as the two groups of gangsters exchanged volleys. The tracer rounds that lit up the night sky looked like a fireworks display. The staccato sounds of the fully automatic machine fire gave the area the familiarity of a war zone. Realizing that the situation had just taken a turn for the worst for he and his men, Lavrov ordered them into full retreat. After he and the widows jumped in their SUV, the vehicle they were in sped away from the scene, followed by the men in the other two vehicles, Angela and Blaze hung out of the windows spraying everything behind them. Cassadine, Tony, Macky and the others walked forward returning fire at the fleeing vehicles knocking out the back window of the last vehicle and hitting one of Lavrov's men in the shoulder.

For the first time since Tony took over Ike's diamond trade, Lavrov had made his presence known and in a big way. Although he failed to take the diamonds from Tony, this was his coming out party, and Tony had just gotten a taste of the kind of man he was dealing with….a man like himself who took care of his own business, personally.

Chapter 20
Ain't Shit Soft About Us

The incident with Lavrov the night before forced Tony to call a meeting with Genie and the muscle. Something had to be done, even if Tony went on the offensive, which was something he was previously reluctant to do because of the political situation that existed, due to Lavrov's Russian mafia ties. Tony knew that no matter how connected Lavrov was, the Russians were not about to lose money over him. The coke they received from the cartels and sent throughout eastern and Western Europe was their main cash crop. If Tony could interrupt that by somehow convincing Mando and the others to cut them off, on the condition that they disown Lavrov, his ass would be all his. Tony would have the green light to go after him full force without causing a war in the streets that no one needed. But he knew that was a long shot since Lavrov's uncle was the boss of bosses.

In the meantime, Tony concluded that he could at least make his own presence known to Lavrov. He could hit his assets and cause him some discomfort. If not, Lavrov would only become emboldened by the mistaken belief that Tony was soft.

Inside the conference room in the back of the grocery store, which is the organization's traditional meeting place, Cassadine and the muscle sat congregating amongst themselves as Tony, Genie and Macky walked in past the soldiers standing guard at the door.

"Gentlemen, let me have your attention," Genie said. "We have a situation that we have been forced to focus our attention on. Some extracurricular shit that we need to handle. Tony's going to explain to you what's going on." Tony took the podium.

"Gentlemen, as you already know, Genie took control after I touched down from Rikers. I have now transitioned into another venture that I plan on making a success. There is a man who

191

stands in the way of me making that transition and having that success. And that man's name is Yuri Lavrov. Nicknamed the Reaper. He is a Russian mafia muthafucka." The mention of the Russian mafia caused some of the men to mumble amongst themselves. Everybody knew the brutal reputation of this relatively new mafia organization from Eastern Europe. Macky and Cassadine, however, looked straight ahead. They were totally unmoved by the mention of the Russians. These were real niggas out of Yonkers who didn't see any of that shit.

"Yes. The Russian mafia," Tony continued as he recognized the anxieties of a few of the men. "It appears I don't have to remind you of their reputation. They are much more brutal and blazoned than the Italians. The Italians have rules and these muthafuckas do not. But that's okay. This is our turf. We have home field advantage, and most importantly, we have some real niggas on our team. We know the streets and they do not because they are the foreigners here. This business with Lavrov threatens not only my new business venture, but it threatens Genie's. It threatens you. He already hit one of Genie's stash houses and killed two of his men. Your homies. We cannot continue to let some shit like this ride. So like past situations, we are going to have deal with this shit, but not like before. Anything that we do will have to be surgical due to the political ramifications behind this. Eventually, we are going to have to isolate ole boy to avert a full blown war. But that doesn't mean that we can't in the meantime make him suffer some. What I'm saying here is not a declaration of war, but a declaration of hostilities. We are going to go on the offense and hit that muthafucka to let him know ain't nobody soft here. Okay. That's all," Tony said before Genie took the podium.

"Alright, gentlemen, you heard the man. We know what we gotta do. This meeting is adjourned." After the muscle and the other members of Genie's organization filed out, Cassadine remained behind with Tony, Genie, and Macky.

"Cassadine, I want you to find out where this Russian mutha-fucka lays his head at and where he tricks at," Genie said. "I need to know his whereabouts, you dig?"

"Consider it done," Cassadine said before walking out of the conference room.

"Genie, I really hate that you've got caught up in this shit." Genie took out his flask and downed some of its contents.

"Look, bruh. We are still in this shit together from day one. Your trouble is my trouble. Drama come your way, it comes my way. Ain't nothing changed. We just gone have to deal with this shit like we always have." Tony nodded his head and gave him dap.

"I can promise you the shit will get dealt with," Tony said looking straight ahead.

Every early Monday morning around 3 am, a Brink's truck carrying Lavrov's weekend earnings to his own personal vault inside of a heavily armed office building, pulled up to dump millions into it. Lavrov had his hand in damn near everything that went on in the city and beyond. He shook down pimps, dope dealers, legitimate business owners, shop owners, unions, and on top of that he had his own cut up, garbage coke and heroin on the streets. Some of the things he was into were not approved of by the Russian mob bosses back in the Fatherland. Selling bad dope, which often killed scores of junkies, was one of them. It wasn't good for public relations and it often brought the heat down on them.

After the Brinks truck pulled onto the curb and parked, two armed guards hopped out in the city darkness and began surveying the area far and near. One of them went inside the building while the other remained standing outside the truck with his 12 gauge shotgun in hand on red alert waiting for any bullshit to pop off. Immediately after the guard inside returned, a massive explosion engulfed the building behind him blowing him off his feet. The powerful blast shattered all the windows in every nearby storefront. As the two guards scrambled to their feet and ran for cover, a rocket propelled grenade whizzed through the air passed them and hit underneath the truck sending it 30 feet into the air. When it landed, it settled on its side. Seconds later, machine gunfire rang out followed by the beautiful tracer rounds illuminating the night sky, that left the two guards bullet riddled bodies stretched out on the streets.

Immediately, the sounds of roaring engines of two black Escalades and the song *War,* by local artist Drae Ross, blared from the speakers as they rushed up and came to a screeching halt. The men inside wearing ski masks quickly hopped out stepping over the bodies of the guards and began quickly unloading the huge money bags filled with Lavrov's cash. After the last money bag was liberated, the men hopped back in their rides and sped away. In five more synchronized attacks across the city, five more of Lavrov's money houses were hit. Later that afternoon, two men on a motorcycle raked one of Lavrov's bars with automatic weapons, killing five of his men. Prior to that, one of his restaurants in Brighton Beach exploded before it opened for business. All over the city, Lavrov's men and business interests were attacked with a total lack of regard for him or his Russian mafia ties. Tony was making his presence known. He was letting Lavrov know there wasn't shit soft about him.

Chilling in the pool inside his penthouse, Lavrov laid back on his float chair, taking sips from his fruit cocktail drink while Angel and Blaze swam gracefully from one end of the pool to the other like two mermaids. Vitaly, who was the head of Lavrov's security, walked in hesitantly to be the bearer of bad news regarding the hits on his boss's business interests. He knew better than anyone that Lavrov wasn't the one to take too kindly to bad news, especially when it involved the loss of his money.

"Sir, I have some…"

"You have bad news, Vitaly," Lavrov said, cutting him off.

"Yes sir. Do you already know?"

"No, I don't already know. I just know you coming here was to give me bad news. Why else would you interrupt my leisure time?" he said just as the widows pulled themselves out of the pool onto the deck and began drying off and eating from a platter of fruit. They both looked at Vitaly intently chewing the grapes as if they too were waiting to hear the news. Vitaly, who knew all too well the reputation of the two sisters, was intimidated by their stares, so much so, he refused to even look in their direction. To him they were the personification of evil.

"Yes, sir. Many of our business interests and stash houses were attacked today." Upon hearing this news, Lavrov showed no emotions. He just continued to lay there on the float sipping on the drink looking straight ahead. Vitaly was unable to read his eyes because of the dark prescription shades Lavrov wore, since his eyes were injured in an explosion during a battle against the Chechen rebels.

"Vitaly, are you not the head of my security?" Lavrov asked him calmly.

"Yes sir."

"Well, why are my business interests being attacked with such ease?"

"I'm not sure, sir. It seems as if someone knows everything about our operation."

"You would think," Lavrov said coldly. "Several of my business interests attacked all at once in the same day. Somebody knows more than they should know."

"Yes, sir, I'm afraid so. But who could it be?" Vitaly asked in a frustrated voice.

"Vitaly, you are the head of my security. These are the things that you should know, correct?"

"Correct, sir. But…"

"And if you don't know these things and cannot protect my interests, you are no good to me, correct?"

"This is correct, sir," he said in a defeated voice. He knew not to argue the point. Suddenly, Lavrov's phone rang perhaps momentarily saving Vitaly's ass. One of the widows answered it and gave it to Lavrov.

"This is Lavrov speaking."

"Mr. Lavrov, how are you this evening?"

"Well, I was doing fine prior to receiving some bad news," he said, looking over at Vitaly who dropped his head towards the ground.

"Oh. Wait a minute! Are you talking about the news of your business interests being hit early this morning while you were still in bed?"

"Yes, as a matter of fact, that is exactly what put a damper on my evening. What did you say your name was again?"

"Stallworth is the name."

"Okay. And I'm Yuri Lavrov."

"I know who you are. I'm the one who called you."

"Oh yeah. You did call me. And how did you get my number, again?"

"I got it from a close relative of yours," Tony said, looking down at Lavrov's brother who was still hogtied, bound and gagged. He looked up at Tony with an exhausted look on his face. He was still reeling from the ordeal he had endured when Macky forced some important information out of him regarding his brother's business assets and money stash houses. The iron used to brand cows was an effective tool to extract information from wanna-be hard cases. "Never mind all that, Mr. Lavrov. Where are you at right now?"

"I'm lying here kicked back in my pool sipping on a mai tai. Why do you ask?"

"Do you have any windows where you can see outside?"

Gangsta Shyt 2

"Yes, as a matter of fact I do have windows," he said before snapping his fingers and motioning Vitaly and the widows to the window. When they reached it, Lavrov's prized candy apple red Lamborghini exploded, followed by his men's vehicles parked behind it. His men all ran outside of the building across the street, brandishing their guns, while Vitaly stood there with a terrified look on his face. This was more than he had bargained for. No one ever tried his boss like this. *Who is this man?* he thought. Angel and Blaze on the other hand, stood there smiling with a look of amazement on their faces like two kids as the cars burned on. The vehicles set ablaze seemed to excite the pyromaniacs inside them.

"Is that your work out there?" the Russian mob boss asked.

"Yes. Hope you liked it," Tony said smiling. "Just a lil' sumpin' sumpin' to let you know that just because I don't broadcast my intentions, doesn't mean I'm going to let shit ride. I hope this ends things between us. I hope that we will can leave the past in the past, because trust me, this ain't what you want."

"Ha ha ha ha." Lavrov laughed aloud. "This is only the beginning, my friend. You have no fucking idea." Tony smiled.

"I figured that would be your answer. But check this out. The next time you go to a family reunion, you will be minus a family member," he said before hanging up the phone. Lavrov placed the phone down and pulled off his shades. His face showed both anger and confusion. Tony's last words about a missing family member played over and over in his mind. Lavrov was unaware that his brother was a guest of the man whom he just spoken to. The man who had just tried him like no one ever dared to before. Once Lavrov found out his only brother was being held hostage, it would naturally tie his hands, but not before some gangsta shyt between he and his more than formidable new nemesis took place in the streets of New York.

197

Chapter 21
Pussy Brought Him In, Pussy Took Him Out

Cassadine Washington was a former New York State Golden Gloves boxer who was reported to have given Floyd Mayweather a run for his money in the amateur ranks. Legend had it that he even put Floyd on his ass with a classic left hook, right cross during an amateur bout.

When Cassadine turned pro he put together a string of victories going undefeated in his first 18 fights, all by knockout. By most boxing analyst's estimates, he was an up and coming lightweight champion who had fists of steel. In fact, "fists of steel" was his nickname. He was a brutal puncher who carried a chip on his shoulders due to being passed over for the Olympics, and a dysfunctional upbringing by a prostitute mother who had a new pimp slash boyfriend every week.

Unfortunately for Cassadine, this chip he carried on his shoulders he took with him outside of the ring that oftentimes got him into scraps with the law and with other niggas who carried around their own chips.

Another fault Cassadine had was he still hung tight with his homeys. Some of them were well-intentioned. Some were nothing but parasites and leeches looking for a healthy host to suck dry, and others were downright resentful and envious of his skill set that could have taken him out of the hopelessness and despair of Yonkers and into places he never imagined existed. Just after Cassadine knocked out the number one contender, he inked a deal to fight for a vacant IBF lightweight title. That day, however, would never come. One night at a house party in Harlem, he killed a man in a fight and gave his partner a brutal beating that left him blind in his right eye.

After doing ten calendar years in prison, he tried to make a comeback, but by this time his skills had eroded. In the ring, he

CATO

was a shell of his former self. Outside the ring, however, he settled into his new life of mob enforcer and assassin with his reclu-
sive childhood friend, Macky Boy Jimenez. Unlike his best
friend, Macky, Cassadine was a tender dick. Meaning, he loved
pussy and women. Every Friday he would go to the club, grab
himself three or four broads, an ounce of coke and lock himself
away in a hotel. Tonight was no different. There were two bad
ass twin broads in the club who looked like they were 'bout it.
When they walked up to Cassadine who sat at the bar downing
drinks, they boldly kissed him on each side of his neck, whispered into his ear, and began rubbing on his dick.

To a cautious man, this would send up red flags. But to a trick
like Cassadine, this was akin to a mouse being drawn to a cheese
laden trap. He just could not help himself. These two females
were the baddest bitches in the club hands down. And they made
it know that they wanted him.

"Hey, Baby Girl, what y'all doing after the club close? Y'all
wanna go hang out with me at my penthouse?"

"You have a penthouse?" one of the broads asked excitedly.

"I have two of them," he said boastfully with a chuckle.
"Which one do y'all wanna go to?"

"Whichever one we can fuck all night in, daddy?" she said
before they both climbed all over him and kissed him on each
side of his neck. A lump developed in Cassadine's throat and his
dick became rock hard as one of the sisters stroked it softly.

"Well, why put off for later what we can go do now?" he said.

"We're with you, daddy," they both said at the same time.
"When you're ready to go, we're ready."

"Shhhiiiiit. Let's go now then. You ain't said shit!" he said
after downing his drink.

As Cassadine and the two sisters got onto the elevator leading
up to his high rise penthouse apartment, the freak show was already underway. They kissed him wildly all over his face and

neck and rubbed on his dick that was still hard from the club. When they reached his apartment, they briefly marveled over the huge saltwater fish tank and the gigantic python housed inside of the long glass enclosure, while Cassadine turned on some Tupac.

Cassadine's bachelor pad looked much smaller outside. Inside however, it was at least 4,000 square feet, which was pretty large for a two bedroom apartment. Right there in the living room is where the females started to undress. By the time they reached his bedroom, they were butt ass naked. These two women were as fine as they come. Their well chiseled bodies were totally identical. Not a flaw on them. Not even a stretch mark. They were tall and had athletic builds like the black goddess, Serena Williams. One was chocolate like Serena too. Surprisingly, the other was light skinned, yet they were identical. Cassadine was beside himself. He had never seen two freaky ass identical twin sisters this fine who were 'bout it.

When one of the broads removed his pants, his excitement was made manifest. His dick was pressed up against his stomach. The veins in it looked as if they were about to explode. While he took out the plastic bag that contained an 8 ball of raw coke and began Hoover vacuuming the fish scales into his sinus cavity, the two sisters kissed each other. Their tongues slowly intermingled like two snakes in a mating ritual. Seeing this, Cassadine's excitement increased twofold. His heart began to race from the pure coke and the sexual gratification of seeing the two sisters kissing each other, which was something he had never witnessed before in person.

"Damn!" he said as he sat there on the bed naked with his dick hard as old folks toe nails. "Y'all get down like that?"

"Yes, daddy, we get down like this," one of them said before opening the others legs and started sliding her tongue over her clit. The sister moaned, closed her eyes and pushed her sister's head down deeper in between her legs. Cassadine got on his knees and straddled over her and positioned his dick in her face. She took the cue and grabbed a mouthful. While the sister took care of the other, the other sister was taking Cassadine's manhood in and out of her mouth in a seductive rhythm. As he sat there on his knees and resting back on his legs, he breathed heavily while looking down at her soft tongue slowly sliding down the sides of his dick. Anxious to take in this massive dick, the other sister pushed him over onto his back, mounted him and began riding him furiously as the other sat on Cassadine's face and kissed her passionately. As she rode Cassadine, she shrieked and talked to him.

"You like how I'm riding this big dick, daddy?" she said as her ass moved back and forth, taking in every inch of Cassadine. "Oh fuck! Fuck! Fuck! Oh shit! Fuck this pussy good, daddy!" she said as the dick began to hit its mark.

"Let me get some of this dick too," the other sister said excitedly as she rubbed her breasts as if she was in a trance. The sister ignored her and kept riding until she reached her climax. She screamed as she bore all the way down on Cassadine. Her body tensed up from the pleasure. Relieving herself of the last drop of her juices, she panted as she thrust her hips forward.

"Damn, bitch! Let me get some of the dick!" the light skinned sister said before she literally pushed her off Cassadine. His dick which was covered with her cum, hit his stomach like an ironing board after she was pushed off him. The sister who felt left out mounted him, quickly stuffed it inside of her and resumed where her twin left off. She clutched the headboard for leverage and began gyrating and moving her ass back and forth, taking deep digs onto Cassadine's pole. Cassadine's toes had begun to curl from the pleasure. He was really feeling this sister who moved with a rhythm that the other didn't seem to have. She was more sensual and took her time. The other was a wild cat who wanted it hard and rough. The steady eye contact she maintained with him turned him on even more. There was something in her eyes that was sensual, dreamy and yet dangerous.

Damn! I'm digging this bitch, he thought to himself as he looked up at her. He was so into her he rolled her over on her back, pent her feet up near her ears and began pounding her.

With each deep incursion inside of her bald pussy, she screamed, "Fuck me! Fuck me hard! Fuck me hard, daddy!" Her eyes rolled around and around like pinballs. "Oh yes! Give me this big dick!" she yelled. She carried on so that the entire complex could hear her ordeal loud and clear. And this only seemed to encourage Cassadine to beat it even harder.

The bed's headboard that slammed into the wall continually sounded like a Native American war drum. While the constant pounding took place, the other sister caressed her breasts and nestled her body against Cassadine like a cat while running her tongue all over his ears and neck. When she suddenly raked his throat with something in her hand, the muscles in his ass relaxed as he immediately ceased pumping. His eyes bulged and his body bristled as if he busted a nut. When the sensory nerve centers in his spine transmitted the pain signals to his brain, then came the extreme burning sensation. He looked over at her and clutched his neck just as the blood began to squirt all over her sister underneath him, and onto his satin sheets. The room became dark as the sudden loss of blood caused him to collapse to the floor. Surprisingly, his dick remained standing at attention.

"Bitch! What the fuck?" he said as the widow held the bloody knife in her hand, looking down at him with a menacing, but lifeless, look in her eyes. Looking up at her and trying to maintain his consciousness, his heart began to pound out of control as it struggled to pump his dwindling blood supply to the rest of his organs. Seeing his dilemma, the light skinned sister rose up in the bed and licked his blood off her fingers.

"Mmmmmmmmmm," she said as she hopped down off the bed onto the floor in front of him. Her cold eyes were trained on him without blinking. Holding his neck tightly in an attempt to tourniquet off the blood flow, he managed to get to his feet. He held up his off hand in vain to fight off the advancing widow to his left, but she and her sister quickly repositioned themselves. Their movement was swift, decisive and in sync. At this time his wide eyes shifted down to the knives they now clutched in both hands. They quickly closed in on him like two attack predators. When his back hit the wall and he had nowhere to go, this is when the vicious attack began from both sides like it normally did. They were unmerciful in their bloodletting. With the massive blood loss from the initial slash of his main artery, Cassadine wasn't able to fight them off. The widows soon made short work of him. Standing over his bloody body, Angel and Blaze kissed before throwing on their clothes and leaving him laying there sprawled on his bedroom floor, still clutching his neck with his eyes wide open. Pussy brought Cassadine into this world and pussy took him out.

Chapter 22
Lavrov Strikes Back: No More Rules

The one rule that most gangsters consider sacred not to be violated, transgressed, compromised or abridged is not to go after or target the family members of someone on their shit list. The Italians. The Irish. Even the Chinese mafia have prohibitions on targeting family members, particularly the elderly and children. That isn't to say others like the Jamaican posse, the Colombian cartels, the Mexican cartels or the Haitian Zoe Pound haven't violated this age old rule. The Russian mafia however, who was the relatively new underworld organization on the block, had not adhered to the traditional rules of gangsterism either. When they come for someone, they had been known to kill everyone, including children. Their logic was, if they couldn't get their target, they would get to those who are close to him. Even when they could put forth the effort to find the target, they would still go after the person's folks who were considered soft targets, just to make the target suffer.

Yuri Lavrov was one cat who played by his own rules. To him, nothing was sacred. To him, everyone and everything was on the table to be touched. Finding his new nemesis, Tony, and those close to him had proven to be elusive. But when Lavrov found out about others who were close enough, who were not surrounded by a vanguard of security, he concluded that they would do.

***

Damn, I wish this broad would hurry the fuck up. Genie thought to himself. *This is why I hate coming to the store with broads.*

"Hey, Bae, you like this?" his girl, Sissy, said excitedly standing at the dressing room door modeling an outfit.

"Yeah. Yeah, I like it," Genie said in a rushed tone.

Bitch, just hurry up already, he thought to himself.

Genie and Tony were like night and day when it came to patience with females.

"I kinda like it too! But I think I like the other two outfits better," she said before heading back in the dressing room to try on the outfits. Genie impatiently looked at his diamond studded gold Rolex watch, sighed and sat down in the chair near the dressing room. Genie's two hulking bodyguards standing inconspicuously outside of the store near a bench, watched back and forth as the crowds of people walked passed them. Occasionally, they would take a break from their serious business of protecting Genie and his woman to flirt with the fine ass young females prancing by.

"Okay, Bae, what about this one?" Sissy said, displaying the new outfit she tried on.

"Yeah, it's nice, baby," Genie said in the same rushed tone. Sissy smiled like a fat kid locked in a candy factory.

"Thank you, Bae! I knew you would like it. I know you ready to go. But can I just try on one more?" she asked in a whiny voice.

"Yeah, okay, I guess," Genie said reluctantly. "As long as it's the last one, baby. I gotta go meet up with some folks in a little bit."

"Okay, Bae!" she said before she took off to the dressing room with the other outfit in hand.

"Hey, sweetie, I may be running a few minutes late, but I will be there soon," Genie said into the cell phone. "Yeah I got held up handling sumpin.' Okay. See you soon," he said before hanging up. Sissy was one of two broads Genie was involved with. She often complained about what her role was in his life. When she asked Genie when she would be number one in his life, he told her that she was his number one. When she reminded him that she knew of his other girl, Tracey, he told her they were tied

206

for first place. What she didn't know was, Genie was the type of cat who would probably wait until he was in a nursing home to settle down. He wasn't going to be settling for one woman any time soon and he made it known to everyone.

In that regard also, he and Tony were like night and day. The only woman for him was Sugar. Genie would tease him that he was one Hail Mary away from being a Catholic Priest who vowed celibacy.

"Okay, Bae, this the last one. How you like it?" she said, walking around in front of him like a fashion model on the runway.

"Yeah, I like it, baby. How much is it?" he turned and said to the older black sales lady.

"I gotta ring up it up first, man," she said frowning. The whole time she was rolling her eyes at Genie because of his impatience with his broad. She was an old seasoned vet who recognized the sugar daddy/young girl situation going on. Then again she was probably motivated by hate. After Sissy placed her outfits down on the counter, Genie pulled out a wad of money, peeled off five bills and handed them to her.

"Go ahead and pay for your clothes, baby. I'm going to run to the restroom. Go ahead on to the car and I will catch up. I should beat you out there."

'Okay, Bae." She gave him a kiss. "Muah. I love you, Bae."

"Yeah, okay," Genie said before walking away.

The sales lady looked up and rolled her eyes at him as he walked out of the store. *Sorry, no good ass nigga couldn't even tell the girl he loved her back,* she thought.

One of the bodyguard's escorted Sissy and her two hands full of bags to the Bentley. After she climbed into the backseat, he closed the door behind her. He then went and sat down in the front passenger seat next to the driver to wait for his boss to return. In the backseat, Sissy bragged over the phone to one of her home girls about her new outfits. She even took pictures of a few of them to show off, knowing full well this would evoke even more hatred from them. The Bentley's stereo played the song *Pull Up On Yah* by a local artist Tru Dru The Fam.

Just as Genie and the other bodyguard got onto the elevator to head to the Bentley, two females on a pink motorcycle wearing black leather jackets and matching pink helmets sped through the intersection and both peered at the Bentley as they drove passed it just as Genie and the bodyguard walked out of the mall passing by the people going to and fro. The motorcycle with the two riders continued on for a couple hundred yards before hooking a u-turn. Pulling back up next to the Bentley, Angel and Blaze smiled and winked their eyes flirtatiously at the driver and the bodyguard who smiled back. Blaze, who was sitting on the back of the motorcycle rolled something underneath the Bentley and waved before they quickly sped away.

Curious as to what she had rolled under the ride, the driver foolishly opened the door and as soon as his foot came into contact with the concrete, the Bentley exploded sending a fireball rushing through its interior blowing out all the windows including the windshield. The concussion of the blast knocked Genie to the pavement. With his pistol drawn, the bodyguard laid on top of Genie to shield him. As the frantic, panic stricken bystanders screamed and scrambled to safety for their dear lives, Genie looked on in horror as the Bentley burned on with three charred bodies inside.

***

When Tony woke up to the familiar sound of the ringtone *Forever* by Regina Belle, he was surprised since this was a sound he hadn't heard in a minute. It was Angela Washington. He hadn't heard from her in over a year. Out of the blue she called. Tony pressed ignore on his phone just before Sugar walked into the room with his brunch. They had slept in late, which was unusual for both of them. Tony's body was trained to wake up at 5 am every morning, but last night's intense love making session with Sugar, in addition to the 20 hour flight from Africa, the jet lag and the gun battle the night before, had taken its toll on him. So the rest was just what his body needed.

"Hey, Bae," Sugar said, giving him a kiss before laying the platter of waffles, salmon croquettes, home fries, scrambled eggs, coffee and orange juice down on the bed. Tony smiled.

"Hey, sweetie. I see my exhibition last night paid off. I get breakfast in bed again." Sugar chuckled.

"Well, I can't let things like that go unrewarded, you know. So now you know what you need to do if you want breakfast in bed more often." Tony laughed.

"Yes, I do," he said before taking a sip of his piping hot coffee. Just as he started to eat, there were rings and knocks at the door that sounded urgent. In fact, it sounded like the police. Tony looked at his watch. It was 2:27.

"I'll get it, Bae," Sugar said before rushing off to answer it. The knocks and rings persisted as if someone was growing impatient. "Okay! Okay! I'm coming, damn it!" Sugar said frowning.

"Who the fuck is it?" she asked before looking at the video monitor. It was Genie at the door, and three of his men standing near a white Expedition parked across the street. Genie was clearly shaken, his white shirt had black stains with a couple of rips in it. Sugar quickly opened the door.

"You alright, Genie?" Sugar asked with concern.

"No, I'm not. Where's Tony?"

"What's going on, bruh?" Tony asked standing at the top of the winding staircase near the bedroom door.

"Where is that muthafucka's, brother?" Genie demanded. His eyes were bloodshot red.

"Who's brother? What the fuck is going on, man?" Tony asked as he made his way down the stairs.

"Lavrov! Where the fuck is his brother?"

"Why, what's up? He's at Macky's crib now. What's up, my brother? Talk to me. What the fuck happened?" Tony said as he walked up to him. After having heard what he needed to hear, Genie turned and began walking away.

"Bruh, you still haven't told me what the fuck is going on. What's up?"

"Sissy is dead! They killed her!" he yelled. Sugar gasped and covered her mouth.

"Oh no, Genie," she said, shaking her head in disbelief.

"My brother, hold on. Let me get dressed. I'm going with you," Tony said, before making a mad dash upstairs. Throwing on his clothes, he grabbed his two pistols and looked under the bed for his shoes. Downstairs, Sugar began consoling Genie as his men stood at the door looking helpless as they felt their boss's anguish.

"Genie, I am so, so sorry. What happened?" Sugar said rubbing Genie in the middle of his back.

"They just killed her, Sugar. They probably thought I was in the ride and they just fucking killed her," he said as his bloodshot eyes seemed to become even more so.

"I'm ready, bruh," Tony said as he ran downstairs. "Baby listen, I will be back in a few." He placed a kiss on her lips before walking outside with Genie. "I want you to step up security and keep your eyes peeled," Tony said to Yancey, the head of his security.

"Yes, sir," he said before directing the guards to the different parameter points of the huge mansion. The men followed his orders and posted up in their positions with assault rifles in hand, and mean mugging. After Tony and Genie got in the ride, the white Expedition blasted off from the curve.

"Bruh, what the fuck happened?" Tony asked. Genie took out his silver liquor flask and took a long swallow from it.

"As far as I could see as I was coming out of the mall, a motorcycle with two bitches on it rode passed the Bentley, turned around and came back and parked next to it. The next thing I know, the ride exploded just after they sped away. I believed they hit it with a grenade or sumpin.'"

"Damn!" Tony said looking off. "Well, where the fuck was Cassadine?"

"I don't know. No one seen or heard from him since Friday." Tony continued to look off in space

"So was Sissy inside the car?"

"Yeah."

"Are you sure, bruh?"

"Yeah. I saw the bodies burning with my own eyes and hers was one of them," he struggled to say as a lump settled in his throat. Genie then took another long swallow of the yack. His bloodshot eyes had welled up slightly. He was both angry and sad that this young beautiful girl who was only six college credit hours from being an RN was now dead. Deep down inside he had already begun the process of self-pity and blaming himself. However, the self-pity would have to wait. He now had vengeance on his mind and no one to exact it on except Lavrov's brother. And it was time to go see that muthafucka.

When Genie and Tony walked into Macky's crib, Genie looked at Macky.

"Where the fuck is he?" he demanded with a deadly serious tone.

"Who?" Macky asked looking at Tony with a confused look on his face.

"Lavrov's fucking brother! You know who the fuck I'm talking about!" Genie shot back angrily.

"He's down in the basement," Macky replied, his eyes questioning Tony. Without any delay, Genie rushed off in the direction where the Russian was held up at. "What's going on?" Macky asked Tony as he rushed in behind his partner and best friend.

"They murked his girl," Tony replied. When Genie reached the room where Lavrov's brother and his broad were handcuffed to a pole that went up to the ceiling, the switch blade in his hand popped open. Rushing straight for Vladimir with his cold eyes trained on him and donning the knife so he could see it, the Russian and his girl muffled a scream, but their screams went unheard. When Genie grabbed the Russian by his long blonde ponytail pulling back his head, right before he could raked the knife across his neck, Tony grabbed his hand that held the blade. The Russian closed his eyes as the tears streamed down his face. His body tensed up. He looked as though he had accepted his fate.

"No, my brother!" Tony said as he grabbed hold to Genie's hand. Without Tony telling him, Macky moved quickly and stood in front of the Russian to shield him.

"Bruh! Get the fuck out of my way!" Genie said in a no nonsense tone.

"Genie! I can't let you do it, bruh! You are not thinking clearly right now," Tony yelled, looking him in his eyes.

"I'm thinking clear enough. I know what the fuck I'm doing! Now get the fuck out of my way, T," he yelled. By this time the Russian's broad had tears coming down her own face as she looked at her old man who was scared shitless as he looked at this crazed nigga a few feet away from his throat with a very long switchblade in his hand.

"No! You are not thinking clearly and you don't know what you are doing right now! Step off, bruh!" Tony said as he struggled to hold him back. "Now I know you are upset about Sissy, but you cannot let it cloud your thinking! We have a bigger plan here and a lot at stake. And I can't, and won't, let you fuck it up!"

Genie broke loose from Tony's grip, took a step back and charged with the knife towards the frightened Russian. Tony pushed him back so hard he flew into the door and lost his balance. After gathering himself, he charged again. This time Tony placed a kick to his chest that flipped him onto his back.

"Bruh! Chill! Don't make me do this!" Tony said as he jumped into the martial arts stance. With the blade still in hand, Genie popped to his feet before attempting another lunge at the Russian. He was met with a straight right to the jaw that dropped him to the hardwood floor, causing him to lose grip on the blade that slid across the floor. Macky moved quickly and grabbed it before Genie could recover. Groggy from the hard shot to the jaw, Tony grabbed his friend and walked him out of the basement and into the living room. The Russian's eyes showed relief as Macky followed in behind them. He took a deep breath as he closed his eyes. When Tony and Genie reached the huge red sectional sofa, he dropped Genie down on it.

"My brother," Tony said to him softly with his mouth close to his ear. "I know you are pissed beyond measure right now and you have every right to be. I know how you truly felt about Sissy. But we have to use our heads here. We will get that muthafucka soon enough. But we are still playing chess here until we can go full guerilla on these muthafuckas."

Genie was still trying to shake off the blow to the jaw. Macky walked back into the living room folding up the knife and placing it into his pocket. He looked at Genie with both caution and compassion for his loss. He thought about his own girl, Nicola, and how he would react if she was killed by someone. Though he couldn't blame Genie for his reaction, he wouldn't have reacted in the same manner. He was disciplined enough to never make a move unless it was on Tony's orders. He never allowed his emotions to get the best of him, which was a testament to the training he received from Tony. As Genie sat there with his head in his hands, Macky walked into the kitchen to retrieve an ice pack.

"Bruh, are you okay" Tony asked.

"Yeah, I'm good. Nigga, you almost broke my muthafucking jaw!" Genie said, holding the right side of his face. Tony smiled.

"Nigga, you know damn well, can't nobody break your hard ass jaw. But real talk, bruh. I wasn't trying to hurt you. I just wanted to knock some sense into your hard-headed ass. I have mad love for you and would never intentionally harm you, bruh. But you know what we have to do here. We can't act on impulse and go straight gangster. At least not yet. You're a boss now who has many lives you are responsible for. We must continue to play this thing like I designed it."

Macky returned with the ice pack and handed it to Genie who placed it on his jaw.

"But that's not to say we're going to let this shit ride and not send this muthafucka a real message. That ain't how we operate," Tony said as he stuck his hand out for Macky to hand him the knife. When the Russian and his broad saw Tony walking straight towards him in a straight line with the knife in his hand, their eyes stretched wide. Without breaking stride, and without hesitation, Tony walked menacingly up to the Russian popping out the knife, grabbed his ear and raked the knife over it. The blade cut through his ear with ease like soften cream cheese. The Russian's eyes bulged as his breathing became rapid. He and his broad attempted to scream, but the gag completely suppressed it. As Tony turned and walked away with the bloody ear in one hand and the knife in the other with blood dripping to the floor like rain drops, the Russian collapsed from shock.

214

Chapter 23
My Brother's Keeper

Cassadine's disappearance puzzled some and angered others. There were some like Tony and Genie who believed that he had abandoned his post. And that if he had been there that day in front of the mall, Sissy would still be alive. Others, like Macky, who truly knew him, knew he wouldn't flake on his responsibilities. The kind of cat Macky was, however, he felt responsible for Cassadine since he was the one who brought him in.

Ever since they were shorties in Yonkers, they were best friends. Cassadine was the only kid who could understand Macky, who was his own best company, being the target of bullying by some of the more hardened kids. His junky parents, however, contributed to much of his reclusiveness and introversion. He wasn't allowed to have company over and even if he did, the shame of having parents who had long gone over the deep end in their addiction would only cause him more grief from his peers. His parent's chronic addiction became worse after his older brother, Raheem, was murdered by the Ricans. But Cassadine understood Macky due to his own dysfunction at the crib. His mother was a junky and a whore. So these two kids brought together by a neighborhood fight and a shared commonality would create a bond for life.

After no less than 100 calls, texts, inboxes, and checking everywhere at Cassadine's hangouts and the places he frequented, Macky was all out of answers as to where his friend had gone. Knowing the kind of cat he was, death before dishonor, like himself, he feared the worst. It wasn't a dereliction of duty on Cassadine's part that was behind his absence. There was something foul and far more sinister about his disappearance. The last lead Macky had was from one of Cassadine's men who once hung out at the bar with him.

When Macky arrived at the bar in the Bronx, where Cassadine was last seen, the first thing he noticed were security cameras. The only two people in the bar this early in the morning was the bartender, who was helping unload beer and liquor off the liquor truck into the cellar and coolers, and the bar's owner, a short stocky man who had a strong Italian accent.

"May I help you, fellow? We're not quite yet open for business," he said, looking over his glasses with a printer and a spreadsheet in front of him and a cup of coffee with the steam emanating from it off to the side.

"Yes, sir. I have a friend who's been missing since last Friday," Macky said as he pulled out a picture of Cassadine and placed it down in front of the owner. "This is his picture. Thus far, he hasn't shown up for work, or his girl's crib, and his phone is going straight to voicemail." The owner studied Macky carefully before he took the picture into his hand.

"Oh sure. I know this fellow. The boxer. We call him Champ. Comes in here damn near every Friday, and sometimes on Saturday. Always leaves with at least two beautiful women at the end of the night."

"Was he in here last Friday?"

"Yes. He left with two black women who were so beautiful, they make your eyes water and the front of ya pants harden up. The kind I would take home to momma, even when I know I'd get cut out of the will and disowned. No offense," he said with a chuckle. "Are you a cop or something, fellow?"

"No. Not at all," Macky said, looking up at the security cameras. "Do those work?" he asked nodding to them.

"Yes. They better! I paid two months profits for those expensive motherfuckers."

"Can I take a look at the feed?" Macky asked politely.

"And you said you're not a cop, right?" Macky nodded his head. "So who are you with then?" he said with one eyebrow raised over his glasses after sipping his coffee. "There are only two people who would be this interested in finding a man. A cop and hitter. So if you are not a cop, then who do you work for?"

"I'm with Antonio Stallworth, and he would be most appreciative in your cooperation."

"Oh okay. Well, that's all you had to say then, young man. I know Mr. Stallworth well," he said before heading to the office. "Follow me, buddy." When the owner rewound the video feed, Macky saw his friend being smothered by the two beautiful twin sisters, Angel and Blaze.

"Yeah. There they are!" the owner said as his eyes lit up. Macky shook his head as he looked at his childhood friend's carelessness. He violated an age old street rule. Beware of the big butt and a smile. *Forever weak for pussy,* he thought.

"Can we get a close up on the females' faces?" Macky asked as he looked on intently.

"Oh yeah. This thing can do every fucking thing," the owner boasted. As the video zoomed in on the two females, Macky noticed one was light skinned and the other dark. There was no doubt in his mind that these two sisters were not only responsible for Cassadine's disappearance, they were at the attempted hijacking last week and were more than likely the two broads on the motorcycle that killed Genie's girl, Sissy.

"Do you need a photo of them, too?" the owner asked.

"Sure," Macky said as he stared at the twins leaving the club with Cassadine. His mind then drifted back to Ike's grandmother's strange admonition. *Beware of a pair of women you have never met. Like you, they have killed many men.*

Macky had already been to both of Cassadine's penthouses, but had only knocked before. This time he felt no other choice but to go inside. Using a tool to access the house he's often used to gain access to hit marks inside their home, once the door popped open, he walked inside. Before he could get in the door good that familiar putrid odor of decaying flesh hit him in the face. Death was definitely present inside the apartment. When Macky looked on the floor he saw Cassadine's clothes that he stripped out of during the freak session.

Noticing the glass on the snake's enclosure was broken and the snake missing, he pulled strap and walked cautiously to the back bedrooms. When he nudged opened the door, there was blood everywhere. Walking in a little farther, on the far side of the bed he was shocked to see the huge African Rock Python with the bottom half of Cassadine's body protruding from his mouth. The snake had dragged the body out of sight to perhaps get some privacy while it fed. A few minutes later, it would have swallowed Cassadine whole.

Macky looked down at the snake and put his pistol back into its holster. He then pulled out a switchblade, knelt down to the snake, aimed the blade at the top of its head and came crashing down on it with all his weight. When the 8 inch blade penetrated the massive serpent's skull and into its brain, its gigantic body immediately began thrashing about furiously as it instinctively regurgitated Cassadine's partially decomposed body. Almost immediately, Macky noticed his throat had been slit damn near from ear to ear, in addition to the hundreds of other cuts to his body. Every inch of Cassadine's lean, once chiseled frame, bore a cut. The defensive wounds on his left arm proved he tried to fend off his attackers. Macky knew him better than anyone that he was the type of cat who handled himself quite well. And in order for those two she-devils to get the drop on him and catch him slipping, they had to have ambushed him, which was easy since he was lured with pussy. The brutality that he could only imagine took place in this room, didn't faze Macky nor catch him off guard, for he had seen his share of violence of all types for various reasons in his young life. But this was different. He had never seen such brutality, calculation, callousness, and viciousness from women, especially from twins. All he knew was, those two deranged bitches had to be stopped.

Chapter 24
Dear Sir: Shit Just Got Real

When Lavrov, got a note tied to an ear that once belonged to his brother that said,

Dear Sir:

Shit just got real for you and especially your brother. He's out of his sickle cell meds, and we are not going to contribute to his addiction by giving him his much needed fix of the boy. Try us again and we will put him out of his misery, but not before we mail you the rest of his remaining body parts piece by piece. You've been warned.

Yours truly, a real life Gangster

Lavrov literally became ill at the sight of his younger brother's ear. Vladimir was his only living sibling. More than that, he was the only relative, besides his dear mother in Russia, whom he had love for. Anyone who saw Yuri and Vladimir back in St. Petersburg, Russia, automatically assumed they were twins due to their likeness and closeness. And perhaps it was because their mother dressed them alike. When Stallworth advised Ike to spare Vladimir and keep him as a bargaining chip that was the smartest move he could have made in this entire debacle with Lavrov. Like most men, Lavrov had a huge weakness. He was now reduced to a caged dangerous animal rather than one on the loose wreaking havoc.

Looking at his brother's severed ear he was now helpless. Soon he would become withdrawn and sullen. With his family in his custody, Tony had pretty much bitched him up. Seeing their man's anguish, Angel and Blaze tried to console and comfort him, but he would have nothing of it. He told them to get the fuck out of his presence. For him to tell them that was akin to a master giving a loyal dog, who would gladly give its life just to impress, a boot to the ass. And like that loyal dog, they were willing to do what it took to get back into their benefactor's good graces.

Chapter 25
Watch Out Lil' Bitch

When Tony left in haste to accompany his grieving friend and partner, he inadvertently left his cell phone on the bed. Almost from the time he left, the phone had been going off. At first Sugar ignored it. She even grabbed it to put it into the drawer next to the bed until he returned. When she picked it up, a text was coming in with a picture contact on it. The face belonged to a beautiful light skinned girl with long dark hair. At first Sugar refused to be taken by jealousy and curiosity and thus resisted the urge to read the texts.

In her mind, she totally trusted Tony. The two years they had been together, he never gave her any reason not to trust him or at the very least suspect him. He often told her that he was a one woman type of cat and she believed him wholeheartedly. But the text from this broad who she had never seen or heard of before, who was just as beautiful as she was, was something she needed to know about. She could call Genie's phone and talk with Tony about it, but that wouldn't be cool at all in a time of crisis like this.

As she laid there flipping through the TV channels, she tried to ignore that drama queen voice in her head. Like her old man, Sugar was a boss in her own right and had proven such. However, she was still a woman. And one that wasn't about to let any man fuck over her and play her like a sucker. Not even Tony, who could have any woman he wanted. The more and more she thought about the text, however, that woman side of her was taking center stage. After the ringtone went off again, she jumped up and immediately went to the bar to get herself a stiff drink.

While the song *Watch Out Lil' Bitch by* 2 Chainz played from the wall speakers, Sugar poured a shot of hen with no chaser, just as the No Drama voice reasoned. *If there was something going on with this woman, Tony wouldn't dare leave his phone here. Cheating men take care and concern not to leave behind any evidence, especially a phone.* Sugar quickly downed her drink as if her body called for it.

Bitch, please! That nigga was in a hurry and under duress, Drama Queen said. *And that's why he left his phone. Men do dumb shit sometimes and get caught up.*

Girl stop that shit, No Drama said. *That man ain't never gave you any problems, Sugar, or even made you think he was out there slinging dick.*

Get the fuck out of here. He doesn't have to be out there slinging dick, Drama Queen shot back. *Maybe he's just giving the dick to one thirsty side bitch like the one on his phone.*

Awww come on. This female don't look nothing like side chick material, No Drama said. *She looks upscale and siddity.*

Really bitch? Really? You ain't never seen a thirsty siddity bitch before? I have. There are thirsty siddity bitches out there too, Drama Queen said. *Just waiting to run cross a swagged out gangsta ass nigga like Tony. He would be a siddity bitch's dream. A nigga like that would bring excitement to her boring, dry ass life.*

Sugar downed another drink that made her resolute on what her next move was. On this rare occasion Drama Queen won the argument. And perhaps it was due in large part to the two straight shots Sugar took to the head with no chaser. *I'm 'bout to call this bitch. Better yet, I'm 'bout to Facetime this bitch. That's my man's phone, I got papers on him and I wanna know why she's frantically trying to contact him like she ain't got no damn sense.*

That's right bitch, Drama Queen said. *Facetime that ho.*

"Hello," Sugar said into the phone. The two women momentarily stared at one another.

"Hello?" the proper voice responded. "Do I know you?"

"Who are you?" Sugar shot back.

"Wait a minute. You called me. Do you always call people then asked who they are?"

"Do you always blow someone else's man's phone up?" Sugar said, popping her neck. The two shots of hen were now in full effect.

"Excuse me?"

"You heard me! Why are you blowing my man's phone up?" she said sternly.

"Lady, who is your man? I don't have the slightest idea what you are talking about. You must have the wrong number or something." She popped her own neck.

"No bitch! I got the right number! You just got the wrong woman fucked up! You been blowing my man's phone up all morning! Tony Stallworth is his name!" Sugar who was normally restrained and cool headed, had now reverted all the way back to the projects.

"Wait a minute. Bitch? I'm not anyone's bitch! Bitch! Now if you just give me a second to explain to you why I've been trying to contact him, I can clear this up so you can rest your nerves."

"Oh Bitch! Now the real you coming out, trying to look all siddity and sophisticated on your picture!" Sugar said laughing. "As far as my nerves they are made of steel! You better ask somebody! I would never let a thirsty trick, side piece material bitch like you penetrate them!"

"What? Side piece? Honey, you have me totally confused with someone else. I have never been a side piece to anyone, not even Tony the entire time we were together. Speaking of Tony, the man that I once knew better than anyone, including your tired ass, wouldn't have a woman of your ilk, not even as a side bitch….a hood rat who flies off the handle over something that isn't even that serious. Now is Tony there? If he is put him on the Goddamn chat! I'm through talking to your silly ass!

225

"What bitch?" Sugar yelled. The echo traveled all throughout the house. The soldiers downstairs could hear her. "Where the fuck are you at, bitch? I will come see you!" Sugar was so animated she was now standing up in the bed.

"Hahahaha." She laughed at the top of lungs. "Bitch, I'm in Europe right now, but I will be home next week. You can bet your tramp bitch ass on that! And if I just so happen to run into Tony, which I know I will, first I'm going to ask him has he lost his Goddamn mind fucking with someone like you! Then I just may fuck him for old time's sake to make him forget all about that annoying noise in his ear!" She hung up the phone and turned off her chat.

"Bitch! Bitch!" Sugar yelled looking at the phone. Realizing she got hung up on, she immediately called back. She called back again and again and each time the phone ring. She called back one last and the message came on saying her number had been blocked. This only infuriated Sugar even more. She snatched the nightstand drawer open so hard it flew onto the floor and Tony's phone slid across the other side of the room.

She walked over and picked it up and began reading the text messages from Angela Washington. The more she read, the further she was convinced that there was something going on between them. The two shots of hen didn't help matters either. Tony never told Sugar about Angela and there was no need to because they were history before they became serious. He also never told Angela about Sugar because it never came up. During the past two years she had relocated to Europe, Angela spoke with him a couple of times, but it was harmless small talk like *how is Europe treating you?* Or *how is your mother?*

On Angela's part there was the typical, *I miss you so much.* Or, *do you miss me?* Tony would never feed into it, though. However, to a female like Sugar who was not only a proud sister who did everything with class and carried herself like a Queen at all times, but a boss and a killer like her old man, she wasn't trying to hear that shit that this correspondence was something harmless. Tony needed to tell her something, but not right now. For weeks she had put off a trip to Orlando to settle her grandmother into a new home in Poinciana Springs that she purchased for her a couple of months ago. Now was as good a time as any to make that happen.

After months of wooing and convincing her grandmother to move into a new home she purchased for her, Sugar's grandmother had finally relented. As a compromise, however, Sugar promised her that she would move her back into the old home after it was remodeled. She also promised to allow her brother Horace could move into the new home once he jumped from prison. Other than Tony, Horace, her Uncle Roy, and a few other relatives, Sugar's grandmother was the one person in this world she truly cared about and would kill or die for. Tony once told her that *if there is no one in this world you would kill for or die for, this life just ain't worth living.*

***

When Tony returned to the crib, he walked slowly up the winding staircase deep in thought about the death of Genie's girl. He too had begun to blame himself. Maybe if he hadn't taken Ike's offer, this drama with Lavrov wouldn't have happened and Sissy would therefore still be alive. Tony had never seen his friend of 25 years that hurt before. To know Genie was to know a cat who wasn't fazed by much. He was also the type of cat who never became emotionally attached to any broad. His reaction to Sissy's death was either he truly cared about her or he felt some embarrassment that someone close to him was touched, which shouldn't happen to a boss. This is probably why he wanted to strike out at anyone close to Lavrov without thinking shit through.

227

When Tony slumped down and laid across the bed with his pistols still in their shoulder holsters, he didn't even notice his phone with a note attached to it. He also didn't notice Sugar's absence. This day was perhaps the most trying since his Uncle Walt was killed outside of his club. Lying there, Tony's mind began to drift back to that night he was informed by the chaplain that his Uncle Walt had died. At first he thought that his death was natural. But when he came home on emergency leave and went to the funeral home to view his uncle's body and make funeral arrangements, the multiple bullet wounds told another story. Walt was murdered. Less than a year later after Uncle Walt's funeral, and a week after Tony's time in Afghanistan was up and he retired to the civilian life, his murderers met the same fate. He killed them all to make sure the Stallworth curse, initiated by his father, wouldn't be repeated. At least not from the same people.

As Tony snapped back to reality, he began to miss his wife. When he sat up in the bed to place his .45s down on the nightstand to go look for his baby, he finally noticed the note attached to his phone. Immediately, he knew there was a problem.

"Shit!" he yelled.

Your bitch and me had a very deep conversation. She's trying to get in touch with you. Hope y'all have a blast. I'm out.

"Fuck!" he yelled again closing his eyes. He then looked through his phone and saw the texts From Angela that he ignored earlier.

Hello Tony. I just wanted to let you know that my mother isn't doing well at all. The doctors have given her 2 weeks. They said there was nothing else they could do for her, but make her as comfortable as possible. I'm really in a bad way right now because she didn't tell me she was this sick. I'm so hurt right now, Tony, I don't know what to do. I wish you were here with me to help me deal with it. When you get this message please call me. I will be there in a few days. Love always.

Though Tony's thoughts were with Angela, and more importantly, her mother, his first concern was for his wife whom he loved more than anything or anyone in this world. So naturally, the first call he made was to her. After he got her voicemail on the third ring, he realized that she was ignoring his call. He then placed another call as he ran downstairs to ask the soldiers if they saw her leave. Again, the phone went to voicemail. This time he decided to leave a message.

"Baby Girl, please give me a call back. We don't ignore each other's calls. Call me back, baby, okay?" he said before he put his phone in his pocket.

"Hey, Yancey, did Sugar tell you where she was headed?" he asked the head of his security.

"She didn't say where she was headed, but she had the driver to take her to the airport. She seemed pretty upset when she left, though."

"Did she take any security with her?"

"No. That's what I'm saying. When I insisted that I should go with her, she told me she could take care of her damn self."

"And so you just let her go anyway!" he said angrily.

"Well, sir, I insisted and she wasn't having it. So I had a couple of men to follow her to look after her anyway."

"Okay. Good thinking, Yancey," Tony said before running back into the house to get his pistols and suit jacket. As he ran upstairs, he called Sugar again, and again, her voicemail picked up.

"Fuck!" he said as he grabbed an overnight bag and began stuffing clothes into it. "Fucking women!" he yelled.

Running downstairs, he placed a call to Macky for him to meet him at JFK. For the first time since she and Tony been together, Sugar allowed her emotions to get the best of her. In this current climate of hostilities with the most dangerous people they had ever encountered, that kind of mistake could prove fatal. Tony had trained her to never think and act on emotions. But what he failed to realize was, though Sugar was a boss, she was still a woman….subject to mistakes and lapses in judgment just like her man. But this time was a whole different ballgame where the stakes were far too high to be slipping. With this new brand of enemy who often went on the offense, Tony was well aware that there was always someone watching and waiting in the cut for one slip up.

***

Sitting in a Black Hummer in the parking area at JFK airport, Angel and Blaze stared intently, without breaking their gaze, at the beautiful black woman with the long braids being helped with her luggage. As Sugar walked inside the airport check in, Angel pulled out a phone and placed a call.

Chapter 26
Grandmotherly Wisdom

When Sugar boarded her flight after a short delay, she was still fuming from the exchange with Angela. This is why when Tony attempted to contact her for the tenth time, she looked at his text coming through and without reading it, she turned her phone off. The flight attendant, a pretty dark skinned girl walked up to her smiling.

"Ma'am, can I get you a complimentary drink for your short delay?

"Sure," Sugar said without hesitation. "I'll take a Hennessy and coke."

"Okay. One Hennessy and coke coming up. I hope you enjoy your flight," the young flight attendant said before walking off. After the other pilot finally stepped onto the plane after being caught in traffic, the plane's engines started. Not long after the announcement protocol, the plane lifted from the runway into the heavens. A few minutes after Sugar downed her drink she drifted off to sleep.

Just before the plane touched down at Orlando International Airport, Sugar was awakened by the pilot over the loudspeaker.

"Ladies and gentleman, we are on our final descent and about five minutes from touchdown on Orlando International Airport. Today's weather forecast is sunny skies with very little chance of rain. We ask that you remain in your seats until the plane has landed. We hope that you enjoyed your flight with us today. Thank you for choosing Delta Airlines."

Once the plane landed and its tires came to a screeching halt on the runway, Sugar grabbed her tote bag and began leaving the plane with the other passengers.

Behind her a voice yelled, "Ma'am! Ma'am! You left your iPad!" After hearing this, Sugar remembered she'd left her iPad on the seat and turned around.

"Ma'am? Is this your iPad?" the tall light skinned blonde girl asked politely.

"Yes, it is. Thank you so much," Sugar said smiling.

"Don't mention it," Blaze said as she and Angel smiled with their eyes lowered on Sugar's ass as she headed for the plane's exit doors.

After grabbing a rental car from Budget, Sugar set off for her grandmother's crib. Seeing the familiar landmarks in her hometown again seemed to put her troubled mind at ease. Perhaps this is what she needed all along - .a getaway from the hustle and bustle of the city. She never thought, however, not even in her worst nightmares that she would be on a getaway from the man should loved more than anything in the world. Already she had started to miss him dearly, so much so that she began to question her decision to leave. And worst yet, not tell him where she was going and ignoring his many calls and texts on top of that.

Maybe I acted rashly, she thought. *I certainly shouldn't be ignoring him. That is something I promised to never do. Let me at least see what he's saying. All this shit could just be a big misunderstanding on my part. If so, how foolish I'm going to look in his eyes now.*

When Sugar turned on her phone to read the texts and listened to her voicemail, the phone died.

"Shit!" she yelled. "Now you wanna die on me, you piece of shit phone!" She tossed the phone in the backseat.

After reaching her grandmother's crib and pulling into the granite rock driveway, the usual excitement of seeing her granny began to build. Smiling, she quickly grabbed her luggage, hopped out of the white Range Rover and headed into the house. After ringing the doorbell a familiar male voice answered.

"Who is it?" She heard followed by someone looking through the peephole.

"Sugar," she answered. When the door slung open her brother Horace grabbed her and literally picked her up off the porch into the air.

"Big sis!" he yelled.

"Horace!" she yelled back. "I'm so glad to see you! So you got out on time!"

"I'm glad to see you too, sis! And yes. I made sure I got out on time by staying out those fools way. When they tried to let me out of lockdown after I stuck that fool who tried me over the phone, I told them to let me end of sentence from the box so I wouldn't get into anymore shit." Sugar laughed.

"Well, you just going to stand there and not help me with this luggage?" Sugar asked before punching him in the chest.

"Oh my bad, sis," he said before grabbing her heaviest suitcase.

"Where's granny at?" Sugar asked eagerly

"Where you think she at? In her normal place. The kitchen."

"In the kitchen? Like she in there cooking something good to eat?" Sugar asked excitedly.

"You don't smell that?" Horace asked as they walked into the living room.

"Yeeeessss! I smell it!" she said smiling. "And it smells like collard greens?"

"Yep. My favorite. She promised she would hook her favorite grandson up when once he jumped."

"Okay. Let me go in here and surprise her," Sugar said in a whisper as she crept towards the kitchen. When she walked in, granny was just getting ready to fry some cornbread.

"Hey grandmomma!" Sugar said with her arms outstretched.

"Hey baby!" granny screamed. "Why you sneak in here on my like this? You know I don't like surprises. You should have told me you were coming! Where is my grandson-in-law?" Sugar's smile dropped a notch. The mention of Tony made her remembered to charge her phone.

"Oh grandmomma, hold on a sec. Let me put this phone on the charger," she said before she hooked the charger to her iPhone and plugged it into the outlet. "I came by myself, grandmomma. Tony was kind of busy and couldn't make this trip. I had some off time, so I came home to make sure you make it into that nice home that's been waiting on you to move in going on four months now."

"I don't know why grandmomma acting like that," Horace said before going to the fridge. "It's a nice crib in a super nice, secluded neighborhood where you don't have all those nosey neighbors and the trifling negroes. I saw the picture of it. It's two stories with a balcony and an elevator in it. In Poinciana, right?"

"Yes, Poinciana where granny grew up at." Sugar sat down at the table.

"I know I need to go 'head on and move in it. Y'all showl right. This here old house is in need of some serious repairs. I'm ready to move. But remember what our agreement was. As soon as the renovation is finished, I come back home," granny said as she placed the cornbread batter into the hot grease.

"Look at her. Just hate to leave this house," Horace smiled and said before he sipped on a glass of sweet tea.

"Yeah grandmomma. I remember the agreement. But hopefully once you start living in the house, you will wanna stay there permanently. It's really a nice place."

"I know. I know, baby. And I appreciate you getting it for me, but I have been in this house going on 50 years," she said as she flipped over the fried cornbread patties. "When you live in a house that long, you become a part of it and it becomes a part of you."

"I understand, grandmomma. Part of me miss this house too. Horace, you remember how you used to believe there were tiny people inside the attic?" Sugar said laughing.

"Yes. And who told me that? Y'all really had me going with that. Up until I was 15 I believed that shit."

"Hey! Watch yo language," granny turned around and admonished him.

"Yes, ma'am," he said sheepishly.

"You remember that time the dog down the road chased me all the way inside the house into my room and granddaddy got his gun to shoot it?" Sugar said laughing out loud.

"Yes, do I? When the owner Mr. what's his name came to get that mutt, granddaddy told him I ought to shoot your ass along with that mangy ass, shit eating dog," Horace said laughing.

"Alright. Watch yo language," granny warned again with a chuckle.

"Sorry, granny, but that's what granddaddy said. Boy granddaddy didn't play nothing."

"He showl didn't," granny said as she removed the last remaining cornbread patty from the hot grease. That man could be one mean soul, especially about his loved ones and friends. And Sugar knew it too. She was messing with that dog that day like she always did. I used to watch her out the living room window picking at him. He just got fed up that day and got loose on her. " Sugar smiled and put her head down. "All that darn screaming she was doing that day. I was certain somebody was trying to kill her," granny said laughing. "When I saw that it was that lil' ole bitty dog I nearly hit the floor laughing. He wasn't studdin' us. He was just standing at Sugar's bedroom door barking and carrying on. I guess he had had enough of your bad behind." They all started laughing.

"Grandma, I wasn't that bad," Sugar said.

"Child, please. You were as bad as they come. Stayed into something," granny said as she flipped over the new batch of cornbread. The aroma of the fried cornbread and the collard greens, totally permeated every inch of the house.

"Sugar, you was bad, though," Horace said smiling with one eyebrow raised.

"What a minute! I know, you ain't talking!" Sugar said with her hands on her hips. "Who used to set dog poop on fire in front of Mr. Johnson's door, knock and run and the poor man would yell fire and stomp on it to put it out?"

"You did that to Mr. Johnson, Horace?" granny asked, looking over at him with a chastising look on her face. Horace laughed so hard he nearly fell from his chair.

"Nah grandmomma! Sugar lying!" he said as she continued to crack up laughing.

"Wait a minute! I'm lying? I'm lying?" Sugar asked, raising up from her chair. "Do I need to call Uncle Roy over here to be a witness to your many past misdeeds?" Horace laughed even harder.

"Horace, I know doggone well you didn't do that to poor Mr. Johnson. You know the man was shell shocked from the war. And so your uncle even knew all about it, huh?" Horace was laughing so hard he could no longer defend himself.

"Yeah grandma. Uncle Roy caught him in the act and grabbed him by his shirt. But he couldn't get on him like he wanted to, because he was trying to keep from laughing himself."

"So you did that to Mr. Johnson and your uncle didn't tell me about it?" granny said as she removed the remaining cornbread patties from the grease and placed them on the plate covered with a paper towel.

"Grandma, you know Uncle Roy would never tell on us. He's from the streets and he would consider that snitching. But he would get on to us when we did something he thought would really get us into trouble," Sugar said smiling as she looked over there at the cornbread. Her stomach had begun to growl like that dog who chased her to her room as the last of the Hennessy started to leave her system. She had also begun to think about Tony. By now her cell phone should be charged up enough to call him.

"Sugar, where is Tony now? Did you say he couldn't make it?" granny asked.

"He's back at home. Nah. He couldn't make it." Granny gave her granddaughter, who she'd raised from a child, a discerning look over her glasses.

"Yeah where is this man of yours I keep hearing so much about?" Horace asked. "I heard about what he did to old boy in the bathroom. I like that," he said with a grin. Sugar smiled and didn't say anything. Granny continued to monitor her while she floured the chicken. She knew her granddaughter better than anyone and she was not about to give in so easily to the story she gave her. She knew something was wrong.

"Sugar, is everything alright between you and Tony?" she asked as she immersed the floured chicken parts into the cast iron skillet of hot grease.

"Uh oh," Horace said, rising from the chair. "I guess this is where the only man in the house leaves the ladies to have their female conversation." Sugar smiled and gave him a playful punch him to the chest.

"Ummm hmmm. That chiseled granite hurt ya hand, didn't it?" he said smiling. He then kissed her on the cheek before kissing granny. "Just call me when the food is done. That's all I need y'all to do," he smiled and said before walking out of the kitchen.

"Okay. What's going on, Suge?" granny asked before washing her hands and sitting down in the chair in front of her granddaughter.

"Awwww grandma. I'm okay," Sugar said as her shoulders lurched down towards the floor.

"Child, no you not. Look how you slouching right now. You know I know every little quirk you have that says something is wrong with you." Sugar smiled and tried to straighten up her posture. "Now tell grandma what's going on."

"Okay. I got upset with Tony and came here sooner than I had planned. I just needed to get away, grandma."

"Okay. Now we getting' somewhere. What did he do to upset you? Or better yet, what did you think he did to upset you?"

"Grandma, it was really just stupid on my part. I think it just may have been a case of me overreacting."

"Okay. And why you think you overreacted?" granny said, looking over her glasses.

"Well, some female from Tony's past was blowing his phone up and I called her."

"Ooooo-Kay. You call her and then what happened?"

"We ended up getting into a heated argument," Sugar said as her face began to wrinkle up as she began to recall the exchange.

"And you lost your temper, right?"

"Yeah. Kinda. I had every right to," she shot back.

"You had every right to? But did it make it right that you reacted the way you did?"

"Grandma, you sound like you are taking her side," Sugar replied in a frustrated tone. "Of course I was right to go off on that wench!" she said angrily. Granny laughed and stood up from her chair.

"Child, did you call that girl a wench?"

"Kinda. I actually called her much more than that," Sugar said, mischievously grinning to herself.

"Ummm hmm. You called her out her name, she called you out your name and out went the civility and the ladylike behavior. If there is one thing in this world I taught you and that was to be a lady at all times." Sugar nodded her head in agreement and thought to herself just how ladylike she's been as she had a flashback with her standing naked over the hitters, the Shadow Twins, with her nickel plated .38 just before she unloaded on them and brought their assassin days to an end.

"I know, grandma. But she just rubbed me wrong." Sugar's body language suggested she was becoming upset all over again.

"Okay. But did you give her a chance to say what she wanted with Tony? I mean, she must have had a good reason for trying to contact him, baby." Sugar immediately thought back to Angela's words. *Now if you just give me a second to explain to you why I've been trying to contact him, I can clear this up.* Granny picked up on it.

"Ummm hmm. So she did try to explain to you what she wanted with Tony, huh?"

"Yes. As a matter of fact she did," Sugar said in a low voice as she began to realize the part she played in the contentious discussion. Then suddenly, just as it seemed Sugar had reached a peaceful resolution, Drama Queen resurfaced and whispered in her ear. *Hell naw! You wasn't wrong! Fuck that bitch! She had no business calling your man's phone no matter what the reason!*

"Yeah, but none of that matters! She didn't have any business calling my husband's phone!" Sugar said defiantly. Granny laughed.

"Still the stubborn, bullheaded one, I see," Granny said flipping the crispy golden brown chicken with the long fork. "You know what I think? I think she had a good reason to contact him and you just overreacted, baby. Have you spoke with Tony to see if he could shed some light on this matter?"

"No." Sugar rolled her eyes.

"And why not? I'm sure by now he's wondering where his wife done gone to," granny said as she flipped over the last piece of chicken.

"Because I overreacted," Sugar said putting her head down. She had finally relented. The voice of reason won out this time, like it did most of the time with her. Granny smiled and touched her on her head and looked down at her endearingly.

"Baby, you need to call that man. Call your husband and at least give him a chance to explain. More importantly, let him know where you at. I'm sure he is worried sick right about now. You know he worships the ground you walk on."

***

After the dreaded take off, that sent Tony's heart rate back down to normal, he and Macky were finally in the air after a somewhat long delay caused by a diverted flight. Macky had filled him in on what had happened to his friend and understudy, Cassadine. And they both concluded that these were the same two women who had murdered Sissy outside the mall. Tony had also figured Sugar had gone back to the crib to move her granny into her new place they had purchased for her, since she had mentioned it several times. This is the one thing that gave him comfort about the situation. At least in Orlando, and away from New York, she would be relatively safe from the drama that was well underway. He had even considered having her go back home until this whole Lavrov thing blew over, but he knew she wouldn't have it.

While Macky was busy locked in a heated battle with the game on his cell phone, Tony thought about how bad he slipped leaving his phone behind. *How the fuck could I slip like that and leave my damn phone behind? But it ain't like I had anything to hide. Well, I guess I kinda did. I should have told Sugar about Angela a long time ago. And I should have told Angela about Sugar as well. I guess I never got around to doing the shit. But fuck all that. Sugar knew better than to fly off the handle like that and just jump up and leave, especially without at least getting an explanation from me. If she knew about all the drama back in the city she wouldn't have just left like that without the soldiers. I should have filled her in on everything. Well, none of that shit matters now. I just need to catch up with her to make this shit right again.* After a few more minutes of beating himself up over his bad decisions, Tony drifted off to sleep.

A couple of hours after a lunch of fried chicken, collard greens, fried cornbread, potato salad, sweet tea and peach cobbler on the side, granny went to a church meeting while the movers began removing the last of her things she wanted to take with her. Since the new crib was already completely furnished all the way through with brand new expensive furniture, she only decided to take a few things with her. Everything else would go in storage while the old home was being renovated.

After noticing Horace in her old room doing something, she decided to investigate. When she walked in, he closed the two long suitcases shut as if he was trying to hide something.

"Alright, Bug. What you doing in here?" she asked, standing at the doorway to the room with her arms folded.

"Why?" he asked before picking up the two suitcases.

"Ummmm why. Because, first of all this is my damn room," she shot back. "Second of all, I hope you ain't got any shit stashed off in grandmomma's house."

"First of all, this ain't your room no more, nosey. Second of all, it ain't dope. It's just a few things I collected before I went down the road. I hid them here, and yes. They're clean." He stood up with the two suitcases in hand. "I didn't want those movers to steal them, so I decided it was time to move them."

"So what are they?" Sugar asked with her arms still folded. Horace paused momentarily to decide whether or not he was going to answer. He knew however, Sugar wasn't leaving or wouldn't even allow him to leave without an explanation.

"Well, if you must know," he said as he knelt down to open the suitcases.

"Yeah. I must know," she shot back with her hands on her hips. After opening the suitcases, Sugar looked down to see a small arsenal of weapons. There were two AK 47s, two M-16s, an AR 15, several pistols that included Glock 40s, .45s, a couple of nines, a .380, a couple of knives, piano wire and about half a dozen hand grenades.

"Boy! What the fuck are you doing with all that shit up in here?" Sugar demanded.

"These are my tools," he said, quickly closing up the suitcases.

"Your tools? Boy, you ain't no damn carpenter! So why do you have them here?"

"I left them when I caught the case. And I didn't have anyone I could trust to move them for me. You know I don't fuck with anybody."

"So you mean to tell me all this time that shit been up in here? Hand grenades, Horace? Really nigga?" she said getting in his face. "What if that shit had gone off in here while grandma was moving something around?"

"Sis, chill the fuck out, okay? You know grandma never come into this room. She hadn't been in here since you been gone. I know you noticed how she left everything in place just like you left it. My stash is even where I left it. I had it under the floor in a small space under the house. She wasn't in any danger."

"Yeah, okay," Sugar said just as the movers walked in. "You and me will talk about this shit later." she whispered to him before he picked up the two suitcases and headed out of the room.

"Ma'am, we are ready to go now. Is there anything else?"

"Nah. That's all," Sugar said as she watched Horace walk out of the room with the two suitcases in hand.

Chapter 27
Ain't No Mountain High Enough

When Tony found out about the hour layover in Atlanta, he was pissed. The only tickets he could get on such a short notice were the one with the one connection. The old school joint *Aint No Mountain High Enough* by the immortal Marvin Gaye blared from the speakers inside the Hartsfield Jackson airport terminal as Tony and Macky waited. While Macky displayed his typical stoicism and patience that belied his young age, his mentor and boss, paced back and forth impatiently when suddenly his ringtone went off. Beyonce's song *One Plus One*. It was Sugar.

"Baby Girl! Where are you?" Tony said trying to suppress his excitement.

"I'm in Orlando moving grandmamma into her new home," she replied nonchalantly.

"Okay, but why didn't you at least let me know you were going? And why wouldn't you at least let the soldiers go with you?"

"I didn't want anyone tagging along with me. Besides, I was pissed off after talking to your bitch," she said as she continued on with her hardcore act. She knew she had softened her position the moment she heard his voice.

"Baby Girl, listen. You got it all wrong. She's not my bitch or anything else," he said as Sugar rolled her eyes on the other end. "She's an ex who reached out to me because...... Hello! Hello! Damn!" he said looking at his phone. "I know damn well she didn't just hang up on me." he said out loud catching the attention of the bystanders. On the other end, Sugar looked at her own phone and became livid.

"Goddammit!" she said as the movers moved granny's last belonging into the house.

"It's the coverage area," one of the movers said smiling as he recognized her dilemma. "I've had three dropped calls since I been here. You must be with T-Mobile?"

"Yes, I am, unfortunately," she said angrily looking at her phone hoping Tony would call back. "Shit!" she said as she realized her hardcore act had just caused her to miss her opportunity to make up with Tony.

"Is there anything else, ma'am?" the mover asked.

"Huh?" she asked with a bewildered look on her face.

"Oh. No. We good," she said. "How much do owe you?"

"$400," he said before Sugar peeled off five one hundred dollar bills.

"Keep the change," she said.

"Thank you, ma'am." He handed her a receipt. "Oh yeah. Upstairs in the bedroom on the left is where you can get a good signal."

"Thank you," she said before he and the other two movers walked out. Sugar then immediately made a mad dash upstairs to call Tony back. When she called him, his phone went to voicemail on the first ring. "Shit!" she yelled.

After trailing Sugar to her granny's new crib, Angel and Blaze peeled off and went back to a shopping plaza down the street a couple miles away and posted up in the parking lot. It was the nearest plaza to the home. As the two widows sat in their rental listening to the song *She Wolf* by Shakira while waiting for Lavrov and his men to show up, the many dudes passing by, black, white and Latino were flirting with them. The men cat called and whistled at the drop dead gorgeous twins, while the widows smiled and flirted back. Little did those men know, however, these two women were the last females in the world they wanted to fuck or be fucked up with. The nickname, widows, they were given was well earned. Just like the Black Widow spider who is infamous for devouring her male lover once she is done fucking his brains out, these two widows have on many occasions left their share of men's naked corpses behind.

The small Lhasa Apso dog in the car next to them, his instincts must have picked up on something unnatural about them. He barked incessantly at them while his master was trying to calm him down.

"I'm so sorry," she said to them. Her face had turned red with embarrassment. "He's never acted like this in public. I don't know what has gotten into him. Rocket! Calm down!"

The two sisters smiled at her and the dog and nodded their heads. Blaze, who was the more brutal of the two, stared directly into the dog's eyes with such coldness he retreated from the seat whimpering, hopped down in the floorboard and went into hiding.

***

When Sugar made another call to Tony, the call went straight to voicemail which was now saying it was full. Frustrated, she laid across the king sized bed and just stared up at the ceiling. *How could I have acted like that with Tony? He didn't deserve that from me,* she thought. After a few minutes of trying to replay and block the events of the last 24 hours out of her mind, she drifted off to sleep.

After the plane's tires finally touched down on Orlando's International Airport tarmac, sending Tony's heart rate back down to normal again, he and Macky left the plane with the rest of the passengers. A tall man wearing dark shades was awakened by two men, while four more walked up from the rear of the plane. The men spoke to him in Russian. "Ser, pora exit." *Sir, it's time to unboard.* The tall Russian awoke and stood to his feet before he and the men, two in front and four behind him, were the last to leave the huge plane.

After Tony and Macky went to the Hertz rental car company and found out there was a wait, Tony's frustrations returned. He again picked up the phone and called Sugar, but the phone went to voicemail. He then thought to call her Uncle Roy whose number was still on his call list. After the third ring and just as Tony was about to hang up, someone picked up.

"Hello," a deep raspy voice said.

"Is this Big Roy?"

"Big Roy speaking. Who wants to know?"

"Hey what's up, Roy. This is Tony. Sugar's old man."

"Oh okay. Stallworth, the man with the plans and the fast hands. What's good partner other than that long money you got in your bank account?" Tony cracked a smile.

"Man, I need a solid."

"What's up, man?" Roy asked as he recognized the frustration in Tony's voice.

"Maaaaan, me and my partner are up here at the airport and can't get a rental car right now. I was wondering if you could give us a lift to granny's new crib."

"For show. I'm about 30 minutes from the airport. I'll be there in a minute." Tony was somewhat relieved. There was no way in hell he was going to wait 4 hours for a rental. Good thing he had kept Roy's contact info. *But why the hell does Sugar's phone keep going to voicemail like that?* he thought.

Not long after Lavrov and his men walked out of the terminal, some of his Russian mafia contacts had a ride to pick them up before they set out to meet up with Angel and Blaze who made a quick drive by to scope granny's new crib to make sure Sugar was still there.

As Lavrov passed by the city of Orlando on I-4 en route to his destination, his mind played back the moment he received his brother's severed ear. It was then and there in the black Expedition that he made up his mind that no matter what happened tonight, Stallworth's bitch was going with him in one piece or many pieces. And anyone who got in his way would die.

***

When Sugar finally woke up from what sounded like her granny and Horace moving around downstairs, she looked outside to see that darkness had fallen. She then looked at her watch and couldn't believe she had dozed off that long. After that flight, that meal granny put together that would give anyone the itis and not to mention the most trying day in she and Tony's marriage, she needed the rest.

After she was now fully awake, and saw that Tony had called, she immediately placed a call to him. When he answered, her eyes lit up.

"Hey, Bae," she said as she walked out on the balcony where it was pitch dark. The balcony's light bulbs had blown some time ago after being left on for over a month.

"Hey, Baby Girl!" he said excitedly as he looked at the Disney World and Universal Studios signs they passed. "Did you hang up on me earlier?"

"No, Bae, I would never hang up on you. You already know how I feel about that type of thing as do you. I just lost the signal here at grandma's new crib."

"Okay. So y'all made it over there?"

"Yes. We finished moving her in earlier. We didn't have to move much because remember I told you that I had it completely furnished all the way through. She just brought some things she said she wanted here."

"Okay. Cool. Baby Girl, we really need to talk when I get there. I need to clear some things up with you I should have done a while back. Shit that has come back to bite me in the ass now."

"Umm Okay. You sure do. But hey. Did you just say when you come here?" Sugar paced about on the balcony. She was so glad to hear from him she could hardly contain her excitement.

"Yes, Baby Girl. I had your Uncle Roy pick me and Macky up from the airport. I didn't wanna wait on a rental they said would take a few hours."

"So you decided to come after me and you caught up with my uncle Roy, huh?" Sugar asked smiling."

"Yep. Of course I came after you. And yes, I caught up with Uncle Roy who's driving the hell out of this Cadillac of his as we speak," Tony said smiling.

"Is that my spoiled rotten niece on the other end of that phone?" Roy asked."

"Yes, sir. This is your spoiled rotten niece," Tony replied with a chuckle. Sugar laughed.

"Tell him that's right. Spoiled rotten because he and granny made me that way."

"Oh and I'm glad I did not play a part in that," Tony said smiling.

"You sure did play a part. You played a big part in it. And that is why I love you all so much. Y'all sure know how to spoil a girl." They both laughed.

"Bae, why are you bringing Macky with you? Is everything okay?" Sugar knew whenever Tony brought his number one killer with him there was some possible drama looming.

"Yes, Baby Girl. That is something else I needed to speak with you about. Shit has gotten serious back at the crib which is why when you left without the soldiers I became super concerned."

"Well, you know if I had known this, I wouldn't have just up and left like that. You really shouldn't keep things from me, Tony. I have proven I'm worthy to know everything there is to know, haven't I?"

"Yes, Baby Girl. You have. I just didn't have time to brief you after everything happened so fast. But listen. We will discuss all that and more when I get there. In the meantime, I want you to remain at the crib and take all precautions. The people who we are beefing with are extremely dangerous. They killed Cassadine and Sissy and tried to kill us and hijack the shipment a few nights ago. There is nothing these muthafuckas won't do at this point. We should be there in less than thirty minutes so sit tight till we get there, okay?"

"Okay, Bae," Sugar said as she peered down the dark road. "I love you, Tony."

"I love you more, Baby Girl. See you soon."

Chapter 28
We Are Who We Have Become, and Nothing Will Ever Change That

When Sugar walked downstairs, she saw her cousin Trent, Horace, one of Horace's homies Marco and his girl, and granny.

"What's going on down here?" she asked smiling.

"Sugar gal!" Trent said. "Give me a hug, girl." The two hugged tightly as granny smiled from her brand new red leather reclining chair. Seeing family together was one of her favorite things in life as it was with most mothers and grandmothers.

"It's been a while," Sugar said.

"You ain't lying. I think it's been since spring break in your senior year when y'all came to the beach in Panama."

"Yeah, that has been a while then. How's everybody in Panama City?" Naturally, Sugar didn't dare mention she was just there a little over a couple months ago when that gangsta shyt took place on the beach.

"Everybody's good. Same ole, same ole. I just moved to Sanford with my girl a couple weeks ago. When I heard Horace had jumped and you were in town, I thought y'all was having a family reunion or sumpin.'" Sugar laughed.

"Well, it ain't an official family reunion, but when my old man and Uncle Roy get here we can have an unofficial one."

"Tony and Roy on their way here?" granny asked excitedly.

"Yes, ma'am. They are about half an hour away, but with that traffic it'll probably be more like an hour."

"Sugar, why you didn't tell me? I could have put something on to eat."

"No, grandma, I just found out right before I walked down stairs."

"Okay. So you and your husband did have a chance to talk with one another?" granny asked.

"Yes, ma'am," Sugar said smiling.

"Well, good! All's well that ends well. Now what are we going to do about dinner? I know that man of yours will want a hot meal after that long flight."

"Yeah, that's a damn good question. What are we going to eat?" Horace asked. "'Cause y'all know I just jumped and I'm trying to eat everything on every occasion." The room filled with laughter.

"We'll order out on me," Sugar said laughing and shaking her head at her brother who was always the skinny one in the family with the biggest appetite.

***

When Lavrov arrived at the shopping center with his men, where Angel and Blaze were waiting patiently for him, they were laid back in the seats relaxing listening to *Pretty Hurts* by Beyonce. When they laid eyes on Lavrov they perked up as did he. He was a totally different person now than the man they left back in Manhattan, who looked as if he was at the end of his life. He was now back to the man they had known ever since they met him in a bar as teens, not long after they killed their abusive adopted father and burned and disposed of his body which still had not been found to this day.

"Alright," he said, kissing them both. "Let's go do what we were born to do. They all armed up to the teeth before setting out for granny's crib a couple miles away.

***

After everyone had decided what they wanted to eat, Sugar ran upstairs to grab her credit card to call in the order. When she grabbed her purse which was lying across the bed, she caught a glimpse of two black SUVs just sitting ominously down the road one behind the other. Her instincts told her either that was the

Feds or some other unknown enemy like jackers or even the people Tony had mentioned earlier. Either way she felt in her heart that it was some sort of drama coming her way. She remembered what Tony had said about how dangerous the people were who had already killed Cassadine and Sissy and how there was nothing they wouldn't do at this point. Thinking about what was a stake and how dare these muthafuckas come to her granny's crib, all of a sudden that old her began to resurface. That dangerous part of herself she thought she put back into its deep dark small space in her memory. She then recalled what Tony said as she looked at the ominous vehicles. *We are who we are. We are who we have become, and nothing will ever change that.* Sugar was now a killer just like her old man. And tonight, she would possibly have to prove this once again.

As Sugar walked down the winding staircase, the family continued to laugh and reminisce about old family while some old school music played on the brand new stereo that had a sound system that sent tunes throughout every inch of the huge mansion. The old school song, *The Closer I Get To You* by Roberta Flack and Donnie Hathaway played softly in the background as everyone continued to laugh and congregate.

After Sugar ordered the food, she pulled Horace off to the side while Trent, his homie and his girl who had just arrived all talked amongst themselves. Granny seemed like she was in her own world as she smiled and listened to the music.

"Bug, listen," Sugar said to Horace by his nickname.

"What's up, big sis? Is everything alright?" Her grim facial expression told him something was wrong.

"Where are those tools you had earlier at granny's crib?"

"Now, sis, don't trip. I brought them here until tomorrow. Okay? Don't start in on me again."

"No. Good. Where are they?"

"They upstairs in the bedroom," he said with a puzzled look on his face. She had just gone off on him about having the guns at granny's old crib. "What's going on, sis? What's up?" he said holding her shoulder.

"Not down here," she said. "Come upstairs with me. I don't want grandma startled." The two walked upstairs without the others noticing them.

"Listen," Sugar said as they reached the bedroom where Horace's arsenal was stashed. "I really don't have time to fully explain everything, but there might be some drama popping off here tonight." She nodded her head to the ominous vehicles down the road. Horace looked at them intently. "How long have they been there?

"I'm not sure. But all you need to know is if anything does go down, we have to play for keeps, because there is too much at stake. Now my old man, Tony, Uncle Roy and one of Tony's soldiers are on their way here. But until then, we handle shit ourselves if need be."

"Okay," Horace said monitoring her. "Well, that's all you gotta say. Enough said," he said as he began to open the suitcases.

"Your partner and Trent, are they stand up? They know about the gangsta shyt?" Sugar asked as she loaded up an AK.

"Show you right! My nigga, Marco, got him a couple of bodies back in the day and you already know how cuzzo, Trent, carry it," he said as he loaded a couple of Glocks and an AR 15.

"Okay, listen carefully, Bug. When I had this house built, we put an escape route in each closet in the rooms even in the living room closet that leads to a bullet proof room, fortified by steel, that leads to the outside. If anything goes down and something happens to me, make sure grandma get to it, okay?" Sugar said, before putting a Glock underneath her shirt, a small .380 in one of her boots and laying AK with the banana clip on the bed.

"Okay. Already!" Horace said as he put the two Glocks underneath his shirt, one in the small of his back and the other in the front.

"Now this may not be anything at all. But we are going to play this shit on the safe side," Sugar said. Horace looked at her with amazement, after watching her load that AK like she was an expert. This wasn't the same big sis who was only a year older than him that he remembered before he left to do the ten calendar. There was something deadly serious about her now.

"Sis, we really need to talk later," he said. "You've changed."

"Lil' bruh, trust me. You don't even know the half," she said with a wicked grin as they headed back downstairs where everyone was still laughing and congregating without a care in the world and totally unaware of the storm coming their way. When they made it downstairs, the lights and the music went off.

"Wow! Somebody musta forgot to pay their light bill?" Trent said jokingly.

"Grandma, I need you to come with me," Sugar said after she caught a glimpse of four shadows scurrying around back. The light from the full moon outside gave them up.

"Baby, what's the matter?" granny asked with concern in his voice. "It's probably just the breaker went out."

"Granny and Trent's girl, what's your name, sweetie?"

"Aryanna," she said in a startled voice.

"Okay, Aryanna. You and grandma come with me."

"Sugar, baby, what's going on?" granny asked again. This time her voice displayed a greater urgency. Sugar noticed granny fidgeting with her hands, which is something she always did when she became nervous.

"Granny, just trust me. Come with me and I will explain when we get where we're going," Sugar said calmly. "Horace take Trent and Marco upstairs. Remember what I told you."

"Okay," Horace said as he kissed her cheek. "Y'all come up here with me. Watch ya step."

"What's going down, homey?" Marco asked as they made their way upstairs. "Is it 'bout to be some drama or sumpin,' 'cause you know that's down my alley?" Marco, a former gang member seemed excited about the prospect of some shit popping off. He was a cold blooded killer, just like Horace, who was trying to go on the straight and narrow, but shit just seemed to keep coming his way.

"Yeah, bruh. Fuck it. Let's do this shit if need be," Horace said.

Inside the living room closet, Sugar instructed a frightened Aryanna and her granny, "No matter what happens or what you hear outside remain absolutely quiet. If need be, this room leads to an escape route to a clearing outside surrounded by huge pine trees only a couple of hundred feet from the house."

After giving Aryanna a loaded Glock, she looked her directly into her eyes.

"Anyone come through that door other than one of us, you fire and keep on firing until they're dead. You understand, sweetie?" Sugar said with a serious look on her face. Aryanna just nodded her head as she held the Glock 40 with both hands. Her eyes were as big as saucers. Sugar then kissed her granny on the forehead. "I will be right back in a few minutes, granny. Everything will be alright. I love you." She kissed her again and exited the closet. Granny continued to fidget with her hands as she rocked back and forth. She had no idea what was going on with her granddaughter, who she thought was an accountant.

After Horace handed her the AK, Sugar dialed Tony to see where they were. As soon as he answered, a battering ram crashed into the fortified back door, but the door withstood the blow. Waiting there in the dark behind the huge wall unit, Sugar laid the phone down and took aim at the back door. Horace was also in position and ready to fire. Amidst the curses outside, again, the battering ram crashed into the door, but to no avail. The door stood tall like an oak tree. Thanks to Sugar's security mindedness she learned from Tony, she made sure that when the house was being built the doors installed would be the ones which were impervious to break in by criminals and Pigs alike.

The first flash grenade crashed through the kitchen window and exploded inside the huge kitchen and dining room, shattering glass and windows, then came the automatic gunfire from Sugar and Horace that lit up the inside of the entire pitched dark house. The tracer rounds gave a beautiful, but deadly light show that illuminated all the combatant's positions as they scrambled to keep from being searched out by the infrared scopes that guided the deadly flying projectiles. The return fire raked the inside of the house as Sugar and Horace scrambled for cover. When Trent made it midway downstairs in a crouch with an AK in his hand, bullets started whizzing by from each direction, sending glass and other debris all across the room as if a tornado had been unleashed. Some of the glass from the shattered chandelier caught him in the face, causing him to tumble down the remaining stairs. Horace saw his cousin's dilemma and ran and grabbed him by his shirt and dragged him to safety, while Sugar lit up the kitchen window up with full automatic fire. The barrage from the 7.62s cut out a new window as the intermittent volleys of gunfire from Lavrov's henchmen spoke back.

When the back door blew completely open from a small plastic explosive charge, all hell broke loose inside the once immaculate crib that was now beginning to look like one of those gutted out buildings in war torn Syria. The Russian, his men and the widows bolted inside with guns out in front of them blazing as Sugar and the home's other occupants ducked before returning fire.

When two of Lavrov's men made a mad dash for the living room to get a better position in which to fire on their targets, Sugar sprung out from behind the colossal redwood wall unit and sprayed them with the AK as she yelled, "Die muthafuckas!"

The two men's flesh absolutely exploded with each impact of the tiny missiles. Their bullet riddled bodies hit the floor with a thudding sound right where they once stood. They never moved again. Not even so much as a twitch. Granny and Trent's girl, Aryanna, held their hands tightly over their ears to keep out the eardrum shattering sounds as their hearts skipped a collective beat with each burst of the deafening gunfire that echoed throughout the huge mansion. Being that granny's crib was the first and only house on the block that had been built in the new secluded subdivision, which was at least two miles away from town, no one nearby could hear the gunfire to call the police. So Sugar and her people were on their own this night. When Tony called back and Sugar picked up, to his horror he could hear the raging gun battle in the background. The gunfire was so loud, it sent a sharp pain surging through his eardrum causing him to momentarily drop the phone.

"Shit!" He yelled. "Hey, I need you to step on it, Roy! Something is going down at the granny's new house!" The valves on the CT6 engine of Roy's brand new Caddy sedan opened up and roared as it was about to be put to the test.

As Lavrov and his people continued to rain down gunfire inside the dark living room and ducked when the fire came back their way, Marco opened up from upstairs with two Glocks, killing one of Lavrov's men before Angel returned fire and hit him in the shoulder, causing him to tumble down the stairs near her position. Before he could regain his composure from the fall and the impact of the bullet and get to his feet, Angel dove from her position on top of him and viciously slit his throat almost in one lightning quick motion. Marco sat there slumped over at the foot of the stairs with his eyes wide open and his gun still in his hand, taking his last breath as his lifeblood flowed heavily from the gaping surgical wound to his neck into the cracks of the hardwood floor.

Horace saw his homey laying there lifeless and started firing wildly spraying the kitchen which was now totally destroyed.

"Muthafuckas! Fuck y'all!" he screamed in a death yell as he darted to the other side of the room just as Sugar laid down cover fire. He was barely missed by a hail of bullets that would have taken him out the fight for good.

"Listen, Trent! I want you to stay right here, okay?" Sugar said calmly. "I have to go help Horace.

"Okay, cuzzo," the wounded Trent said. "I'll be okay." His blood covered face had now impaired the vision in his other eye. After Sugar quickly crawled off leaving him there, and almost immediately, Blaze slipped up on him. When Trent looked up at first he thought she was Sugar due to his now impaired vision. "Hey cuzzo. You back already?" he said as he tried to wipe the blood from his eye.

"Yeah, baby, I'm back." When he realized it was rather odd for Sugar to call him baby, he again attempted to wipe the blood from his good eye to see the widow crouched over him grinning with two knives in her hands. His death was quick.

When Sugar made it over to where she last saw Horace, exchanging gunfire as she moved across the room, she stopped dead in her tracks. She was horrified at what she saw that took all the fight out of her. Angel had a gun to her brother's head. Lavrov was standing by with his HKK trained on her as he and his three remaining men cautiously emerged from behind the kitchen's island countertop, where they had taken cover from the flying heat rocks. Lavrov smiled as he moved forward with his gun trained on her.

"Are you the Queen?" he asked still smiling.

"Let him go!" Sugar demanded as she was mad dogging Angel.

"So you are the Queen," Lavrov said as he moved closer with his gun still trained on her, "and one bad bitch I might add. You took out two of my best men." He looked down at the bullet riddled bodies of his two soldiers whose eyes were wide open. "Your husband trained you well."

"Let him go I said, bitch!" Sugar again demanded with her AK pointed at her as she pressed her gun to Horace's temple and used him as a shield.

"Listen, Mrs. Stallworth. I know you are a Queen in your kingdom, but look where you're at. You in a house away from your soldiers and your King with the enemy who has at least five guns trained on you and one on your relative here. So you are not in any position to be demanding anything. Now if you don't want this man, who is obviously someone you love dearly, dead, I suggest it is you who should drop her gun. Now!" he said sternly. "Or I will have her blow his fucking brains out all over this lovely hardwood floor!"

Realizing this tall white man with the long pony tail was dead serious Sugar relented and complied by placing her gun on the floor. Lavrov smiled as Blaze walked up behind her and rubbed Sugar on her cat. Sugar immediately spun around as her hand cut through the air like a blur and slapped the shit out of her before Lavrov's men grabbed her. Blaze quickly popped up on her feet like a martial arts action figure with the knives brandished and smiling with that familiar deadly look in her eyes. When she moved towards Sugar in a predacious kill mode, Lavrov quickly grabbed her.

"No!" he said to her. "Go to the fucking truck!" Clearly pissed, she wiped the blood from her mouth, and licked and smiled at Sugar before storming out of the once beautiful, now destroyed home.

When Tony, Roy and Macky arrived at the mansion with their guns drawn, it was dark and eerily quiet. After cutting the mansion's power back on, one by one they all cautiously slipped through what was left of the backdoor taking every precaution. Once inside they could clearly smell the gun smoke. The remaining chandeliers and the powerful ceiling spotlights shined a light on the destruction that belied the seemingly peaceful view of the front of the home. Although all three men had experienced their share of death and mutilation over the course of their lives, they were nonetheless taken aback by what they saw.

"Sugar!" Tony called out as he, Macky and Big Roy walked pass the bodies scattered throughout the living room. By now the stereo came back on with the power and the old school joint *Walk On By* by Isaac Hayes played from the surround system and echoed off the walls. Somewhat distraught at the sight of his blood kin lying there dead, Roy knelt down over his nephew Trent and gently closed his eyes with his hand. The scene bore witness to an intense gun battle that took place in which both sides took it to one another with the utmost viciousness. Though Sugar and her people were outmanned, it appeared they gave as much hell as they caught.

After scouring the huge mansion's bedrooms, Tony remembered the home had an escape route upstairs and downstairs that led to the outside. Running back down the winding staircase past Macky and Big Roy, Tony went into the living room closet and opened the secret door as Roy walked over to the stereo and turned it off. Before Tony crept inside with his gold-plated four fives drawn, he cautiously inspected the door jams, the floor and the ceiling above him for any explosive booby traps. Once he concluded it was clear to proceed, he pressed onward to the safe room and then down through the corridor that led outside followed by Macky and Big Roy. Outside in the clearing surrounded by huge pine trees, a few hundred yards from the house is where he found granny and Aryanna huddled together. Aryanna was shivering and pointing the Glock at him. Her eyes told a tale of sheer terror.

"It's okay, honey. I'm Sugar's husband," Tony said softly as he knelt down and removed the gun from her trembling hands, just as Roy and Macky walked into the clearing.

"Auntie!" Roy said to granny as knelt down over her. "Are you okay?" Granny sat there on the ground as if she was trying to catch her breath. She only nodded her head to acknowledge that she was fine. "Don't try to speak, auntie," he said as he rubbed her head gently. "Are you hurting anywhere?" She pointed to her chest. "Okay! We are going to get you out of here!" Roy said as he helped her to her feet.

"Where is Sugar?" Tony asked Aryanna. Seemingly in shock, she just shrugged her shoulders to say she didn't know. Almost as soon as he inquired about his Queen, Sugar's *One Plus One* ringtone by Beyonce rang. Tony frantically reached into his pocket and grabbed his cell phone.

"Hello! Baby Girl! Hello!" he said excitedly

"I have your bitch," a voice with a Russian accent said. "I will be in touch." He hung up.

For the first time in Tony's life as a gangsta, he was now in the most uncomfortable position of feeling a sense of helplessness. His Queen was now in the company of his greatest adversary to date and by far his greatest challenge, an unpredictable, sadistic and depraved man, along with his two widows, who had no boundaries and played by nobody's rules. What happened inside that mansion was a game changer that would no doubt alter the lives of all involved forever, including Tony. The chapter that he had long closed had now been reopened as the gauntlet had just been thrown down. What happened inside that mansion just ensured more *Gangsta Shyt* to come.

Gangsta Shyt 2

To Be Continued...
Coming Soon
Gangsta Shyt 3

Stay Connected with Us!

Text **LOCKDOWN** to 22828 to stay
up-to-date with new releases, sneak peaks,
contests and more…

Thank you!

Submission Guideline.

Submit the first three chapters of your completed manuscript to <u>ldpsubmissions@gmail.com</u>, subject line: Your book's title. The manuscript must be in a .doc file and sent as an attachment. Document should be in Times New Roman, double spaced and in size 12 font. Also, provide your synopsis and full contact information. If sending multiple submissions, they must each be in a separate email.

Have a story but no way to send it electronically? You can still submit to LDP/Ca$h Presents. Send in the first three chapters, written or typed, of your completed manuscript to:

LDP: Submissions Dept
Po Box 870494
Mesquite, Tx 75187

DO NOT send original manuscript. Must be a duplicate.

Provide your synopsis and a cover letter containing your full contact information.

Thanks for considering LDP and Ca$h Presents.

CATO

<u>Coming Soon from Lock Down Publications/Ca$h Presents</u>

BOW DOWN TO MY GANGSTA

By **Ca$h**

TORN BETWEEN TWO

By **Coffee**

BLOOD STAINS OF A SHOTTA **II**

By **Jamaica**

WHEN THE STREETS CLAP BACK **II**

By **Jibril Williams**

STEADY MOBBIN

By **Marcellus Allen**

BLOOD OF A BOSS **V**

By **Askari**

BRIDE OF A HUSTLA **III**

By **Destiny Skai**

WHEN A GOOD GIRL GOES BAD **II**

By **Adrienne**

LOVE & CHASIN' PAPER **II**

By **Qay Crockett**

THE HEART OF A GANGSTA **III**

By **Jerry Jackson**

LOYAL TO THE GAME **IV**

By **T.J. & Jelissa**

A DOPEBOY'S PRAYER **II**

By **Eddie "Wolf" Lee**

IF LOVING YOU IS WRONG... **III**

By **Jelissa**

BLOODY COMMAS **III**

SKI MASK CARTEL II

By **T.J. Edwards**

BLAST FOR ME **II**

RAISED AS A GOON V

BRED BY THE SLUMS

By **Ghost**

A DISTINGUISHED THUG STOLE MY HEART **III**

By **Meesha**

ADDICTIED TO THE DRAMA **II**

By **Jamila Mathis**

LIPSTICK KILLAH II

By **Mimi**

THE BOSSMAN'S DAUGHTERS 4

By **Aryanna**

Available Now

RESTRAINING ORDER **I & II**

By **CA$H & Coffee**

LOVE KNOWS NO BOUNDARIES **I II & III**

By **Coffee**

RAISED AS A GOON I, II, III & IV

CATO

By **Ghost**

LAY IT DOWN **I & II**

LAST OF A DYING BREED

BLOOD STAINS OF A SHOTTA

By **Jamaica**

LOYAL TO THE GAME

LOYAL TO THE GAME II

LOYAL TO THE GAME III

By **TJ & Jelissa**

BLOODY COMMAS I & II

SKI MASK CARTEL

By **T.J. Edwards**

IF LOVING HIM IS WRONG...I & II

By **Jelissa**

WHEN THE STREETS CLAP BACK

By **Jibril Williams**

A DISTINGUISHED THUG STOLE MY HEART I & II

By **Meesha**

PUSH IT TO THE LIMIT

By **Bre' Hayes**

BLOOD OF A BOSS **I, II, III & IV**

By **Askari**

THE STREETS BLEED MURDER **I, II & III**

THE HEART OF A GANGSTA I & II

By **Jerry Jackson**

CUM FOR ME

CUM FOR ME 2

CUM FOR ME 3

An **LDP Erotica Collaboration**

BRIDE OF A HUSTLA **I & II**

THE FETTI GIRLS **I, II& III**

By **Destiny Skai**

WHEN A GOOD GIRL GOES BAD

By **Adrienne**

A GANGSTER'S REVENGE **I II III & IV**

THE BOSS MAN'S DAUGHTERS

THE BOSS MAN'S DAUGHTERS II

THE BOSSMAN'S DAUGHTERS III

A SAVAGE LOVE **I & II**

BAE BELONGS TO ME

A HUSTLER'S DECEIT I, II

By **Aryanna**

A KINGPIN'S AMBITON

A KINGPIN'S AMBITION **II**

I MURDER FOR THE DOUGH

By **Ambitious**

TRUE SAVAGE

TRUE SAVAGE II

TRUE SAVAGE **III**

By **Chris Green**

CATO

A DOPEBOY'S PRAYER

By **Eddie "Wolf" Lee**

THE KING CARTEL **I, II & III**

By **Frank Gresham**

THESE NIGGAS AIN'T LOYAL **I, II & III**

By **Nikki Tee**

GANGSTA SHYT **I II &III**

By **CATO**

THE ULTIMATE BETRAYAL

By **Phoenix**

BOSS'N UP **I , II & III**

By **Royal Nicole**

I LOVE YOU TO DEATH

By Destiny J

I RIDE FOR MY HITTA

I STILL RIDE FOR MY HITTA

By **Misty Holt**

LOVE & CHASIN' PAPER

By **Qay Crockett**

TO DIE IN VAIN

By **ASAD**

BROOKLYN HUSTLAZ

By **Boogsy Morina**

BROOKLYN ON LOCK I & II

By **Sonovia**

GANGSTA CITY

By **Teddy Duke**

A DRUG KING AND HIS DIAMOND

A DOPEMAN'S RICHES

By Nicole Goosby

BOOKS BY LDP'S CEO, CA$H

TRUST IN NO MAN

TRUST IN NO MAN 2

TRUST IN NO MAN 3

BONDED BY BLOOD

SHORTY GOT A THUG

THUGS CRY

THUGS CRY 2

THUGS CRY 3

TRUST NO BITCH

TRUST NO BITCH 2

TRUST NO BITCH 3

TIL MY CASKET DROPS

RESTRAINING ORDER

RESTRAINING ORDER 2

IN LOVE WITH A CONVICT

Coming Soon

BONDED BY BLOOD 2

BOW DOWN TO MY GANGSTA